# Glossolalia
# New & Selected Stories

Also by David Jauss

Fiction
*Crimes of Passion*
*Black Maps*

Poetry
*You Are Not Here*
*Improvising Rivers*

Nonfiction
*On Writing Fiction*

# GLOSSOLALIA
## NEW & SELECTED STORIES

*For Lois —*

*with hopes you like some of
the tongues I've spoken in
here —*

*and with best wishes
to you and work, now and
forever —
David Jauss*

## DAVID JAUSS

**Press 53**
Winston-Salem

Press 53, LLC
PO Box 30314
Winston-Salem, NC 27130

First Edition

Cover design by Kevin Morgan Watson

Cover art, "Alone," Copyright © 2013 by Jack L. Geiser,
used by permission of the artist.

Author photo by Alison Jauss

Printed on acid-free paper
ISBN 978-1-935708-84-1

*for Galen and Ethan*

# ACKNOWLEDGMENTS

Earlier versions of these stories, sometimes under other titles, appeared in the following magazines:

*California Quarterly*: "Shards"
*Crazyhorse*: "The Stars at Noon"
*CrossConnect*: "Brothers"
*Denver Quarterly*: "Misery"
*Great River Review*: "Deliverance"
*Indiana Review*: "Hook"
*The Iowa Review*: "The Bigs"
*Iron Horse Literary Review*: "Tell Me Something"
*The MacGuffin*: "The Sacred Drum"
*New England Review*: "Freeze"
*Northwest Review*: "Torque"
*Prairie Schooner*: "Beautiful Ohio" (reprinted by permission of the University of
    Nebraska Press; copyright 1989 University of Nebraska Press)
*Puerto Del Sol*: "Apotheosis"
*Shenandoah*: "Constellations," "Glossolalia," and "What They Didn't Notice"
*StoryQuarterly*: "Rainier"


"Shards" also appeared in *Prize Stories 1983: The O. Henry Awards* and in *Best Short Stories from the California Quarterly, 1971-1985*. "Freeze" also appeared in *The Pushcart Prize XIV: Best of the Small Presses, 1989-1990*. "The Bigs" was reprinted in *Bottom of the Ninth: Great Contemporary Baseball Stories*. "Glossolalia" was included in *Best American Short Stories 1991*; *The Pushcart Prize XVI: Best of the Small Presses, 1991-1992*; and *The Pushcart Book of Short Stories: The Best Short Stories from The Pushcart Prize*.

Earlier versions of some of these stories also appeared in previous collections: "Hook," "The Stars at Noon," "Apotheosis," "Shards," and "Deliverance" in *Crimes of Passion* (Chicago: Story Press, 1984) and "Torque," "Freeze," "Beautiful Ohio," "The Bigs," "Rainier," and "Glossolalia" in *Black Maps* (Amherst: University of Massachusetts Press, 1996).

I am grateful to the National Endowment for the Arts, the James A. Michener/ Copernicus Society of America, the Minnesota State Arts Board, and the Arkansas Arts Council for fellowships that enabled me to write many of these stories. My thanks also to the teachers and friends whose advice and support have meant everything to me: Frederick Busch, Philip Dacey, Stephen Dunn, George P. Elliott, James Hannah, Bret Lott, Dennis Vannatta, David Wojahn, Deb Wylder, and Edith Wylder.

# GLOSSOLALIA
## NEW & SELECTED STORIES

# TORQUE

The day after his wife left him, taking their three-year-old son with her, Larry Watkins took out his circular saw, attached the metal-cutting blade, and carefully sawed his 1974 Cadillac Fleetwood in half. It was not an impulsive or crazy act, as his neighbors might have supposed. He had spent almost four hours the day before making the proper measurements, drawing the cutting line with a magic marker, and chaining one bumper to the garage wall and the other to the Chevy so the two halves wouldn't spring together when he cut the frame. And in a way, he had been planning this moment ever since 1985, when he came back to the U.S. after two years of guard duty and beer drinking for Uncle Sam in Germany. To celebrate their release from the service, he and his buddy Spence had rented a limousine for an hour and cruised around Virginia Beach, drinking Scotch from the limo's bar and looking at girls through the tinted glass. Spence was talking away about his plans: he was going to catch the next bus to Albany, marry his girl, and go to work in her father's office supply store. Larry hadn't given much thought to his future, so when Spence asked him what he was going to do when he got back to Minnesota, he said the first thing that came to his mind: "I'm gonna get me one of these limousines."

They had both laughed when he said that, but the more Larry thought about it, the more he liked the idea of owning a limousine.

He remembered Arlen Behrens, an acne-faced kid he'd known in high school. Arlen hadn't had a date in his life, but after he got a red Trans Am for his birthday, he started going steady with Karla Thein, one of the homecoming princesses. Larry could only imagine what the girls in Monticello would think of a limousine. He pictured himself sipping champagne in the back seat with a pretty redhead while his chauffeur drove them down Main Street. Everybody would gawk at them, even the rich kids passing in their Corvettes and Austin-Healeys, but he'd wave or smile only at those he considered his friends. If he had a limo, everyone would see that he wasn't who they'd always thought he was; they would see that he was someone else entirely, someone mysterious and admirable.

Larry knew he could never afford a limousine, of course, but he thought he might be able to build one. So after he returned to Monticello, he started collecting articles about limos and writing to *Limousine and Chauffeur* magazine for information about how they were made. He had six manila envelopes full of blueprints and suggestions by the time he met Karen at Shopko, where she worked in ladies' apparel and he worked in electronics. She was a tall, slim blonde with green eyes and a crooked smile, and he was amazed that such a beautiful woman would go out with him. He told her about his plans to build a limousine, but she only laughed and called him a dreamer. When he picked her up for a date in his Impala, she'd say, "Oh good, we're going in the limo again tonight." And on his twenty-third birthday, she gave him a blue chauffeur's cap, climbed into the back seat, and said, "Once around the park, then home, James!" She teased him, but Larry knew she was looking forward to the day when he'd build his limousine and drive her around town like a queen.

Then, a few months after he and Karen were married, he bought the Caddy from Hawker's Salvage and had it towed to his garage. He thought Karen would be pleased, but when she came home from work and saw the rusty, battered car, she demanded he take it back.

He was so surprised he couldn't say anything for a moment. Then he said, "You can't take it back. It's not like a pair of pants that don't fit or something."

"Well, you've got to sell it to somebody else then. We can't afford a second car, especially one that won't run. What did you pay for it anyway?"

"Just five hundred dollars," he said.

"Five hundred dollars! How could you do such a thing?"

"But I told you I was going to build a limo."

She fixed him with a look he had never seen before. "Well, I didn't believe it. I thought that was just you talking."

He stared at her a moment, then went over and stood beside the crumpled hood. "I know it doesn't look like much now," he said, his voice trembling a little, "but wait till I fix it up. You'll have the nicest car in town. And we'll go places. We'll go all over. It'll be as comfortable as sitting in your living room, only you'll be going somewhere."

"Fix it up?" she said. "You think you can fix *that* up?"

In the weeks that followed they continued to fight about the car, but Larry would never agree to sell it. Once Karen went behind his back and put an ad in the paper, but Larry found out about it and told everyone who called that the car had already been sold. After that, Karen didn't say anything to him about the Caddy, at least not in words. If he mentioned it, she'd just shake her head and look away. Even then, he didn't give in. He wanted to prove to her that he was the kind of man who made his dreams come true, the kind of man who *deserved* a limo. But he didn't have enough money to start working on the car yet, so he just kept on collecting articles and blueprints. At least once a week he'd take out his envelopes, spread them across the kitchen table, and spend a couple of hours going through all the information.

The summer their son turned two, Larry talked Karen into taking a trip to Disney World. "Randy would love it," he said, and though Karen worried he was too young to appreciate Disney World, she finally agreed. They packed up the Chevy and left Monticello just after dawn that Saturday. It took them two long days to drive to Florida, but they managed to make the trip fun, playing License Plate Poker and I Spy and singing songs from Disney movies. But when they finally reached Orlando and Larry mentioned there was a limousine factory nearby that he wouldn't mind touring, the fun stopped. No matter how hard he tried to convince Karen that he hadn't planned the trip just to see the factory, she wouldn't believe him. While they were eating dinner at McDonald's, he asked her to listen to reason, and that made her so angry she went into the restroom and stayed there for almost half an hour. When she finally came out, her eyes were red and puffy, but there were no tears in her voice: "Take us to the airport," she said. "Now." Two hours later, she and Randy were on a flight to Minneapolis, where her parents lived. She was planning to get a lawyer and file for divorce as soon as she got there.

Larry checked into a Motel 6 near the airport and stayed up late drinking Jim Beam from a pint bottle. The more he drank, the crazier it all seemed to him: he'd actually let a car, a *junk heap*, come between him and his family. What was wrong with him? There was only one thing to do: sell the damned car and toss out his box full of blueprints and articles. And that's exactly what he'd do, the minute he got home. As soon as he made that decision, he felt as if a terrible burden had been lifted from him, and he lay back on the bed and closed his eyes.

The next morning, Larry started back to Minnesota. He hadn't intended to stop at the limousine factory, but his route took him near it and since he'd already decided to sell the Caddy, he figured it wouldn't hurt anything to take a look. Once he was there, he had such a good time watching the workmen convert ordinary Cadillacs into customized stretch limos that he decided to go through the tour again, this time taking notes. He hadn't changed his mind about selling the car; he just wanted to compare the factory's methods with those recommended by *Limousine and Chauffeur* magazine. After he did that, he'd throw the notes out along with everything else. So he took the tour again, and when he came back out to the parking lot, he stood there for a long moment, looking at the Chevy's rusted fenders and torn vinyl seats, before he unlocked the door and got in.

Two nights later, back in Monticello, he sat down at his kitchen table and dialed the number of Karen's parents. By then, he had decided not to say anything about the Caddy unless he had to. He'd just ask Karen to come home, and if she said yes, he wouldn't even bring the car up. But if she said no, he'd promise to sell it and never mention a limo again. It was all up to her. He listened to the phone ring, then she answered, her hello cool, preoccupied. But when she heard his voice, she started to cry, and he knew he wouldn't have to sell the car. "I'll drive up to get you and Randy in the morning," he said, after she finally stopped crying.

That was over a year ago. They'd had many fights after that, and every one ended with her crying and forgiving him. But after a while—he didn't know exactly when or why—they stopped fighting. They spoke politely to each other and never even mentioned the limo, yet somehow Larry felt worse, as if they were arguing in a deeper, more dangerous way than before. And then, yesterday morning, Karen looked at him across the breakfast table and said she was leaving, and he knew this time she would not come back.

Now Larry stood in his garage, sweating in the intense July heat, the saw whining in his hand, and looked at the two halves of his Cadillac. He had been preparing for this moment for six years, and for the life of him he couldn't remember what he was supposed to do next.

The next day, when Larry didn't report for work, his boss called him and asked if he was sick. Larry told him about Karen, and he said Larry should feel free to take the day off. Mondays were always slow, and they could get by short-handed for a day. But they'd need him back tomorrow. Larry said no problem, he'd be there. But he didn't report to work the rest of the week, and though the phone rang every morning shortly after the store opened, he did not answer it. The next Monday, he received a registered letter notifying him that he'd been terminated. He sat at the kitchen table strewn with breakfast, lunch, and dinner dishes and looked at that word: *terminated.* It had a finality that he liked. He said it aloud and listened to it in the quiet house.

Although he had only a few hundred dollars in savings, Larry was glad he'd been fired. Now he would finally have the time he needed to work on the limousine. But it was too hot to work outside just then, so he spent the next few days sitting in front of a fan, watching TV. He watched everything, but he liked the nature shows on the Discovery Channel best, especially the ones about survival in the wild. Though these shows were full of conflict and danger, there was something comforting about the simplicity of the animals' concerns—food, shelter, a quiet moment in which to lick their wounds. Sometimes he'd tape a show and watch it several times.

Larry didn't do any work on the Cadillac, but almost every day he went out to the garage to look at it and plan his course of action. One morning, about two weeks after Karen and Randy had left him, he was surprised to find someone sitting in the back of the severed car. It was Elizabeth, the retarded woman who lived across the street with her elderly mother. She was a big, heavy-breasted woman with red bristly hair and splayed feet, and she was always talking to herself. The words didn't make any sense. They sounded foreign, even alien, and Larry always wondered if her mother could understand her. He remembered how Karen had been able to understand Randy's babble when he was a baby. He had been jealous of that ability; it had made him feel like an outsider in his own family.

Larry leaned over and looked in at Elizabeth. She was wearing a loose-fitting flowered dress—the kind Karen called a muumuu— and holding a red purse the size of a small suitcase on her lap. Her mouth was moving continuously, chewing words as if they were gum.

He cleared his throat and said, "Can I help you?" It was what he'd said to his customers at Shopko, and he felt strange for having said it now.

Elizabeth turned her moon face to him and abruptly, for the first time in his presence, went silent. But then she immediately started talking again. She was looking at him, but somehow he could tell she was still talking to herself.

"What's wrong?" he asked. But that, too, was a stupid question: she was smiling and every now and then a giggle broke into her babble. He stood watching her for a moment, not knowing what to do. Then he opened the door and said, "I'm sorry, but you'll have to leave." But she didn't move. She just opened her purse a crack, put her eye right down to the opening, and half giggled, half jabbered some strange phrase over and over. Then she suddenly snapped the purse shut and looked at him as if she thought he were trying to peek.

Larry didn't know what to say. "If you want to go somewhere," he finally said, "you picked the wrong car. This one doesn't even run."

Just then, Elizabeth's mother came huffing up the driveway in her housecoat. "Oh Mr. Watkins, you found her!" she said, trying to catch her breath. "I was so worried. I was just about to call the police." She came up beside Larry and looked in at Elizabeth. "You naughty girl!" she said. "You know you aren't supposed to go outside by yourself." Her scolding didn't seem to bother Elizabeth; she just sat there, chattering away happily and peeking every now and then in her purse.

The old woman turned back to Larry and, wiping her sweaty face with a handkerchief, said, "I don't know what's gotten into her, Mr. Watkins. I've been up and down the block looking for her, but I never thought to look in your"—she paused, as if she wasn't sure what to call it—"your car."

She went on talking, but Larry was only half listening to her. He was watching Elizabeth bounce up and down on the back seat like an excited child. "You know something," he interrupted the old woman. "I think she thinks she's going somewhere."

❖ ❖ ❖

That night, Larry called Karen for the first time since she left. "Oh, it's you," she said.

"What's the matter?" he said. "Can't I call?"

"Yes, you can call. Just don't think you'll change my mind."

"I'm not calling about that," he said.

"Then what are you calling about?"

For a moment, he didn't answer. He was listening to Karen's mother, in the background, talking to Randy. She was using the high, sing-song voice grown-ups put on to talk to children. Larry strained to hear what she was saying, but all he could make out was "grow up big and strong." Then he realized Karen was on the phone in her parents' kitchen, and for a second he was standing where Karen was, looking across the room at the kitchen table, where her mother was sitting beside Randy's highchair, poking a spoonful of something at him. He felt a sudden ache, like hunger, in his stomach, and he gripped the telephone.

"You remember that retarded woman across the street?" he finally said.

"Of course I do. How long do you think I've been gone? Forty years?"

He gritted his teeth a moment, then went on. "Well, this morning she was sitting out in the Caddy," he said. "Her mother was looking everywhere for her. She was about to file a missing person report. And here she was, just sitting there in the back seat, smiling and jabbering like nothing in the world was wrong."

"If this is about that stupid car . . ."

"No. Really, I just wanted to call. I thought you'd want to hear what happened."

"Now why would I want to hear about that woman sitting in your worthless car?"

"I don't know," Larry said. And now that he thought about it, he didn't know why he'd wanted to call and tell her. It all seemed so stupid now. Of course she wouldn't care. And why should *he* care?

In the background he heard his son say "Grandma" and

suddenly he had to sit down. The last words Randy had said to him before he and Karen got on the bus were, "Grandma's gonna take me to the zoo."

Larry sat there, staring across the kitchen table at the sink where Karen used to give Randy a bath when he was a baby. He felt very tired all of a sudden. He wanted to put his head down on the table and go to sleep.

Then Karen said, "Are you still there?"

"Yes," he answered. "How's Randy?"

"He's fine. He's made friends with the neighbor's little four-year-old, and he's been playing with him all day in his sandbox."

"Tell him I'll build him a sandbox in the backyard if he wants."

"I told you, Larry. I'm not changing my mind."

"I know," he said. "I was just thinking about when he comes to visit. You know, on weekends or whatever."

"All right," she said. "I'm sorry. I didn't know what you meant. Listen, do you want to talk with him for a minute?"

Larry was quiet. Then he said, "No, I guess not."

"Are you all right?" Karen asked.

Larry stood and looked out the window at the garage. Then he said, "I've been working on the car. You should see it. It's looking pretty good. I hung the new drive shaft and split the door posts the weekend you left, then last week I finished bending the new side panels and installed the window frames."

"Larry," she said.

"It took me forever to run the wires from front to back," he went on. "Over fifty wires in all. But everything's electric now: the locks, the windows, you name it. And I just finished installing the extensions on the gas lines, brake lines, and exhaust. It's been a lot of work, but it's been worth it. I'm just about ready for the paint job. I've decided on a royal blue Corvette finish. I tell you, it's gonna be beautiful, Karen, really beautiful."

"Larry, I'm not going to listen to this."

"I'll take you for a ride in it when it's finished," he went on. "You'll be the first one in it, you and Randy."

"Larry, I mean it."

"Okay," he said. "Okay. I'm sorry." Then they were silent for a long moment.

Finally, Karen said, "When will you understand? Even if you had done all of that, it wouldn't mean anything to me. I don't know why it's so important to you. Why can't you just let it go?"

"What do you mean, *if* I had done it?"

"You know what I mean."

"No, I don't," he said, his voice rising. "Why don't you tell me."

Karen sighed. "I don't want to sit here and fight with you, Larry. Randy's right here, and so's my mom."

"If you don't think I've been working on that car, you're wrong," he said. "Dead wrong."

"Okay. Okay. You've been working on it."

"Not just working on it, I'm damn near finished with it."

"I said okay. Don't get mad."

"I'm not mad. Who said I was mad?"

"Okay, you're not mad. You're not mad, and the limo's almost done. And I've changed my silly little mind and I'm not going to file for divorce after all."

"Don't talk to me that way."

"Why not? That's how you talk to me."

"You know what?" he said, pacing beside the table now. "You think you know everything. You think you're so smart. Well, you don't know shit. You understand? Not even *shit*."

"Larry, listen to yourself. You sound like—"

"You listen to yourself!" he shouted, then hung up the phone so hard it rang.

He stood there a moment, trembling, then went to the refrigerator and opened it. He stared inside for several minutes, not seeing anything, before he finally closed the door and went out to the garage. It was dark outside, and it'd be hard to work, even with utility lights, but he had to get busy. He had wasted too much time already. It was still terribly hot, and the weathermen were saying the heat might not break for another week, but he couldn't wait any longer. He took off his shirt, gripped the rear bumper, and pulled the back half of the Cadillac about six feet away from the front half. Then he began to align the frame, pausing every now and then to towel the sweat from his face and arms.

When he finished aligning the frame, he took an imprint of the end of the frame section, then stood and stretched his aching back. There was nothing else he could do now. He'd take the imprint to Hawker's the first thing in the morning, so they could begin building the frame extensions he needed. On his way back from Hawker's, he'd stop at Eriksen's Welding Supply and buy welding rods—about twenty pounds should do it—then swing by Vern's Sheet Metal to see about renting their break to bend the side panels. Hawker should have the extensions for him by the end of the week, so if he worked steadily he could be done welding the frame by the weekend. Then the next step would be installing the drive shaft. That was the trickiest part, according to the tour guide at the limousine factory, because the longer the drive shaft was, the greater the amount of torque it had to bear. Larry was planning to add at least one more hanger bearing, but still he was worried that the shaft would vibrate or even twist out of its supports. Several times he had imagined driving down the highway with Karen and Randy, the three of them talking and laughing as if nothing had ever been wrong between them, when all of a sudden the shaft would lurch out of the hanger bearings with a sound like the end of the world. Whenever this thought had come to him, he had forced himself to think of something else. But now he stood there between the two halves of the Cadillac and watched the shaft drag beneath the swerving car, spewing sparks.

The next morning, Larry was too exhausted to take the imprint down to Hawker's. He didn't even have the energy to watch TV, so he just lay on the couch and stared out the window. Birds flew by, lighting on the branches of the sycamore, and squirrels chattered and chased each other in the yard. He watched all this

for a while, but he wasn't really seeing it. He was wondering what
would have happened if he hadn't been born. Who would be
living in this house, looking out the window? Who would Karen
have married? And what would her son be like? The more he
thought, the more he felt insubstantial, as if he had only been
dreaming all these years that he existed. He looked around the
room, and everything seemed simultaneously familiar and strange.
He remembered how once, when he was a child, he had lain on
the floor of his bedroom and imagined that the ceiling was the
floor of an upside-down house and he was somehow stuck on
the ceiling. Nothing was different—there was the same light
fixture, the same posters on the walls, the same bed and carpet—
but everything had changed.

Now he lay on the couch, watching the dust swirling in the
light slanting through the window. It looked like snow. He watched
it fall for a long time, wondering if it would ever stop. It didn't. It
kept falling, but as it fell out of the light, it disappeared.

Then he held his hand up to the light and turned it back and
forth. *I'm here*, he thought. *I'm alive and I'm here.*

Later that morning, the doorbell rang. It was Elizabeth's mother,
her face a knot of worry. "I'm afraid she's in your car again, Mr.
Watkins, and I can't get her out."

Larry was dizzy from standing suddenly after lying down so
long, and he hung onto the doorjamb. In the bright sunlight, the
old lady's wrinkled face looked as if it had been burned, and it
occurred to him that that's what aging was: a gradual kind of fire
that ate your flesh. He shivered, even though the air coming
through the screen door was oppressively hot.

"I'm sorry to bother you," she said, and took a step back down
the stairs. "If this isn't a good time . . ."

Then Larry realized he had been staring at her for some time
without speaking. "Excuse me," he apologized. "I just woke up,
and I'm a little groggy. I'll be happy to help you."

He slipped on his tennis shoes and followed the old woman out to the garage where, as before, Elizabeth was sitting in the back seat with her purse on her lap. But this time she wasn't just jabbering; she was singing. Larry couldn't recognize the song, if it was a song. He remembered how Randy would make up nonsense songs, and it occurred to him that children—and maybe retarded people, too—didn't know that words existed. Maybe they thought words were only sounds, meaningless noises people made back and forth, to pass the day. Or maybe it was the other way around and they thought every sound was a word. And maybe they were right, maybe every sound *was* a word, and they weren't speaking nonsense after all.

Elizabeth's mother said, "I've tried everything, but I can't get her to budge. She can be very stubborn, you know."

Larry opened the door and said, "Elizabeth. It's time for you to go home." She stopped singing for a second and looked at him, then opened her purse a crack and peeked in. Then she smiled and started singing again.

Her mother shook her head. "Who knows what all she's got in that purse this time. Yesterday I found my missing bottle of perfume in there, and her toothbrush, and a pair of socks. I'd been looking for that perfume for a week."

Larry turned to her. "When was the last time you took her somewhere? You know, on a trip."

"Oh, once in a while I take her with me to the grocery store. And every other Sunday we go to church. But otherwise—well, you can see how much trouble she can be, and I'm not strong enough to make her behave."

"Yes," Larry said, "I can see that." Then he looked in at Elizabeth and said, "Where're you headed today?" Elizabeth babbled excitedly and clapped her hands. "No kidding?" Larry said. "Me, too." Then he climbed into the front seat and took the wheel in his hands.

"Mr. Watkins?" the old lady said, clasping the collar of her dress with a bony hand.

"Don't worry," he answered. "I'll have her back before lunchtime."

❖  ❖  ❖

Every morning after that, Elizabeth spent a few hours in the car, and each day her purse got a little fuller until finally she couldn't close it anymore. Eventually, Larry began to get up before she did, and he'd be waiting in the limo when she crossed the street, chattering and waggling her arms. She'd sit in the back and he'd sit behind the wheel, watching her in the rearview mirror as she bounced up and down on the seat and pointed out the window at the world passing by. For hours at a time, he didn't think about Karen or Randy or the threatening letters from the bank and the electric company. He was not happy, but he was not unhappy either. He was Elizabeth's chauffeur, nothing more, and he just sat there, his mind empty. And it wasn't until after they'd finished their drive and he'd helped her across the street to her house that he would come back to who and where he was. When that happened, he'd stand there a minute, in her yard or in the street or on his steps, before he could bear to enter his empty house.

Toward the middle of August, a man came to serve divorce papers on Larry. He started up the walk, then heard strange noises coming from the garage. Crossing the yard to the driveway, he saw the rear end of a car sticking out of the garage. As he reached the door, he saw that the car had been sawn in half and there were two people sitting in it. "What the hell?" he said. Then he called out Larry's name, but Larry didn't seem to notice; he just kept looking out the windshield at the garage wall. He was silent, but the woman in the back seat was jabbering in some strange language the process server couldn't understand. But Larry seemed to understand. He nodded as she spoke, said something back to her, then turned the wheel carefully to the left, as if rounding a dangerous curve.

# FREEZE

At first Freeze Harris thought Nam was a crazy nightmare, an upside-down place where you were supposed to do everything that was forbidden back in the world, but after a while it was the world that seemed unreal. Cutting ears off dead NVA had become routine; stocking shelves at Kroger's seemed something he'd only dreamed. Then, on a mission in the Iron Triangle, Freeze stepped on a Bouncing Betty that didn't go off and nothing seemed real anymore. It was like he'd stepped out of Nam when he stepped on the mine. And now he wasn't anywhere.

The day after Freeze stepped on the mine, the new brown-bar reported for duty. His name was Reynolds, and from the moment he arrived at Lai Khe, he had it in for Freeze. Freeze had just come in off the line that morning, and he was stumbling drunk outside the bunny club, wearing only his bush hat, sunglasses, and Jockey shorts. He had a bottle of Carling Black Label in one hand and a fragmentation grenade in the other. He was standing there, swaying back and forth, when Reynolds came up to him, his jungle fatigues starched and razor-creased, and stuck his square, government-issue jaw into Freeze's face. "What the fuck are you doing, soldier?"

Freeze looked at the brown bar on Reynolds' collar and saluted with the grenade. "Drinking, sir. Beer, sir."

"I'm not blind, Private. I'm talking about the frag."

Freeze looked at the grenade. He had pulled the pin after his first six-pack. If he let go of the firing lever, he'd have only four and a half seconds to make out his will. *I, Mick Harris, being of unsound mind and body . . .* He laughed.

There were red blotches on the lieutenant's white face now. "What's so funny, hand job?"

Freeze laughed again. He closed his eyes, woozy, and shrugged his shoulders. "You," he said. "Me."

Reynolds stiffened. "I'm ordering you to dispose of that frag immediately and safely."

"Can't," Freeze said. "Beer tastes like piss without it." He raised the bottle to his lips.

When he lowered it, the lieutenant had disappeared. Freeze looked around but didn't see him anywhere. Maybe he'd never been there. Maybe he'd imagined it all. He took another long drink from the bottle, concentrating on his sweaty fingers gripping the firing lever. His hand was starting to go numb. It was almost like it was dissolving, disappearing. When he finished his drink, he looked at his hand. It was still there.

As he tilted the bottle back to take another drink, he heard someone say, "Here's the son of a bitch." He squinted toward the voice. The brown-bar was back, a sneer on his face. There was another face too, but this one was grinning. It was an MP. He had a harelip that made his grin look like it was splitting his face. Freeze imagined his face cracking like an egg and laughed.

Then the MP lunged at Freeze, grabbing his hand and twisting it behind his back. The sudden pain made Freeze groan and drop the beer in his other hand. While he looked down at the bottle foaming on the red dirt, the MP pried his fingers open. Then the pain was gone and Freeze looked up. The MP stuck the grenade in Freeze's face and grinned. "My turn to play with this," he said.

Reynolds said, "Cut that shit. Just toss the frag out on the perimeter, then take this soldier to the stockade and let him sleep it off. I'll deal with him in the morning." Then he turned and strode away.

*Frigging brown-bar*, Freeze thought, and imagined him stepping on a mine and blowing into a hundred pieces.

Only later, after the harelip had hauled him to the stockade and asked him his name, company, platoon, and squad, did Freeze find out that the brown-bar was his new platoon leader. "Your ass is gonna be grass come morning," the MP said, laughing. "Reynolds, he's your new LT." But Freeze didn't care. What could the bastard do to him? Send him to Nam? All he wanted to do was sleep. Sleep and dream. When he woke up, everything would be clear again, everything would be back to normal.

But the next morning he felt worse. He'd been dreaming about a mummy he'd seen in a museum when he was a kid. The mummy was the color of caramel, and in his dream he'd broken off one of its toes and taken a bite. Then a gum-chewing guard woke him, and for a moment he thought the guard had taken a bite too. "Feeling all bright-eyed and bushy-tailed this morning, Private?" another voice said, and Freeze turned toward it: Reynolds, grinning.

The lieutenant tossed some wrinkled fatigues onto Freeze's cot. "Get up and get dressed," he said. "You've got a party to go to, and you're the guest of honor." Then he told Freeze that he and Konieczny were to report to the privies by 0700 for shit-burning detail.

Freeze sat up slowly, his head heavy and aching. "*Konieczny?*" he said.

Konieczny was the big, red-haired recruit just off the bus from Bien Hoa. It was bad enough to put him in the stockade, but to treat him like that twink Konieczny . . . He'd spent ten months in-country—*ten fucking months*—and he'd walked point for the first three. Nobody in his company had walked point that long, and they gave him a badge just for having survived. And now this new brown-bar was treating him like a goddamn twink.

"That's right. Since he's a new recruit, I thought you could teach him some of the finer points of shit-burning. Now chop-chop," Reynolds said, then turned and left.

"You heard the man," the guard said, then went back to chewing his gum.

Freeze watched the guard chew. *Eat death*, he thought, and smiled to himself. *Chew that gristle down.*

He tried to stand then, but his head was pounding so hard he sat back on the cot with a moan. He stayed there, dizzy, for a moment, then stood slowly and dressed. Each movement made his head throb.

When Freeze finished tying his boots, the guard escorted him back to barracks. Though it was still early, it was already so hot that Freeze's shirt had soaked through by the time they got there. The guard said, "Enjoy your party," and left. Freeze opened the screen door and went inside. It wasn't much cooler in the hootch. All the men were shirtless, but their chests were still wet with sweat. Some of them had pulled their footlockers out into the middle of the wooden plank floor and were sitting on them playing cards and drinking Cokes or smoking joints. A few were lying on their racks reading magazines or letters. Others were talking and laughing about some photograph they were passing around. When they looked up and saw Freeze, they went quiet for a moment. Then Jackson put down his cards and said, "You okay, man?"

That's what he'd said after Freeze had stepped on the mine. He'd come up to him, put his hand on his shoulder, and said, "Hey man, you okay?" Over and over, "You okay?" When Freeze had finally been able to answer, he told Jackson to fuck off, he was all right, leave him alone. But Jackson didn't back off. None of them did. For the rest of the patrol, they all stayed close to him, thinking they were safe if they were around him. He had the magic, they said, the luck. He wasn't going to get greased. The mine had proved that. So they stuck close to Freeze until finally he turned his M-16 on them and said he'd shoot the next mother who came near.

Now Freeze looked at Jackson, then at the others. Once he had been closer to these guys than to anybody in his whole life.

But ever since he'd stepped on the mine they had seemed like strangers. He felt like he'd walked into someone else's barracks, someone else's life.

"Yeah," he said to Jackson. "I'm okay." Then he crossed over to his rack and pulled off his drenched shirt. Kneeling down, he started to dig through his bamboo footlocker.

"I hear you and Konieczny are going to a party," Clean Machine said, then laughed. "Some people have all the luck."

Freeze looked at him, but he didn't say anything.

Duckwalk sat down on Freeze's rack. "I hope you're doing all right," he said. "We been worried about you, bro."

Freeze didn't answer. He was trying to remember what he was looking for in his footlocker. Then it came to him: cotton. He found some in the neck of an aspirin bottle and tore off two chunks. Then he stood and turned to Konieczny, who was waiting in front of his rack, smiling uneasily. "What're you laughing at, twink?" he said. Konieczny just stood there, looking confused.

"Ain't nobody laughing," Boswell said, and pushed his Stetson back on his head. "Ain't nothing funny here." Then he looked at Jackson. "You want to finish this hand, pardner? 'Cause if you don't I'll be plenty happy to pick up that pot."

Jackson looked at Freeze, his forehead creased. "You still with us?" he asked.

"What's it to you?" Freeze said.

Jackson looked down and shook his head, then he picked up his cards and turned back to the game.

Freeze went outside then and stood in the heat, his head pounding. He wanted to go back to sleep. Maybe when he woke up he would be Mick again, not Freeze, and the mine would be just a bad dream.

In a moment, Konieczny joined him and they marched in silence up the hill to the latrine, each of them humping a can of diesel fuel. When they got there, Freeze stuffed the cotton up his nostrils, glaring at Konieczny all the while. Then they lifted the shelter off its blocks, exposing the fifty-five gallon drums cut in half, and started to soak the shit with fuel.

"Jesus," Konieczny said. "This is number ten."

Freeze didn't say anything; he was thinking how much he hated Reynolds for making him do this. If the son of a bitch was here right now, he'd throw him into the shit barbecue. Lieutenant Crispy Critter. He smiled as he poured the fuel into the latrine.

"Make that ten thousand," Konieczny said, his hand over his nose and mouth.

Though it was still early, the day was so hot and humid that the air seemed too thick to breathe. Freeze was breathing through his open mouth because of the cotton in his nose, and it felt like he was suffocating. His head throbbed and his stomach felt queasy. Then the smell of the diesel fumes and the shit suddenly penetrated the cotton and made him drop to his knees. With a noise like a bark, he vomited onto the red dirt between his trembling palms.

"You all right?" Konieczny asked, leaning over him.

Freeze wiped his mouth and looked up at Konieczny's face, its freckles and peachfuzz and acne. The twink would be lucky if he lasted a week in the bush. Freeze could see him tripping a mine and blowing into the air, his body cut in half. He remembered how Perkins had looked after he triggered a Bouncing Betty. He'd had his wet intestines in his hands, and he was trying to put them back in. Or had Freeze just dreamed that?

He looked away, squinting in the sun. "Fuck you," he answered.

"Just trying to help," the kid said. He shrugged his shoulders and turned back to the work.

Freeze stood, his legs quivering. He thought about saying he was sorry, but then he'd have to explain and he didn't know how to explain or even what to explain. So they finished soaking the shit without talking, then dropped matches on it. Black smoke curdled out of the pit, and the stench made them gag. Standing there beside the blaze, his eyes burning, head swimming, Freeze almost threw up again. And later, back in the hootch, he lay on his rack, the stink of the burning shit still thick in his nostrils, and heaved his guts into a C-rats can. His heart was beating fast, like it did when they were in a fire fight. What had happened? He'd been a strack soldier for ten months, an assistant squad leader—leader of the first fire team—for the past four, ever since C.B. got zapped. And now he was a shit-burner. God, how he hated that frigging brown-bar.

Hating the lieutenant made him feel better than he had since he'd stepped on the mine; it made things seem more real, more logical. So he stoked his hate, made it grow. Everything was Reynolds' fault. Reynolds was the evil heart of it all. If it wasn't for him, he'd be happy now, he'd be one of the guys again, nothing would have changed. The bastard was worse than Charlie.

Lying there on his canvas cot, Freeze imagined Reynolds walking point through knee-high brush. Then he saw him stop dead. He'd felt something under his boot. For a second, stupidly, Reynolds thought it was a scorpion, or a rock, but then he felt the pin sink and he knew it was the metal prong of a Bouncing Betty. Before he could move, or even think, the mine flew up out of the ground with a pop. Reynolds closed his eyes and covered his head with his hands, and for a moment, a moment that stretched out until it was outside of time, he waited for the explosion of light, the thundering roar, the hail of shrapnel. Then the moment ended and the Bouncing Betty fell back at his feet, dead. The main charge hadn't gone off. Reynolds opened his eyes and stood there for several minutes, panting hard, the sweat rolling off his face and dripping onto the mine, his eyes staring into ozone. *Hey*, his men would say later, *you should have seen the brown-bar freeze.*

Freeze planned his revenge all afternoon. Then, an hour or so before dusk, he saw Reynolds go into the officers' club. After waiting a few minutes to be sure he wasn't coming back out, he snuck into Reynolds' quarters. He had planned to fire a single pistol shot into his pillow and leave, but once he was there, that plan seemed too dangerous, even crazy. He had to do something, though, so he stole the two officer-grade steaks Reynolds had in his refrigerator. He stuffed them inside his shirt and left, almost giddy. He could just see the look on Reynolds' face when he saw the steaks were missing.

Back in the hootch, Freeze put the smaller steak up for auction. He stood on his footlocker and dangled the slab in front of his squad. "What am I bid for this hunk of heaven?" he said.

Duckwalk was sitting on his rack, cleaning an AK-47 he'd souvenired from an NVA. He shook his head. "The LT's gonna fuck you, Freeze," he said.

"You'll have his steaks for supper, but he'll have your ass for breakfast," Jackson agreed. "He's gonna know you swiped his meat." He took another drag on his joint and went back to playing solitaire on his footlocker.

Everybody was trying to act uninterested, but Freeze knew better. He knew how long it had been since anybody'd had a steak. To them, even the warm Cokes they got every stand-down were bennies.

"Let's start the bidding at a bag of el primo no-stem, no-seed, shall we?" he said and grinned. He was having fun. He had crossed over the edge of hatred and now he was having fun. He could barely keep from laughing.

"Are you nuts?" said McKeown. "We buy that hot cow and we're in as much trouble as you."

"Smoke my pole," Boswell said.

"Shit," Clean Machine said. "I wouldn't give one joint for your sister and your mother both."

But before long, McKeown offered a pack of Park Lanes and soon they were all bidding. When it was over, Clean had shelled out four packs of Park Lanes and a handful of military payment certificates for the steak. Freeze stashed his loot under the floorboard beneath his rack, then ditty-bopped out to the perimeter where nobody could see him and hunkered down in some brush to broil his steak. He lit a tin of Sterno and set it over a little stove he'd made by puncturing an empty C-rats can. Then he started to broil the steak on a steel plate he'd ripped off the back of a Claymore mine.

Smelling the steak browning on the plate, he forgot the stench of the burning shit for the first time that day. He leaned back on one elbow, lit a Park Lane, and inhaled deeply, holding the smoke in his lungs. As he smoked, he looked out over the brush at the lead-colored sky and tried to daydream about going back to the world. He imagined he was back in Little Rock, lying on a lounge chair beside his apartment pool, catching some rays and checking out the talent. But the daydream began to unravel as soon as it started. First he couldn't remember what his pool had looked like. Then he wasn't even sure whether he'd had a pool at Cromwell Court or if that was earlier, at the Cantrell Apartments. And the girls that strolled by in their bikinis were faceless, vague. He tried to remember Mary Ellen, the girl he'd dated the fall before he enlisted, but nothing would come to him. He wasn't sure of the color of her eyes or hair, the sound of her voice. He laughed. Then he listened to himself laugh. It was such a strange sound. He wondered why he'd never noticed how strange it was. He tried to remember Mary Ellen's laugh, but it was no use. Ever since he'd come to Nam he'd been forgetting things, and now almost everything was gone. And what he did remember seemed more like something he'd overheard in a bar, some dim, muffled conversation. He couldn't have seen Perkins holding his plastic yellow guts, or C.B.'s brains in his mouth, the top of his skull turned to pulp. He couldn't have seen these things. It was impossible. Wasn't Perkins transferred to another company? Hadn't C.B. gone back to the world?

By the time Freeze finally remembered to turn over the steak, it had burned black.

After lights out, a heavy monsoon rain began to beat against the ponchos nailed on the outside of the hootch. The wind whipped the water against the green plastic, battering the hootch like incoming.

Then it *was* incoming. Duckwalk sat up in the rack next to Freeze's. "You hear that?" he asked.

Freeze sat up, his poncho liner wrapped around him.

"Not tonight, Charlie," Jackson moaned, "I'm having me a wet dream."

They listened as the mortars walked in closer and closer. At first there was only a distant pop, then a closer thud. Then they heard the whistling of a round and the roar of an explosion.

"Shit," Freeze said. And he and the rest of the men scrambled out of their racks, grabbing their M-16s, and double-timed in their skivvies out into the cold pounding rain. Through the rain's thick odor of rot, they could smell the sharp scents of gunpowder and cordite. On the perimeter of the camp, M-79 grenade launchers and mortars were thumping into a sky green with star flares, punctuating the nonstop sentence of an M-16 on rock-'n'-roll.

In the platoon bunker, they huddled behind the wet sandbags, shivering, staring out at the dark. Konieczny was next to Freeze. "Are they gonna come through the wire?" he asked. When a star flare burst, his face turned green, a Martian's, and Freeze felt the urge to laugh. Then he heard the whistle of an incoming round. He ducked and waited for the burst. It seemed to take forever. Looking around, he saw that everyone was still, as if they'd been frozen. He remembered the game he'd played as a kid back in Arkansas. Statues. It was like they were playing Statues.

Then the shell exploded nearby, raining shrapnel into the bunker, and everybody came alive again. Somebody started screaming.

Reynolds stood up at his end of the bunker. "Who's down?"

Everybody looked around. But no one was hurt. Then the screaming started again. It was coming from outside the bunker.

"I'm dying!" the man yelled. "Help me!"

Before anyone could say anything, Reynolds had crawled out of the bunker and started to run in a crouch toward a man lying in the mud halfway between the second platoon hootch and bunker. Under the light of the star flares, Freeze watched the brown-bar drag the man toward their bunker. For a second he admired Reynolds for rescuing the soldier when he could have ordered someone else to do it, but then he felt the comforting return of hate. *The hotdog*, he thought. *He's bucking for goddamn Eagle Scout.*

The moment Reynolds made it back, they heard the whistle of another mortar and ducked, holding their breaths until it exploded. Then they looked up.

Someone shined his flashlight on the man. "Jesus H. Christ," Reynolds said then, and turned away, disgusted. The man was all right. He hadn't been hit at all. Still, he was moaning as if he were dying.

"Save me," the soldier pleaded. "Don't let me die. I don't want to die." It was clear that he wasn't talking to anybody there. He was staring up at the sky, his eyes blank as milk glass, and whimpering. And he wasn't even a twink. He'd been in the bush long enough to get a bad case of jungle rot. It had invaded his face, and though he'd tried to hide it by growing a scruffy beard, it made his skin look raw.

They told him he was okay, but he kept on moaning and crying. Even after the mortars stopped falling and the machine guns faded to random bursts, he would not stop.

The rest of the men looked away, embarrassed, but Freeze couldn't take his eyes off him.

The next morning, the other soldiers were laughing about the man who thought he was wounded, calling him a snuffy, a wuss, and praising Reynolds for risking his butt to save him. They even had a nickname for Reynolds now. "Man, did you see the look he gave that pogue?" Jackson had said. "It was righteous rabid." And it stuck. All the while they prepared for inspection, the men talked about Righteous Rabid and The Wuss. A week before, Freeze would have joined in. But he wasn't one of them anymore.

At inspection, Reynolds stopped in front of Freeze and poked him in the gut with his finger. "Private Harris," he said, "you look like you've put on a couple of pounds since yesterday." He looked Freeze in the eye. "Maybe you had an extra helping of ham and mothers? Or maybe the entire platoon gave you their cookies?"

Freeze stood there a moment. For some reason he was suddenly sleepy. He wanted to lie down and go to sleep right there on the floor of the hootch.

"I'm talking to you, Private," Reynolds said.

Freeze just stood there. He was so tired he didn't even have the energy to lie.

"So you did do it," Reynolds said. Then he put his face in Freeze's. "I'm going to report this little incident to Captain Arnold, and I'm going to recommend that you receive an Article 15. If I have my way, he'll bust your ass to E-1." Reynolds sneered. "But until then you can party. How does filling sandbags sound for starters?"

A mortar shell had blasted through the first layer of sandbags during the attack and ripped into the second layer, spilling sand like guts. It would take hours to fill enough sandbags to repair the bunker, and it was going to be another hundred and ten degree day. Already the sun was burning off the puddles left by the rain.

Freeze stared at the blue vein that popped out on Reynolds' forehead, between his eyes, a perfect target. "It sounds like shit," he heard someone say. It was a second before he realized he was the one who said it.

Reynolds stiffened.

"What did you say, pogue?"

Freeze said, "Cut me some slack."

Reynolds' eyes narrowed. "Maybe one Article 15 isn't enough for you, Harris. Maybe you'd like another."

Freeze stared at him. He was trying to hate him, trying to recapture the way he'd felt when he stole the steaks, but he couldn't get it back. He wanted it back desperately, but it wouldn't come. After a moment he looked down.

"No, I didn't think you'd want any more," Reynolds said then, stepping back and smiling. "I figured you'd had enough."

The rest of that morning, Freeze filled sandbags in the dizzying heat, his back and shoulders aching, while a fat-ass MP named Hulsey stood by the bunker, throwing his walnut baton into the air and catching it. He was trying to see how many times he could spin the baton and still catch it. So far his record was six revolutions. Whenever he dropped the baton, he'd say "Uncle fucking Ho" and spit. Freeze stood, stretching his stiff back, and watched the MP fling the baton. He shook his head. He'd come halfway around the world to watch a man toss a baton into the air and try to catch it. And the MP had made the same trip to watch a man shovel sand. Freeze wanted to tell him how crazy it was, maybe suggest they go get a beer, but the MP caught the baton and said, "*Seven. A new record! Let's hear it for the boy from Brooklyn.*" Freeze turned back to his work.

He finished repairing the bunker just before noon. He thought the brown-bar was done with him then, but after lunch, Reynolds gave him more scutwork to do. He mopped the barracks, unloaded ammo crates from a deuce-and-a-half truck, and then helped carry the wounded from medevac helicopters, humping stretchers down the metal ramp to the deck, where medics sorted the living from the dead. He was so exhausted from working in the heat that he could barely stand in the prop wash of the helicopters. He staggered in the hot wind, gravel swarming around him, stinging like hornets, and felt his hatred for Reynolds rise almost to madness. He knew Reynolds was just making an example of him, using him to prove to the others that he was in charge and wouldn't take any shit, and he knew he'd back off as soon as he felt he'd made his point. But Freeze didn't care. He still hated him. The bastard had treated him like a dead man's turd ever since he came. He'd embarrassed him in front of his best friends, he'd turned them against him. He could hear the men now, talking and laughing about Righteous Rabid and Freeze. Well, he'd give them something to talk about. When they got out in the bush, he'd frag the son of a bitch. This decision made him feel suddenly calm, even happy, but then he saw Reynolds lying dead on the jungle floor, his eyes open to nothing, his face mottled with shadows cast by the sunlight flickering through the trees, and everything was as confused as a dream again because Reynolds was wearing Freeze's fatigues and he was smiling. Grinning. Almost laughing. Freeze stood there in the prop wash until his partner yelled from the chopper's cargo bay for him to hurry up and give him a hand.

A few minutes later, as he bent to pick up his end of a stretcher, he saw that one of the grunt's legs had been blown off just below the knee and that the other was terribly mangled. Someone had laid the severed leg on top of him. He had his arms around it, holding it to his chest, and he was staring off somewhere, a slight smile frozen on his lips, as if he'd just heard something mildly funny.

"Heavy fucker, ain't he?" Freeze's partner said, as they hoisted the stretcher.

The next day the stand-down ended and the company was sent back out on line. They stood inspection, marched to the air field, climbed aboard the choppers and flew north over the jungle, finally setting down in the brush and bamboo of Tay Ninh province. Freeze was glad to be in the bush; he'd rather be in the shit, where all you had to worry about was someone greasing you, than in camp, where pogue officers like Reynolds policed your every move. He figured that Reynolds would let up on him now, but if he didn't, Freeze would pick his moment and frag his ass.

Reynolds didn't let up. The first day after they'd finished carving Fire Base Molly out of the jungle, stripping the foliage down to the bare dirt, digging bunkers, and stringing coils of concertina wire around the perimeter, he dispatched Freeze, Konieczny, and Clean to secure a helicopter supply drop for a tank column—three men to defend thousands of gallons of diesel fuel and tons of ammo.

"One dink with a hand grenade could blow the whole damn drop to Saigon," Freeze complained, though he didn't really care.

Reynolds looked at him. "The tank column is due at 1900 hours. Saddle up." Then he turned and walked away.

Freeze raised his hand and sighted down his index finger at the lieutenant's back. *Bang.*

Duckwalk turned to him, his thumbs hooked behind the silver buckle of the NVA belt he'd souvenired from a sniper. "Relax, bro," he said. "He's just the Army. What you expect him to do—be your friend?"

Freeze didn't say anything. He shouldered his pack and headed out toward the supply drop with Konieczny and Clean. When they got there, Konieczny sat on one of the crates and radioed back to Reynolds. Freeze broke open another crate. "Chocolate milk," he said, taking out a carton and shaking his head. "Chocolate fucking milk."

"What's your problem, Freeze?" Clean said. "I'm getting sick of this shit. We're all getting sick of it."

Freeze looked at Clean. Then he opened the carton and took a drink. When he finished, he wiped his mouth with the back of his hand. "Whatever you do," he said, "don't let this milk fall into enemy hands."

Then he turned and humped off into a stand of bamboo a couple of hundred meters away and crawled down into a crater left by a mortar shell. He lay there, smoking a Park Lane, and thought about greasing Reynolds. He had to be careful; if he got caught, they'd put him in Long Binh Jail and the only world he'd go back to would be Leavenworth. But even that might be worth it. He imagined Reynolds face-down on the ground, his brains leaking out his open mouth. As soon as Reynolds was dead, he could rest. Everything would make sense again and he'd be at peace. He took out another joint and smoked it. The sun bore down on him, its heat a heavy weight, and soon he fell asleep.

He didn't wake until he felt the ground tremble and heard the steel rumble of the tanks. The sun was hovering over the edge of the horizon, staining the countryside a dusty red. Climbing out of the crater, he sauntered back to the supply drop. He came up to Konieczny and Clean just as the tanks rolled over the rise.

Clean looked at him. "Thanks for your fucking help."

Konieczny looked down the road and didn't say anything.

Freeze didn't know Clean had reported him until the next day, when Reynolds led the platoon on a reconnaissance-in-force. They humped through the jungle all morning, sweating under their packs; then, toward midday, they smelled shit cooking in the heat.

It had to be an NVA camp. Through a stand of bamboo, they spotted a row of bunkers. Reynolds ordered Freeze's fire team to go in first, and they approached in a cloverleaf pattern. But the camp was abandoned. Bombers had attacked it, probably no more than a week before, and there were tank-sized craters everywhere. In a few places, the ground was still white from the phosphorous the spotter plane had dropped to give the B-52s their target. There was no sign of the NVA anywhere. Still, Reynolds ordered Freeze to check out a bunker that hadn't been caved in by the bombs.

"It's crawling with fire ants," Freeze said. "There's no gooks in there."

"I said check it out, Harris."

"Why me?" Freeze said.

Reynolds glared at him. "Yesterday I gave you a direct order, and you subverted it. It will not happen again."

Freeze looked at Konieczny, then at Clean. Clean crossed his arms on his chest and looked back.

So Freeze climbed down and checked the bunker out, and when he came scrambling out a moment later, the ants were all over him. He jumped up and down, swatting and swiping at the red sons of bitches, while the men laughed at him.

"You bastard," Freeze said to Reynolds. "You motherfucking bastard. I'm not going to eat any more of your shit."

"Oh yes you will," Reynolds said. "You'll eat it. You'll lick your plate clean, and you'll ask for more."

Freeze stood there, breathing hate, and stared at Reynolds, an animal snarl on his face. He hated him more than he'd ever hated the NVA. He hated him more than the heat and the jungle, the leeches and mosquitoes, the monsoon rains, the smells of sulfur and shit and death, more than his sixty-pound pack, the blisters on his shoulders, the wet socks, the jungle rot and immersion foot, more than the lizards that cried *fuck you, fuck you* in the night, the thump of mortars, the booby traps, more even than the mine that hadn't gone off.

"That's a negative," Freeze said, and before Reynolds could

move, he snapped the bolt of his M-16, chambering a round, and shoved the flash suppressor into his belly, just under his ribs. The blood was drumming in his temples.

Reynolds sucked in a breath. The men stepped back. "Holy shit," Konieczny said.

"Take it easy, bro," Jackson said. "Everybody's watching. You don't want to do nothing when everybody's watching."

Freeze ignored him. He stared at Reynolds. Reynolds opened his mouth to say something, but no words came out. He closed and opened it again. Sweat began to bead on his upper lip. Freeze focused on one of the beads, and waited for it to slide down his lip and break. But it didn't move. It hung there, as if time had stopped, as if there were no more time.

Then everything went out of Freeze. What was he so angry about? It didn't mean anything anymore. It didn't seem real. Nothing seemed real. The drop of sweat. The circle of men staring at him like he was a gook. Reynolds. He looked around at the craters that surrounded them. They could be on the moon. He lowered his rifle and sat down in the red dust, suddenly dizzy. His hands were trembling.

Then Reynolds blinked and swallowed hard. He looked around him and finally found words. "Konieczny," he said, his voice shaking slightly, "get on the horn to HQ. We need to call in a chopper to remove Private Harris to the stockade."

Konieczny said, "Yes sir" and began to call headquarters.

Reynolds looked down at Freeze then and, squaring his shoulders, said, in a voice that shook now more with anger than fear, "Get this son of a bitch out of my sight. Get him out of here before I kill him."

But Freeze didn't hear him. He wasn't there. He had stepped on the mine and he was rising into the air, twisting and turning in the bursting light for one last peaceful second.

# THE STARS AT NOON

## 1

She had been sleeping, it seemed, then she heard someone cough. Who is coughing? she thought. Then she realized: it was herself.

Silly old woman. Silly half-dead old woman.

Then she noticed that she was sitting up. Why? She looked around the hospital room. The vaporizer breathing the menthol odor of death. The late afternoon light on the linoleum like the outline of someone killed in a highway accident.

Anastasia shivered. Why did she have to think such thoughts? This was no time to think like that. This was a time for joy.

She lay back into herself, hugged the chill inside her. It wouldn't be long now.

Now what was that? Nurses talking in the hallway? She raised her head from the pillow and strained to hear what they were saying. But she couldn't make out the words over the hiss of the vaporizer, so she lay back.

Then it wasn't nurses talking. It was cicadas buzzing in the trees around her father's farm.

She'd heard that ratcheting hum every August when she was growing up. Once, she and Tom collected the brittle, umber-colored husks left in the elms after the humming stopped. She stood under each tree holding one of their father's empty cigar boxes while Tom shinnied up and found the desiccated husks. At first he crushed a lot of them, they were so fragile; later, he learned how to cradle them in his palm.

She had that cigar box full of them somewhere. Where?

And who was this?

The nurse's face hung before her like a question waiting to be answered. "Sister Anastasia? Are you awake?"

Why did nurses wear white, nuns black?

"You have a visitor, Sister."

Hovering beside her in the half-light: Sister Beatrice. The children are right. We do look like blackbirds. She watched Beatrice pull a white handkerchief out of her black sleeve and blow her nose. The old nun laughed, then coughed. She hugged her ribs until she stopped coughing.

Was this how Tom had felt? Dry and ready to crumble?

"Sister Anastasia?"

It was that big-nosed nurse again. What do you want now?

"It's time for your afternoon chest rub, but I'll wait till you're through visiting. Whenever you're done, just buzz for me, okay?"

He would drop down from the tree with his hands full of husks.

"I'm dying," she said, but Tom was gone.

"Pardon me?" a voice said. "Did you say something, Sister?"

Anastasia turned to the voice's face: it was Sister Beatrice. Then she laughed. A blackbird with wire-rimmed glasses. She had to tell the children.

The children—she had almost forgotten the children. How they would suffer when they heard she was dead! She remembered how hard they had cried last spring, when the touring company of the Black Hills Passion Play performed the crucifixion at their school, and she imagined them at her funeral: the boys, bravely blinking, and the girls, their faces in their hands.

What was she thinking of? How could she think such a thing?

"I am an old sinner," she whispered. "Forgive me."

"For what?" Beatrice asked. "You've never done anything to hurt me. You know that."

Anastasia looked at the young nun. She was about to explain, but the coughing started again. When it was over, Anastasia was sitting up. Beatrice helped her lie back.

"Are you all right?" Beatrice worried.

"I need a priest," Anastasia said. She'd been asking for Last Rites for two days, but all she'd received were more pain pills. "Call Father Switzer. Please."

"Don't you talk like that," Beatrice scolded. "Dr. Gaertner says you'll be fine in a week or so. You're going to be under the weather awhile, but what do you expect when you don't wear your shawl when you should? You can't say we didn't warn you—and time and again."

Anastasia smiled at her stern look. No wonder her children ignored her when she disciplined them: no matter how hard she tried, she couldn't look angry, not with that baby face.

Then Beatrice's chin began to quiver and the stern look dissolved. Taking out her handkerchief, she turned away. "I'm sorry, Sister," she said. "I shouldn't cry; there's nothing to cry about." Then she began to cry even harder. She turned back to Anastasia. "Oh, Sister, I hate to see you so sick!" she sobbed, and threw her arms around her.

Beatrice's wide wimple blocked the last bit of light from the hospital window, and Anastasia felt the darkness settling around her. She had been waiting for it, and it had finally come. She breathed it in, felt it fill her hollow cheeks and lungs.

But Beatrice rose, wiping her tears, and the light came back.

"I'm not supposed to tell you this," she said, "but I will. We're planning a big birthday party for you when you get back. We're going to decorate the lunchroom with balloons and crepe paper and signs, and the kids are going to sing 'Happy Birthday,' and then we're going to have cake and ice cream and play some games. Sister Rose is going to bake a huge cake, and I'm going to decorate it. I had the best idea ever: I'm going to spell out your name with candles! Can't you just imagine how beautiful it'll look when all the candles are lit?"

If a candle was still burning after you tried to blow it out, that meant you had a secret boyfriend. And if the stem of your apple snapped on the third twist, that meant his name began with C.

A young man was once in love with me, Anastasia said. Or did she? Sister Beatrice did not seem to hear. "I know I shouldn't have told you," Beatrice was saying. "It was supposed to be a surprise and everything, but I just wanted you to know how much we care about you."

She shouldn't be thinking about Carl now: she didn't want to spoil her death with thoughts of old boyfriends. She was a nun, not a housewife. But everyone else who knew her when she was young was dead: Tom was dead, Mother and Father, her friends. Everyone. Carl was the only one left who would remember what she was like when she was a little girl.

Why did that matter?

The fall from innocence was fortunate; it was sinful to regret it. Adam and Eve banished to Heaven. The discarded apple making cider in its bruises.

What now?

Beatrice was patting her hand. Nice puppy.

"All the kids miss you terribly, and so do we," she said. "I know Antoinette Marie is short-tempered with you sometimes, but she doesn't mean anything by it, and she misses you as much as Camilla and Rose and I do. And Father Switzer—you know you've always been his favorite. Just this morning he said he can't wait to see your smiling face again."

Anastasia thought she heard Father Switzer's lisping Latin. She rose to her elbows. He's finally here. It's finally time. She looked around the room for his shock of blond hair and boyish face.

But it was only the vaporizer, hissing its dark litany. What a foolish woman! Anastasia lay back into a laugh. She knew she'd start coughing again, but she didn't care. It was too funny. *She* was too funny.

"What is it?" Beatrice asked.

Anastasia crossed her hands at her neck, trying to strangle the cough before it began. But it began anyway, and she coughed until she was dizzy, until green and gold burned neon under her eyelids.

She thought: so much pain. But what was this compared to the agony in the garden, the sweating of blood, the scourging, the crowning with thorns, the crucifixion and death? No, it was wrong to complain about a little cough. Her suffering was meaningless. She wished she could cough blood, to make herself more worthy of death.

"Are you feeling all right now?" Beatrice said. She was wiping the old nun's face with a hand towel.

Anastasia couldn't speak for a moment, and when she did, the words seemed heavy, as if she had to draw them up from deep in her lungs. "I don't know how to die," she said.

"You're not going to die, Sister. You're just sick and overtired, that's all. You'll be back to normal in no time."

The laity at least had the luxury of making wills, disposing of property. But she had nothing to will, she had given everything, even her will, away. *Be it done unto me according to Thy word.* All these years she had been exhilarated by that surrender, and her subsequent nothingness, but now she was frightened. She remembered the afternoon Tom lowered her into Grandpa Emery's dry well so she could see the stars: only from the vantage point of darkness could you see the light buried within the light. And she had married the darkness, worn its black habit, so she could be reborn into that light. But what if she had not really surrendered but only given up?

After Tom died, she was the dead one. His absence was so complete it was presence, but no one noticed her, the true ghost. Father sat on the porch rocker, smoking and staring into the night, never saying anything about him or even mentioning his name. But Mother couldn't talk about anything else. She'd sit in the kitchen and talk for hours with Mrs. Willoughby about him. He was born to be a priest, she'd say. When he was little, he'd pin a dishtowel around his neck like a chasuble and pretend to celebrate

Mass, distributing cookies to the neighbor children as if they were Hosts. And he was always praying. Sometimes he'd even talk to his guardian angel as if he could really see him.

How could she tell her parents she too was no longer of this world? Something had died in her when Tom had died, but something had been born, too. A vocation. She stood in front of her bedroom mirror and practiced her announcement for days before she finally told them.

"You must be cold, Sister. Your lips look a little blue. Do you want me to get you another blanket?"

Tom had not been afraid of death and neither was she. But she was almost ashamed to die. Tom was so young, he might not even recognize her. He had been only seventeen when he died. A year later, her first in the convent, she was seventeen too, and all that year she had cherished the thought that they were twins, in a way. But now she was old enough to be his grandmother.

"Why, you *are* cold. And it's so warm in here!"

Just then a cough caught in her larynx, choking her. She opened her mouth and gulped, but there was no air. She gulped until her ears rang, until air no longer mattered, and then she lay quietly, watching Beatrice's white hands flutter about her wimple.

What was that silly girl so excited about?

Then Beatrice lifted her up and her breath came back in sobs. Each swallow of saliva scalded her throat.

"Oh, Sister, are you all right?"

She had almost touched bottom that time. She had come so close, so very close, and Beatrice had ruined it.

Beatrice's lip was quivering now. "I hate to see you like this," she said. "You mean so much to me . . ."

Anastasia lay back. I want to die now. Why won't you leave me alone?

"You've been like a mother to me. I don't know what—"

"I'm just an old nun," Anastasia snapped. "I'm not your mother."

"What's wrong?" Beatrice asked. "Did I say something wrong? I didn't mean—"

"Why don't you just go away? Can't you see I'm tired?"

Beatrice took out her handkerchief again. Tears, tears. Won't she ever stop?

"I'm sorry, Sister, it's just that I love you."

"What do you know about love?" Anastasia said. And she remembered how once, when they were playing Statues, Carl kissed her to make her come alive, and she fell giggling into grass so green it shone. But that was before, that was when they were still children. Years later, he took her for a buggy ride behind her father's big chestnut mare and, stopping in the woods, kissed her twice before she could say a word. All the way home, the wind lifted the pale underbellies of poplar leaves, and the woods purred.

But the last time she let him kiss her was the Sunday before Tom died. It had rained while they were in church that morning, and the hay in the loft smelled pungent and musty. It was the smell of loam, of a freshly dug grave, and each time Carl kissed her, he drove her deeper into the hay, deeper into the smell, until she couldn't breathe. She thought of Tom lying in his hospital bed, and asked God to take her instead of him. He was the good one, the holy one: he should live, not her. All the while Carl kissed her, she prayed for her death. She let him kiss her a long time, until he began to moan with the desire to do more. His moans confused her: they sounded like Tom's, though they came from pleasure instead of pain. That didn't make sense to her. But nothing made sense to her anymore, except her desire to die in Tom's place.

After Carl left, she went to her room and waited for her parents to come home from the hospital. By the time they returned, she had a fever, but she did not tell them: it was her secret, her private miracle. She wept herself to sleep, imagining her funeral. But the next day her fever was gone, and four days after that, Tom was dead.

Beatrice was drying her eyes again. "I don't understand," she said. "You've always said you loved me like a daughter. So why can't I say you've been like a mother to me?"

Later she went to the loft alone and lay in the one window's shaft of sun, sweating in the prickly hay. Dervishes of dust spun in the stained light, descending on her with an almost suffocating weight. She had never realized how omnipresent, nor how active, the dust was.

"Maybe you wish I didn't love you," Beatrice sniffled. "But I do, and I always will."

Anastasia looked at her. She was young and pretty, her whole life ahead of her. She'd never pray to die in her place. She'd never beg God to let her lie on this bed, her skin wrinkled and liver-spotted, her lungs congested with pneumonia, her heart running down like a clock.

"No, you don't," she said.

"Why are you saying these things to me? You know I love you."

Anastasia tried to answer, but she couldn't. Where was her breath? She tried to cough, to open her lungs, but the noiseless spasms only made her throat hurt. It ached the way it did when her children knelt at the communion rail for the first time and stuck out their tongues for the Host. There was a throb at the root of her tongue, a desire. But for what?

Then she coughed so hard that something seemed to snap in her chest. A knot of phlegm humped onto her tongue. It tasted like rust.

Beatrice's face wavered in front of her, stippled with sweat. "Please be all right, Sister. Please."

Anastasia spat onto the bedspread and turned to the wall.

At the wake, old ladies dressed in black hovered in the vestibule like crows. They hugged her and said they were so very sorry, Tom was such a fine young man, he would have made a wonderful priest. Their mouths were crumbling, their yellow skin smelled like sour milk.

"I'm sick of your sympathy," Anastasia said. She closed her eyes. "I'm sick of you."

"How can you say such a thing?" Beatrice said. She was wadding Kleenex to wipe up the mucous. "Try to think how *I* feel." And then her thin-glass voice broke: "What have I *done?*"

If he had lived until his ordination, he would have been buried in complete vestments—cassock, surplice, amice, alb, maniple, chasuble, and stole. Not a black blazer and bowtie.

"Why are you so *angry* at me?"

It had to be a mannequin in the casket; it couldn't be Tom. It had to be a mannequin wearing Tom's clothes.

"His skin looked like plastic, but I kissed him anyway," Anastasia said.

Beatrice stopped. "What did you say?"

Anastasia refused to believe the diagnosis. The doctors can't be right. He doesn't look sick at all. See how big and strong he is?

But in his marrow, a blizzard of white blood cells.

"Please tell me what's wrong."

A hand on her shoulder. Anastasia looked up. Beatrice again: her face fish-belly white.

The old nun turned over onto her back. "Leukemia," she explained.

Beatrice put her hand to her forehead. It shook as she rubbed her eyebrows with her thumb and forefinger. "No, Sister, you don't have leukemia," she said. Then: "I think we'd better call the doctor."

"Just let me die," Anastasia said. And then her phlegm-clotted lungs closed up. But this time she did not struggle for air. This time she closed her lips into a thin smile.

Her lungs were gray cocoons about to burst. Inside, the soul's wings beating.

*My Lord, my Lord, take me for Thy most humble bride!*

Beatrice clutched her handkerchief as if it were holding her up. "Oh, Sister!" she cried, and hurried out of the room, her habit scything the last light.

This was it. This was what she had been waiting for all these years, the end of all that passion and memory. She had no fear of dying. She was a bride of Christ: death was her dowry, nothing more.

All day she had been travelling backward, a flower folding back into its bud. For years she had thought only occasionally about Tom and Carl, but today she had returned to that age when she thought about them daily. And now she was almost back to her birth.

Tom: the husks of cicadas' songs in his hands. A touch could shatter them to shards. Oh, what music the soul must make as it shucks the body!

All she had to do was shut her eyes and the earth would close over her, and she would be lost, perfectly lost. She did not need Father Switzer or Carl or anybody. She laid her hands palms-up at her sides and waited for the last ecstatic moment. Then the dark began to murmur as if it had silt in its throat. She closed her eyes. What joy! she thought. And she sank into the darkness until the whining of the winch stopped and Tom's head appeared over the ledge. "Didn't I tell you?" he shouted down the well. "You *can* see them, can't you?" But she didn't answer, couldn't answer. She just clung to the rope and swung there in the darkness, staring up at Tom, his hair blond as an angel's, and beyond him, the stars in the noonday sky.

## 2

Father Switzer drove down the exit ramp of the hospital parking lot, paid the middle-aged woman in the booth, and turned out onto the boulevard.

"The painters just finished today," he continued. "I think they did a bang-up job. They've changed the whole atmosphere of the lunchroom. You wouldn't believe the difference." Then, as if he'd just thought of it, he added, "Say, why don't we swing by the lunchroom before I take you back to the convent? That way you can see for yourself how nice it looks."

Anastasia noticed a smile starting around the corner of his mouth. The smirk of a boy who tells a lie that is technically true. The pleasure of sin without the guilt.

"It'll only take a minute," he persisted.

She looked out the window of the station wagon. The houses they were passing were among the oldest in the city, but none of them had been built before she was born. Some of them had For Sale signs stuck in their brown lawns. She thought of the children in their art smocks, painting signs for her birthday party. She couldn't say no, but neither could she say yes.

"How could we afford to paint the lunchroom?" she asked wearily.

But he was ready for that question. "Some of the parishioners volunteered to do the painting, so it cost us almost nothing," he answered.

She knew he was grinning now. She continued to look out the window. I will do it for the children, she thought. For the children and Beatrice.

But when Father Switzer wheeled her into the lunchroom and she saw the balloons dangling from the undulating rows of crepe paper streamers, the banners that read HAPPY BIRTHDAY!, WELCOME BACK, SISTER ANASTASIA!, and WE MISSED YOU!, the tables set with pink and yellow paper cups and plates, and the children in their party hats leaping up from their chairs shouting, "Surprise!" and twirling noisemakers, she could not act surprised or happy. She tried to clap her hands to her face in a dumb show of shock, but they stopped halfway and fell back into her lap like broken-winged birds.

Rose and Antoinette Marie welcomed her back. Camilla took her hand and pressed it softly between hers.

But where was Beatrice? Anastasia looked around the room and found her standing by the far table, pretending to be supervising her third- and fourth-graders. She put her finger to her lips unnecessarily.

Just then, Father Switzer raised his hands in a pontifical gesture. "Quiet down, children, quiet down." The students sat back in their seats heavily. Father Switzer waited until the chairs quit squeaking, then looked at Anastasia and winked. "Didn't I tell you the painters did a great job? Just look at these signs. The boys and girls spent half the day painting them. Not to mention blowing up balloons and hanging crepe paper and whatnot. And Sister Rose has baked a *gigantic* cake."

At this, one of the boys let out a whoop. Antoinette Marie rolled her sleeves up her plump red forearms and frowned in a parody of discipline.

Father Switzer was getting serious now. He had his hand on

Anastasia's shoulder. "I wouldn't be telling the truth, Sister, if I didn't say we were all pretty worried about you. We spent a lot of time on our knees, especially after you had your close call."

Anastasia closed her eyes. The reflector on the intern's forehead had shone like the eye of a monstrance. She'd heard Beatrice say, "Is she breathing?" and then the oxygen mask descended over her nose and mouth like a new, unwanted face. A horrible face. She tried to push it away, but it fit too tightly. And now the face was hers, though no one else could see it. She opened her eyes and saw that Beatrice was watching her. She tried to smile, but Beatrice looked away.

Could Beatrice see it too?

"But God heard our prayers," Father Switzer was saying, "and now you're back with us and we can finally celebrate your birthday. I know we're a few days late, but we hadn't counted on your illness. In any case, we intend to make up for lateness with style." Father Switzer grinned and nodded at Antoinette Marie. "Ready, Sister?"

Antoinette Marie produced a pitch pipe from her pocket and hummed the key of C. Then, flourishing her arms and vigorously mouthing the words, she led everyone through two choruses of "Happy Birthday." When they were through, some of the children jumped up and swarmed around Anastasia's wheelchair. "I'm so glad you're not sick anymore," a skinny blue-eyed girl said. "Me too," said the boy standing next to her.

Anastasia looked from one face to another. She couldn't remember who they were. She had been away for only three weeks and already she had forgotten their names.

"I'm happy to be back," she managed.

Beatrice stepped into the circle of children. "Let's not tire Sister Anastasia, children. She shouldn't have too much excitement right away." She turned her wrinkled brow to Camilla. "Perhaps we should have the cake sooner than we'd planned."

Camilla looked at Anastasia. "All right," she said. Then she turned to the children. "Let's bring out the cake and ice cream!"

"Yay!" cried the children.

"Take your seats," Father Switzer ordered, and the children scrambled into their places. Antoinette Marie and Rose disappeared into the kitchen.

"Are you all right?" Camilla asked Anastasia. "You don't seem yourself."

"I think she's overcome with surprise," Beatrice answered for her.

The children cheered then, for Sister Rose had just emerged from the kitchen, carrying an enormous sheet cake. Antoinette Marie followed her out the double doors, pushing a cartload of vanilla Dixie cups and tiny wooden spoons.

"Stay in your seats, children," Father Switzer commanded. "Sister Rose, the first slice is for our guest of honor."

They set the cake on the table in front of Anastasia. There was only one candle on the cake, stuck in the middle of waves of chocolate frosting. Rose struck a match and lit it.

Anastasia looked at Beatrice. "Where are all the candles?" she said.

"We wanted to save your breath," Beatrice answered, and looked away.

"Come on, Sister!" some boys shouted. "Make a wish and blow it out."

The old nun stared at the candle. The cake was so big, the candle so small. In the dark frosting, the flame's reflection flickered, a dying star.

"Come on, Sister!"

Anastasia clasped her shawl tighter around her neck and leaned forward in the wheelchair. For a moment, everyone was silent. She felt them all watching her, waiting for her to blow out the candle, and she closed her eyes. Behind her eyelids, the darkness was private and peaceful, a refuge, and she wished everything were so dark that no one could see her, not Father Switzer or the children or even Beatrice. She wished she were invisible, there but not there, a darkness inside the darkness, like Tom, like God.

"Sister?" Father Switzer said.

With an effort, she opened her eyes and looked at the candle's puny light.

"Have you made your wish?" he asked.

She nodded. Then she took a deep breath and blew the flame out.

# SHARDS

Struck by sun, anything's beautiful. A dead cat, calico when I got up close, was fool's gold from across the street. There were maggots more than a few. I was six. I got sick. Even now, I love the sun more than what it strikes.

Light's the only thing to love. First, it lasts. And it's the kiss that stings the eyes closed. To open your eyes means tears. The trick's to keep them open while they're shut, Father says. That's the killer's code.

The first time I saw a corpse it was night. My eyes were open wide, always are in the dark. My pulse goes up, I swear, when the sun goes down. I see everything *clear*, like a cat.

No moon, nor star. Everything dark. The county road rainblack, snakeskin slick. When I saw the cars I swerved, skidded in the ditch. Stepfather's pickup was all right—muffler damage, nothing more—but I was sick. I *knew* someone was dead. I was sixteen and still I felt sick.

Nausea never passes, only changes form. I waited till it turned to numbness, then got out and climbed up the ditch through shin-high weeds so wet they soaked my Levi's. The Pontiac's left turn signal was still blinking. Its reflection in the asphalt: red, black; red, black. For some reason, that light made me sadder than I'd ever been. I couldn't take my eyes off it.

Sometimes the night's a palpable weight. It shoved me to my

knees: I still carry a shard of windshield glass just under my right
kneecap. It floats, like an injured athlete's bonechip. Me, I'm an
athlete of death.

But kneeling's not praying. I wasn't praying, though the highway
patrolman thought so. A hand shook my shoulder as if waking me.
I looked up: the maroon and tan uniform, the gold braid around
the brim of the hat. "I'll need your help, son," he said. "There'll be
plenty of time to pray later." I hadn't even heard him drive up.

The patrolman opened the Pontiac's door with a yank, but we
had to crowbar the Ford's. Both drivers, one no older than I, were
dead. No doubt about it. The patrolman didn't even bother to
check their pulses. Just pushed his hat up his pale forehead.
Whispered "Jesus" like a sigh.

I nodded, but I was barely listening. All I could think about
was the statue of St. Christopher on the Ford's dash. The car was
totaled, the driver's face crushed, but the statue was unharmed.
Not a chip in the paint. Unperturbed, St. Christopher was still
toting the Christ child across the blue waters of the suction cup.

The second the patrolman looked away, I jerked the statue off
the dash and stuffed it in my jacket pocket. I still have it, too, at
least what's left of it. The morning after the accident, I took it to
the quarry where the Rifle Club shot clay pigeons Sunday afternoons
and I blew it into slivers of plastic from a hundred feet with my
.30-06. I'm a crack shot, have been since I was twelve. The Army
didn't know what they were losing when they turned me down.

I would have been a good soldier. Death doesn't bother me,
unless it's accidental. That car accident shook me up a whole
summer. That was seven years ago, but sometimes I still dream
about it and wake so scared or angry or something in between
that I've got to go out and do something. Not drink. Bourbon
blurs the eye and makes me dream awake. What I need, those
times, is to talk, and at three a.m. no one'll listen but prostitutes. I
pay my money, but all I do is talk.

But if a death is planned, it doesn't bother me. At least *somebody's*
in control. Accidents belong to God, Father says; murders, to us.

No killer likes to kill; we do it to prove we're free. As a boy, I used to pray to have this burden lifted from me, but something made me hunt the bottomland along the Minnesota River near Stepfather's farm. Killing made me sick to my stomach at first, but it cured my hunger. When I wasn't in the woods, I was always hungry. I ate and ate, but stayed lean. Even without exercising, I burned everything up—still do. But when I was hunting, I never ate anything from sunrise to sunset, and never got hungry. I was that free.

I'd pretend I was hungry, though. All hunters know nature's a conspiracy of beauty: cottonwood leaves flash scatterfire silver in the sun, and your eyes close from seeing so much. That's when the buck comes down to the stream to drink, but by the time your eyes are open again, he's vanishing into poplars, white tail waving like a mock flag of truce. Hunger's the only way to keep your eyes open once beauty's shut them, so I always pretended I'd starve if I didn't kill something. I crouched in my duck blind or stalked deer tracks for hours, thinking about nothing but translating the slow squeeze of a trigger into food. And when I brought something down, I felt as if I'd saved my life.

Mother always said I spent too much time hunting and not enough dating. But I never felt free with girls: I couldn't keep my eyes open. A simple kiss could fire my gunpowder veins. There was Marcie, skin fawn-tan summer and winter. And Veronica, all bracelets and silk. But mostly, Sharon. Her blue eyes were always bright as if she'd just been weeping. The first time we made love, something crashed in me and lights flared behind my eyelids. And when I woke, my stomach was roiling and my lips numb as after novocaine. As soon as I could I washed myself off.

Father says sex is just another kind of accident, like a car crash. There are never any survivors. I knew that even before Mother's death, but still I made love to Sharon every chance I got. The night Mother died, I was waiting for her and Stepfather to go to a party in town so Sharon and I could make love in my bedroom. While Stepfather dressed in his room and Mother put on her makeup in the bathroom, I sat downstairs in the den and imagined Sharon beneath me. Eyes closed, lips parted. The sudden shudder of her orgasm. Then I heard Mother cough, three or four times, hard, as if she'd swallowed something wrong. The last cough almost a gasp. And then the boneshuddering thud. I stood up so quickly I felt dizzy. Stepfather was already at the door. "You all right, dear?" he was saying. "Are you all right in there?"

That time I did pray. I didn't kneel, just stood there, head swirling, and swore to God I'd never sin with Sharon again if only He would let Mother live. I don't know how I knew she was dying, but I knew. Perhaps it's a killer's gift. Or perhaps Father had already begun his whispering.

Some prayers are answered no. The others are ignored. Who knows which kind this was? It doesn't matter: either way, Mother was dead. But I want it known that I hold God personally responsible for her death. Women her age don't die of heart attacks, nor die, of all places, in a bathroom, wearing a slip, face half made-up, one lip coral pink.

Stepfather, in black trousers and undershirt, stood beside the bathroom door, gulping air. "Help me," I said, but he didn't move.

"You shouldn't—move her," he said. "She might have—broken something."

"Help me!" I said, but he did nothing. He was hanging onto the doorjamb with both hands now. So I lifted Mother myself, hoisted her over my shoulder and, legs trembling under her weight, carried her to the bedroom and laid her down on the yellow chenille bedspread. Her eyes were half-open, so I shut them with my fingertips, and then, then—Father, help me tell this part— then I tried to bring her back. I tried but it didn't work. I tilted her head back, pinched her nostrils, and began to blow my breath into her. Her mouth smelled like Listerine and her lipstick tasted like wet chalk. My brain swung, dizzy. I tried to forget the smell, the taste, even her, and lose myself in the breathing; blowing; breathing; blowing. A kind of ventriloquism, breathing for another body. It's unnatural, maybe even wrong. But I tried to save her. I breathed myself into her until my head was light, ringing, my stomach cramping. A diver down too deep, I swam toward the sky until my lungs clenched like fists. That's when I started to breathe the killing water. I haven't stopped since.

Breath chuffing, Stepfather paced behind me. "You're not—doing it right," he said. I was, but he shoved me aside and took my place over her still body. I watched him, fat and trembling, pinch her nose and blow into her mouth. Under his closed lids, his eyes moved like a dreamer's.

I was dreaming, too. Death is so real it makes everything else a dream. I looked at my mother's body, lying there limp and lifeless, a swarm of meaningless molecules, and I realized she had never existed, that I had only dreamed her. Her body was real, but she, she was as insubstantial as the breath I'd tried to blow into her.

One night, awake, I dreamed I saw her ghost. I knew it was her, though I couldn't see her face: the nimbus was too bright. Since then, I've seen with her light. Every glance sears.

When I said *ghost*, the Army doctor took his glasses off and looked at me as if it took astigmatism to see me clear. Doctors don't believe in ghosts. They know a dead star shines for centuries; why not a soul? But I knew I couldn't persuade him so I didn't bother to tell him the things Father's taught me about death.

A squint's to make you small, to fit you, square peg, in a round hole. That doctor squinted me to a molecule and asked if I was afraid of ghosts. I'm not, and I wasn't. What scared me then were ordinary things, the things of Mother's I'd found everywhere after she died. Under a sofa cushion, the opal earring she'd spent days looking for. Hidden beneath a sweater in her dresser, a snapshot of Father in his Army uniform, the last one ever taken. A brush with some of her meringue-blonde hair still in it. To touch them hurt.

Two weeks after the funeral I left home. I revved the old Chevrolet to wake Stepfather, then sped down the dark driveway onto the country road, tires churning gravel, gearbox growling. I kept my eyes on the road, but felt Stepfather at his window, parting the sheers to see my taillights, my only farewell. I could hear him saying, "No. Don't leave. Not now." Above me, the star-slung sky hung like a spider web around the fat moon. Shifting into fourth, I fishtailed onto the highway, going sixty.

That was five years ago. Since then I've lived everywhere, been everybody. In Minneapolis, I was Roger Holman, night janitor at Berman Buckskin Leather Goods. At the Olympia Brewery in Seattle, I was Alex Carey. In Denver, when I tried to enlist, Burt Loomis. And so on. Outside of a ticket for speeding on the Ventura Freeway, I had no problems with the law, yet I felt like a wanted man. Even before I was, I felt that way. That's why Father gave me the aliases. He said I needed re-christening.

The only time I used my real name was the fall I took freshman philosophy and physics courses at Berkeley, and I was so afraid of being arrested (again and again I imagined the sudden click of handcuffs, the gruff voice and pistol in the back) I almost broke down. My thoughts were riddled with dark; they rose in spasms, fragments I couldn't assemble. Even my vision was splintered, cubist. There was something in me like a prism that broke light into too many colors to decode.

I took physics to study light. A killer's a student of light, Father says. What I learned was this: light's schizophrenic. Sometimes it acts as if it consists of waves; other times, corpuscles. Most people don't know the difference, light's light, but I can tell when it shifts from waves to corpuscles, when it starts to dance like blood gone mad.

I took philosophy to learn to be good. But the more I read, the more I heard death's dull monotone. Peeling syntax like the skins of an onion, I found tears all the way down to the nothing at the core. After an hour or two, the forked vein in my forehead would start ticking like a bomb. Then everything in the room— desk, lamp, chair, bed, walls, everything—seemed wrenched, warped, or shattered into fragments by the skewing light.

I was so scared and confused I went to see the student counselor. Silver hair, pulled back. Glasses on a chain. I couldn't talk to her; I just sat there, sweating in her air-conditioned office, and looked out the window. There were dozens of women walking to classes in tight blue jeans. I closed my eyes, imagining the darkness where they tucked their shirttails. When I looked back at the counselor, she was staring at my face as if it were an X-ray. That afternoon, I moved on.

I moved to keep up with time. Sometimes time warps into space the way outside warps into inside in a Möbius strip. So when time's moving too fast, you have to move too. Only then can you slow it down.

I don't know why I went back to Minneapolis after leaving Berkeley. When I threw my dufflebag in the Chevy's trunk, I thought I was heading for Phoenix. But once I got out on the freeway, the hum of tires was a mad Gregorian chant. It made me drive. I drove all that day and the next. At gas stations I talked nonstop with attendants. Argued politics, religion, weather. I was not in good shape. At night, the sky was so vast and black, I was afraid gravity wasn't strong enough to keep me from being sucked into space.

I'm a weak person, and I admit it. According to the legend, St. Christopher felt the strange child on his shoulders grow heavier and heavier until he was supporting the weight of the world's misery, but he never buckled, never sank under the river rush. That's why he's a saint and I'm a sinner. But remember: he's only a legend, a fairy tale, and I'm real, I'm the evening news. And I've learned to make my weakness my strength.

My first week back in Minneapolis, time slowed and I was all right again. The reason was Cindy. According to the newspaper, her last name was Roberts, she was twenty years old, and she was a part-time student at the University. The paper didn't say anything about her profession. Cindy was the first one, and the only one that's mattered. It wasn't the same with the others. With them, I was just practicing an art. They were faces chosen at random in theatres, museums, department stores. I never read about them in the paper the next day.

But Cindy was different. She chose me as much as I chose her.

There was something in her that demanded I kill her. Father recognized it too. He knew it even before I did.

The night I met Cindy, I had a dream. I dreamed I'd run into the cars that blocked the rainblack county road. I was dead, my face caved in, and yet I was outside too, trying to open the door with a crowbar, and the patrolman, fat and trembling, was pacing behind me, saying, "You're not doing it right, let me do it." When I woke, my mind was a snarl of darkness; I had to think carefully, slowly, one thought at a time, so I wouldn't get caught in the tangle. What I needed was air, sharp slapping night air, to clear my head, so I pulled on my jeans and sweatshirt and went for a drive. Even though it was December, cold, soot-gray snow flanking the streets, I rolled the window down so I could *breathe*.

The drive ended at the Strand. It was the first time I'd been there in over four years, but Henry, the stocky Scandinavian with acne scars who runs the place, recognized me. "Hey, Slim, where you been?" he said. "You get married or something?" He smiled and puffed on his cigarette. The smoke wound around his neck, a noose.

"I've been out of town," I said. "In Nam."

"Yeah?" he tapped his cigarette on the ashtray. "What you looking for tonight? A little 'Johnny comes marching home'?"

"That's right," I said, and set two twenties on the counter.

"Price has gone up," Henry said. "Overhead's higher than you might think. I'll need another ten-spot."

I laid down two fives and Henry took the bills and smoothed them out with his yellowed fingers. "Right this way, General," he said, then led me up the short flight of worn stairs into the mildew of the dim hallway. At the end of the hall, he stopped. Hanging upside down on the door, a gilt number seven.

"One of our new girls," he said with a nod at the door. "Cindy." A quick one-knuckled rap. "Miss Lucinda?" he asked. "Gentleman caller to see you. Are you indecent?"

I couldn't make out what she answered, but I could tell it was a curse.

Henry laughed and puffed on the cigarette. "Go on in, Ike," he said. "She's all yours."

I opened the door and stood there a moment. A black underwater light. Shadows shifting amorphous as fish and anemone along shoals. Cindy, sitting on the edge of the narrow bed, pale, wan-faced, small-chested, wearing only a black slip. Her hair black, too, and in the blue-black light, iridescent, like a starling's wings. Coughing a little. The sound, the scrape of sandpaper on wood. Delicate, as if a sharp cough could shatter her like glass.

I didn't think I knew, then, what I would do, but I must have because I started to tremble. It was like when you fall in love for the first time, but it wasn't love, or it was a kind of love I'd never felt before. I didn't know what it was. All I knew was that I would do something, and then my bad dreams would be over. Father knew too. *Soon, soon, you can rest.* His whisper was almost a song.

Cindy crossed her arms and legs and shivered. "Hurry up and close the door, for Christ's sake," she said. "There's a draft."

I closed the door. It shut on everything I had been. I was someone else, breathing new air. Air so pure it burned my lungs like ground glass.

"Calm down," she said. She glanced at her wristwatch. "You wanna get started?" she asked and, standing, began to pull her slip up over her shoulders.

"Stop," I said.

White skin bruise-blue in the black light.

She lowered the slip and looked at me. "What," she said. It wasn't a question, or the beginning of a curse. Just "what." Whenever I think of her, I think of the way she said that word. As if it had nothing to do with language.

"I only want to talk," I said. The light revealed her skinny body through her slip the way a fluoroscope reveals a skeleton. I stared past her at the cobweb cracks in the wall.

Her hand on my wrist. "Listen," she said, "there's nothing to be nervous about. You're a good-looking guy, and it's all natural. I'll help."

I stepped away, turned my back to her. The hiss of the radiator. The tick of my pulse.

"Look," she said. "If you just want to talk, that's fine with me. But don't go asking Henry for your money back."

Out the window, across the street, a tavern's red neon blinked on and off, staining the sidewalk.

Cindy said something else then, but I wasn't listening. I just stood there and looked out the window. When I finally turned back to her, she was sitting on the edge of the bed watching me. With a delicate white hand, she pushed back a wisp of hair that had fallen onto her cheek.

"You're very beautiful," I found myself saying.

She smiled a little. "Sounds like someone's changing his mind . . ." she said.

"No," I shook my head. "Really. I just want to talk." And, trembling, I sat down beside her.

She looked out the window a second, then tilted her head at me, as if trying to see me straight. "You're really unhappy, aren't you?"

"Yes," I answered. "I am." My voice distant, an underground thrum.

After a moment, she said, "I feel kind of weird sitting here in my slip if we're just going to talk. Do you mind if I put on my dress or something?"

I shook my head and she took a dark dress off a hook, stepped into it, and zipped it up.

"There," she said, and sat back on the bed, her hands folded onto her lap.

I wanted to kiss her then, she looked like such a little girl. But what I did was cry. It surprised me as much as it surprised her: I hadn't felt like crying at all.

I stopped crying almost the second I started. Eyes stinging, my face in my hands, I began to tell my story. I told her everything, but I didn't tell her the truth. I told her Sharon had died, killed in a car accident when a drunk sideswiped our car late at night. And I told her that Stepfather disowned me after Sharon's death, saying I was responsible because I'd kept her out past curfew. And I told her I was thinking about killing myself. By the time I was done confessing, I was crying again.

Cindy took a deep breath. "Boy," she said. "I don't know what to say. I really don't know what to tell you. If you want my opinion, I think you ought to talk about this with somebody else—you know, a doctor or a minister or somebody like that. They'd know what to tell you. Me, I don't know anything about this sort of stuff. I'm all screwed up myself."

I stopped crying. I had imagined her crying with me, putting her arm around my shoulders, kissing my cheek. But she was just looking at me as if I made her nervous, as if she wished I'd leave.

"You can do something," I said. "You can sympathize."

"I do feel sorry for you," she said. "I really do. And if you want I'll give you the name of this doctor I go see whenever I'm having a bad time. But there's nothing *I* can do to solve your problems."

"What makes you so sure?" I said, gritting my teeth.

Cindy looked at me. "Are you all right?" she asked.

"What do you think?" I said. I was surprised at how loud I said it: almost a shout.

She stood up. "I think you'd better go now."

I stood up too. I felt dizzy, as if I'd been drinking. "You haven't earned your money yet," I said.

"What's that supposed to mean?"

I thought of the dark gash between her legs. Now I wanted her beneath me, I wanted to hurt her, make her weep.

"You know what I mean," I said. "I paid my money."

She backed toward the door, keeping her eyes on me.

"Listen," she said, dead quiet, "you're scaring me. If you don't get out of here this minute, I'm yelling for Henry." She put her hand on the gilt doorknob.

Then I started to tremble again, but not because I was afraid, though that's what Cindy must have thought. I was trembling because Father had given me his blessing. *You know what you have to do*, he said. And I knew.

"I mean it," Cindy said. "I'll yell."

I left. If I'd stayed any longer, I would have told her, and that wouldn't have been good. So I left. Driving home, I sang, every song I knew. I sang as loud as I could, until my lungs were raw, my throat throbbing. Sang to the splintered legs and wave-blue suction cup stuck to my dash. Sang to the stars carved in black ice. Sang. Sang.

For the next three weeks, I slept when the sun was up and stalked Cindy at night. I parked outside the Strand until she left, usually around five. Sometimes she left with another girl, a short muscular blonde in a rabbit fur coat; once with a man in a navy parka, probably one of her johns; but usually, alone, in a taxi. Whatever, I kept strict records: dates, times of departure, routes taken, times of arrival. Lights on low, I followed her to her home, a two-story brownstone converted into apartments on Malcolm, just off 17th. In my spiral notebook, I wrote: *Quiet neighborhood. No dogs. One streetlight dead. The moon over her roof like Bethlehem's star.* And drew: diagrams of her building, front, back, and sides; approach and escape routes; bullet trajectories. After her lights had been out for a while, I stepped off the distance from her door to the curb, the curb to the various places I might park my car, and recorded all the figures before going home.

Always, I made it home before sunrise. For three long weeks, I pulled my blinds on the sun. When you love light, its sleights of sun, you have to kill it. A penance. Each day, a bead on a black rosary.

The penance made me free. My hunger was gone: some days I ate only one meal, a bowl of corn flakes or a can of tomato soup, nothing more. The longer I stalked her, the less I needed to eat. And since her death, I've done nothing but stalk. That's why I'm so lean now, almost invisible. You could walk past me on the street and never see me. My victims never do.

One night, after I'd stalked Cindy for a couple of weeks, I woke to minus-thirty wind chill and a landscape lunar with snow. That cold, air is pure adrenalin. Father said the time had come, so

I cleaned and loaded the Springfield. The smell of oil and metal, so familiar, comforting. That night, I waited three hours outside the Strand, watching snow drift across my windshield. Then suddenly, Cindy, loden green camel's-hair coat and upturned collar, hurrying into a yellow cab. The Springfield's muzzle lay cold on my lap. I followed her home.

From the curb to her door: eighteen steps, maybe twenty in the ankle-deep snow. I'd count to ten, then fire. Already I'd imagined her, time and again, tumbling slowly into the snow as if into an embrace. The cab pulled away from the curb, and she started up the walk. I counted to six, then sighted down the scope, hung her on its cross, counted seven; eight; nine.

But I didn't pull the trigger. *This isn't right*, Father suddenly said. *It's too impersonal.* I lowered the Springfield, let Cindy walk to her door, climb the stairs to her room, switch the yellow lights on and, a few minutes later, switch them off. I waited until I thought she was asleep before I went home.

I couldn't sleep, though. I didn't even lie down for the next three days. Day and night, I wrote letters. A long one, to Stepfather, asking for forgiveness, never sent. One to Sharon, hinting at marriage, sent, later returned unopened. Several to old employers, demanding back pay or compensation for injuries. One to the U.S. Army, attacking their biased enlistment policies. An anonymous note to Henry, warning him that one of his girls was in danger.

And then, knowing I'd never sleep until it was done, I went back to Cindy's house, this time with a Charter Arms .44 caliber handgun. You probably think you know this part of the story, but the papers didn't tell this part, never could. There's nothing factual about a murder; murder's fiction, an escape from the fatality of fact. Destruction is a form of creation, after all. Each murder's a way of saying "Let there be light."

That night the sky was stone. So heavy I could hardly walk without staggering. I'd been running on empty so long I was out of breath, an old man, by the time I walked the two blocks from my car to Cindy's house.

The night before, I'd counted her footprints in the snow from the curb to the hedge that fronted her yard: eight. Crouched behind the hedge, waiting for her and my breath, I tried to see through the tangle of leaves and twigs. Nothing. All I could see, if I turned and craned my neck, was her house and, above it, the cusped moon, curved like a machete. I'd have to rely on hearing alone; I'd count seven steps, stand, and shoot.

I must've waited twenty minutes hunched in the snow: Cindy was late. Every now and then, a car slid by on the icy street, but none of them stopped. Occasionally, the blare of their radios, even through closed windows.

I was freezing, almost ready to go home. Then the taxi drove up. Cindy's voice, wordless, a wind chime heard through blowing snow. The cabby's, heavy, flat, ringing like iron on pavement. Then the engine's cold surge, the tires spinning a second on a patch of ice before catching. I looked through the tangle of leaves but saw nothing.

She started up the walk. The click of her heels on the slick ice. One, two. A cough. Three, four.

Though I'd been planning to kill her for weeks, somehow I didn't realize I was going to do it until that moment. I felt a spurt of joy sudden as a struck match.

At six, I stood up and stepped in front of her.

"Oh!" she said, and jerked back. In the dark, her mouth was red, lipstick a running wound.

Then she saw the gun. My hand had raised it. I looked at my hand. It was trembling but I was perfectly calm.

"*No*," she said, her breath a blossom in the cold, and put out her hands like a shield. Her mouth kept moving, but no words came out.

Suddenly her legs buckled and she fell to her knees. At first I thought she was begging me not to kill her, then I thought she was praying, asking God to save her. But when she fell, face-first, on the ice, I knew I had already shot her. There'd been no noise, I hadn't felt my finger squeeze the trigger, but I had done it. Father said, *Now you are free, now you have conquered death . . .*

How long I stood over her, I don't know. Time had warped so completely into space that all that existed was me, Cindy, and the bloodstained ice. I stood there, staring. There was a halo around her body, an aureole like that you see around everything after you've looked at a light too long. Kneeling, I wiped a bubble of spit from her mouth with my handkerchief.

I wanted to stay, to be with her forever, but Father said I had to go. Lights were coming on all up and down the street. Men and women in nightclothes dialing the police.

*Run*, Father said. My legs refused. I walked, underwater, slow, down the street, all memory of escape routes gone. All happiness gone too, left with Cindy's body. I wanted to go back to her, to sit beside her in the snow, alone, forever, to live in the light her body gave off. *You'll be captured*, Father warned. *You'll lose your freedom.* But I didn't care, still don't: if I'm ever caught, I'll be happy, I'll be able to rest, I won't have to be free anymore. I didn't care, but I kept on walking. My legs were not my own.

My hand wasn't mine either. When I reached the corner, it suddenly aimed the gun at the streetlight and shot it twice, square in its heart, before I knew what it was doing. The light burst into a thousand shards that fell like shivers of snow. My hands over my head, I walked through that snowfall. I am still walking through it.

# THE BIGS

I am a baseball player. I come here from the Dominican Republic the home of Juan Marichal because baseball can't make you the same much of money in the Dominican League. That is why I live in the U S of A and play baseball for the Arkansas Travelers which are a team in the Texas League but live in Arkansas. The Arkansas Travelers are a team which is called a Double A team, meaning not so good as Triple A or Major Leagues—what everybody call The Bigs. Everybody here want to make it to The Bigs. There is no Bigs in the Dominican Republic and that is why I am living here so miserable and now that my family leave me I am more miserable ever than before. The only time I smile is after when I win a big game or if I forget for some minute and think my little Angelita is waiting at home for me to kiss her for goodnight. But tonight I am more miserable than I think a dead man because Coach he suspend me off the team and all because they leave me.

I love baseball. I love to pitch the ball. When I am the pitcher everybody depend of me, if I just stand there and hold the ball nobody do nothing. When I throw the ball everything happen. It is a good feeling but not the same as love which is something I have too much of I think. My heart it feel like it is in shreds each time when I think about Angelita and her black braids. And Pilar. I can not even say her name now without wanting to cry. Pilar is so beautiful, sometimes when I was in her I could not breathe right. When I think about her gone and Angelita with her I want to be on the mound throwing hard like Juan Marichal who come from Santo Domingo the same like me. I am a starter so I pitch the ball each four days, no more, and the rest of the time it go by so slow. I want I could pitch the ball each night if I will not tear my shoulder which is what I do at St. Peterburg my year of being a rookie when I try to show off I have stuff. Now my shoulder it hurt when I think about Pilar and Angelita so I try not to think about them when I am pitching the ball. But most of the time it is of no use because I think about them anyway. That is why I get in such big trouble tonight, I think of them when I should be thinking curve ball or slider, down or up.

The nights they are the most bad. I have dreams. Jackie say I grind my teeth when my dreams get so bad and when I wake up I am all wet with sweating and scared. Jackie try to make me all right then but it never work. She hug me and kiss me and say it only is a dream. Then I tell her what I dream and she say what it mean like a *curandera*. Some times I dream Pilar is opening her legs for Antonio who was sent back to Santo Domingo for weak field and no hit. Other times I dream I am pitching the ball when Angelita run out on the field with her arms reaching out for me but I don't see her before it is too late and I have already throw the ball and it hit her in the face and make her be dead. To me the dreams mean I love Pilar and Angelita so much my heart want to die. Twice I almost buy a gun and shoot my head. But Jackie say a gun is dumb, she say my dreams mean I should get married again and show Pilar some thing or two. She tell me to stop being a Mr. Sadface. That's what she call me when she try to make me smile. I know she want to marry with me by these signs but I don't want to marry with her, I want her to go away and leave me to be alone.

Pilar take Angelita back to the Dominican Republic because she don't care about The Bigs. She don't care about Juan Marichal or the Hall of Fame or driving a car with electric windows. She miss her mama and papa and the pacaya grove in her yard in

Santo Domingo. When she look at the photographs of home that was when she would start crying and then a minute later yell at me for taking her to the U S of A. She don't understand English so good and no one except Antonio who play second base like a hole in his glove also speak Spanish. And she don't understand baseball too. To her it make no sense, to her it is crazy to pitch a ball that no one can hit it. She say to watch a game if no one hit the ball is no fun so I should make the batter to hit some home runs. She say Why you keep everybody from having fun, you think the fans pay so much of money to see pop-ups. She is a woman and she think like a woman. Still I did not suspect her to leave me. The trouble I am in tonight is all because she leave me. I try to tell Coach so he understand but still he suspend me off the team maybe for good. He have a wife who never leave and no kids.

The day Pilar go I pitch six and two-third no-score innings against the Shreveport Captains which are a team too in the Texas League, East Division. Then my arm it get sore and Coach say to get a shower and ice my shoulder up. I think now my shoulder ache because Pilar and Angelita are going that same minute. It was a sign but I don't see it then because I am wondering if Parisi will lose my win for me like usual, the rag arm. But this time he is lucky and I don't lose my win but because I am worrying so hard I miss the sign. God give all of us signs like a manager so we know what He want us to do. But now I don't know what to do. I don't see any signs. I think maybe God is mad with me and I am scared.

The night Pilar and Angelita leave I am halfway to almost home when all of a sudden I know what my sore arm mean and I drive fast with my foot down on the floor and run through red lights one after each other and squeal into the parking lot like a madman. I go up the curb and almost into the swimming pool next by the apartment manager's office I am so much scared they have left me. And when I open the door Pilar and Angelita are gone and I can not find them everywhere. I look in the kitchen and living room and both bedrooms even behind the shower curtain but they are so gone I can feel how they are not there. I sit down on the bathroom floor and look at the shower curtain which Pilar buy when Angelita pull the other one down. She buy it because there is parrots on it like in our country and palm trees. I am so much sad I want to hold this curtain against me tight.

I did not think she would leave, I think only she talk about it. But now I see she mean what she say. After when I get up from the bathroom floor I go back in the kitchen and find what I did not see at first, a note sticked on the refrigerator door with a yellow smiling face magnet. It say in Spanish If you don't make The Bigs come to home and be a family again. I sit down then and put my big dumb head in my hands and cry. Mr. Sadface.

I don't know why I stayed in Little Rock. I should have went to Santo Domingo that same minute. Maybe there is something wrong with inside of me that make me stay. Maybe I don't love Pilar and Angelita like I think so. Maybe I want to hurt them like they do me. Or maybe I don't want to be like Antonio and go back to home the same I left, a worthless nothing. When I go back I want to be like Juan Marichal who is a Hall of Fame pitcher with more strikeouts than dogs in Santo Domingo. I want World Series rings on all my fingers and a car so big it have a TV in it and a bar. But I want more my Pilar and Angelita I think. Why I did not go back I am not sure but maybe I should have went before all this happen, before I become this disgrace to my country and my family. Before I have to go back with no choice of my own.

Jackie she think I stay because of her but that is not right. Jackie mean almost nothing to me. She was Willie Williams' girl last year and after he dump her still she come around and ask to go for a ride in his car which he call his Love Chariot. But he always say No and Get lost and one night I am so lonely I get mad and say Manny you don't have to take this shit off of Pilar that bitch you can have some fun too. So when Jackie come around at The Press Box to drink beers and shoot pool after we lose the doubleheader to Tulsa I say Willie that's no way to hurt a lady and make him say he is sorry so I don't hit him. After that she have her hands all over me. Now she stay here and sleep on Pilar's side of the bed but I want her to go because she is not Pilar. She wear a blonde wig and laugh like she is underneath angry. But she love me and go crazy with crying when I say some things like I don't want you to hang your wig on the doorknob. I can't say anything mad or she will cry and want to be dead so how can I tell her to get lost. She laugh a lot but she have a scar on both wrists from when Willie first tell her to go away. The scars look like X's cut so careful and neat, I can see her trying to make them pretty, her tongue sticking out the corner of her mouth while she do it, concentrating. I am scared she will kill herself dead so I make sex with her but I wish she would go away. She scare me with her crazy too much of love, like I scare myself.

Now I don't know what to do. Each day that pass I wait for a sign. But nothing happen. I want one minute to go home, I want that Pilar will lay on top of me and kiss me so I am lost in the dark cave of her so beautiful black hair. And I want to kiss Angelita for goodnight on her little nose and say to her like before the joke about the bed bugs biting. But another minute I want hard to be a baseball pitcher in The Bigs and hear everybody even the white people cheering my name. I want everybody to know I make the money they don't. I want a house with chandeliers and shag carpet everywhere and a swimming pool in the backyard with color lights under the water. I want all these things but I don't want Jackie with her blonde wig and eye makeup and crying. But more than this I don't want her to bleed to death because I leave her like she always threaten without saying. So I want to go and I want to stay. And that make me not want anything anymore.

That is why I don't finish the game tonight. I am pitching the ball so good they swing and grunt at my curve ball which break in the dirt and my slider low and away. It is already inning eight and still I have no hits on me. Only six more outs to a no-hitter which would make Whitey Herzog to see I am ready for The Bigs. My palm it is sweating so I turn to pick up the bag of resin and then I see on the scoreboard all the zeros and somehow it take the breath out of me it all look so perfect. I am so proud because I do it, I make all the zeros. And then I think about Pilar leaving and Jackie's scars and my dream with Angelita running on the field and my pitch hitting her dead. Why I think these things then I do not know but I think them and it make my heart to beat so hard.

When I turn back to the plate my legs they are shaking like in my first game for los Azucareros del Este when Pilar was in the stands to cheer for me and I imagine she is out there now watching me and knowing if I do good I will make The Bigs and marry with Jackie because I am scared to find her in my bathtub, the water turning red. So I look down at Gene my catcher and nod and then I throw the ball and it sail over everybody's head and up the screen, a wild pitch. Gene he signal time and run out to the mound and say Jesus Christ Manny I give you the sign for change-up not fastball what are you thinking of. I can not remember what I say but Gene he go back to behind the plate and thump his mitt and give me another sign. I nod and throw the ball and it hit the batter in the shoulder and he spin around like he want to fight but I stand there only and look at him. Then he go down to first holding his shoulder and swearing at me and Gene he say Don't worry about it kid. You'll get 'em, he say. Just take it easy.

All this time I am thinking If I throw a no-hitter I will never see my Pilar and Angelita again. Not forever. So when Gene throw the ball back to me I am not watching close and it hit the top of my glove and don't go in. I look around quick and it isn't there. Gene he jump up then and yell Second! Second! but by the time when I find the ball and turn around to throw it to Peachy, already the runner he is standing up and brushing the dirt off his uniform. I hear Coach swear loud but somehow I don't care like I should.

Settle down, Gene say then and give me a sign. I start to wind up but then I forget what pitch he ask for and I stop, a balk. The runner he walk down to third laughing. I don't look at him. Gene come out to the mound then. Calm down for Chrissakes, Gene say. If they get a hit they get a hit the main thing is win. So just rare back and hump that ball in there. Okay I say and he go back.

Then he give me a sign maybe for fastball or could be slider. But I just stand there and hold the ball. He give me another sign I think for curve but I just stand there. Then Gene come out to the mound again and Coach too this time and Coach he say What's the problem Manny your arm getting sore again. I shake my head no. Then what gives, he say. What the fuck is going on. I almost can not talk the words are so far down inside of me but somehow I say Nothing but I say it in Spanish—*Nada*. I never talk on the team in Spanish because in The Bigs they want that you always talk American. But I say *Nada*. Then he look at me foreign and ask You all right. I say Fine in American and he say Good let's set 'em down, then he trot back to the dugout and Gene go behind the plate and give me one more time again the sign and this time too I do nothing. If I do nothing nothing happen because I am the pitcher, I am the one who hold the ball. I want then everything to stop, I want time to stop, I want Jackie to stop, I want being alone and sad to stop, so I hold the ball for one minute. For that one minute the world stand still, nothing change, and I can breathe.

Then the umpire step before the plate and say Throw the ball Sanchez or it is delay of the game. The batter he step out of the box and shrug his shoulders to the dugout of his team and spit. I stand there more. Then Gene say What the fuck and everybody in the stands start to yell and boo but I don't do anything.

Then out of the dugout come Coach's face looking red. All of a sudden I feel so sorry for him, so sorry for Gene and Peachy and my teammates and for Jackie and Pilar and Angelita and the umpire and the people in the stands who are booing so disappointed. I feel so bad for everybody I want to cry. Then Coach he say What the hell do you think you're doing Sanchez. I say it again—*Nada*. And he say Don't give me any of that I want to know why you aren't throwing the goddamn ball. His face is close to mine the way he get with a umpire who make a lousy call. I look down and say from somewhere My wife she leave me and my little girl is gone away. Jesus H. Christ he say then and touch his left arm which mean bring in the lefty. Then he say You're under suspension Sanchez now get your sorry ass out of this park and don't come back until your head is on straight. I don't want to see you or hear you or even *smell* you until then is that clear. I just stand there and listen to him, I can't even nod. Everything I live for is disappearing into nothing, I am becoming like a zero, and I am sad but somehow all of a sudden I am so much of nothing I am gone away and I'm there but not there too and where I am is so peaceful I want almost to cry. I want to tell Coach about this place, I want to tell everyone, but there are no words there so I only smile at him. He look away then mad and cursing but still I smile so happy.

And I am still smiling when Parisi come in to take from me my no-hitter and make me a nobody who can not go to home or stay where he is without shame. I am holding the ball and everything have stop and I am so happy and I love everybody even Coach and the fans booing and Whitey Herzog who keep me from being in The Bigs so long and Antonio who steal my wife maybe. I love everybody so much I feel like I am dead and looking down on everybody from heaven, not a man anymore but a angel with no sadness or pain or anything, just love. But then Coach take the ball away from me and give it to Parisi. He take the ball away, he take everything away, and I am standing there waiting and alone and there is no sign.

# APOTHEOSIS

*he following letter, addressed to Cardinal Archbishop Juan Martinéz
Siliceo, Inquisitor General of Spain from 1546 to 1557, is among
ninety-seven documents bearing the seal of the Holy Office of the Inquisition
discovered by Professor Philip Rosen during his excavation of the thirteenth-
century Catedral de Toledo. Little is known about Friar Miguel Sabogal, the
author of the letter, or Eusebio Daválos Hurtado, the author of the historical
memoir Sabogal transcribes in his plea to the Inquisitor, save that Sabogal's
name appears in Document 33, which is a partial list of those excommunicated
by the Holy Office in 1556. It is possible that Friar Sabogal is also referred
to in Document 86, the record of the tribunal's proceedings on the 14th of
August, 1558. According to that document, an "M. Sabegol" was burned
to death, along with twenty-one others, in the* auto-de-fé *of Toledo, following
testimony by a hosteler that he had attempted to convert him to the views of
Martin Luther.*

To His Holiness, the Most Eminent Cardinal Archbishop Siliceo:

With the most sincere of wishes for your good health and happiness,
I address you to inform you that I have received and shall comply
with your summons to appear before Inquisitor Baltasar de Castro
the seventh day of February. I regret that a summons has been
deemed necessary, as I am innocent of the charges made against
me; let me assure you, Your Eminence, that I am not a heretic, that

I, too, deplore Luther and the influence of his evil writings. Brother
de Quiroga's report to the archpriest, in its claim that I furthered
Luther's heresies by reading a "vile and heretical document" in my
retreat sermon, is, without doubt, inspired by his jealousy of my
position in the monastery and my popularity with the other brothers.
The document I shall transcribe here is the one I, as retreat master,
read to the novices and brothers two weeks past, and it is the one I
shall repeat, under oath, before the tribunal in Toledo ten days hence.
As you will see, Your Eminence, the document is merely an account
of the experiences of one Eusebio Daválos Hurtado while among
the murderous Indians of Guatemala. Hurtado was a member of
the Mercedarian Order of mendicants in that colony when the
Cakchiquel Indians rebelled against Spanish rule and religion. Of
Hurtado, I know only that he is a disgrace to the Catholic faith—
the document was presented to me by a friend, the historian Jose
Dávila Garibi (of the Academy in Córdoba), to whom it was
presented by a soldier who had recently returned from the province
of New Spain. It is only because Hurtado's document describes
the dangers God's workers confront in bringing religion to heathens
that I included it in my retreat sermon. I did not read it with heretical
intent. Yet I, a man of God, have suffered the great shame of
being called before the tribunal. I am grateful to you, Your
Eminence, for sparing me the additional shame of being arrested
and taken by cart to the Holy Office like a common Jew or follower
of Luther, and I ask with humility that you examine the document
for proof of my innocence.

### Here Begins the History of Eusebio Daválos Hurtado

I have lived for twenty years subject to the disgrace of being known
as a man who no longer wears the cowl and has taken a wife. My
son, Salvador, has suffered by both loving and being ashamed of
me. The Church would not recognize his birth nor admit him for
learning. When he was young, children called him "the son of the
devil" because he had not been baptized, and when he reached

manhood, no tradesman would take him as his apprentice and no father would allow his daughter to walk with him. It saddened me that he had to leave the home of his parents to live in San Marcos, where no one would know his disgrace, but I was relieved that he would no longer suffer. And now, today, I have learned that his wife has given birth to a son and that the child has been admitted to the church in San Marcos for baptism. This has given my son joy because I, despite my renunciation of the cowl, have always taught him that religion is the highest order of man's thought. Now that my grandchild has escaped the shame that I brought upon his father, I feel I may safely write the history of my life as prefect apostolic of the Mercedarians in the Lake Atitlán district. It is my wish that upon my death this history be passed on to my son, so that he may understand and, perhaps, forgive me.

I have said that I was the prefect apostolic of the Mercedarians. I held this office from the time I arrived in New Spain until the Cakchiquels rebelled two years later, murdering all of the Spaniards in Santiago Atitlán, including the missionaries, and sparing only me. As prefect apostolic, I was overseer of all religious instruction and administration of the sacraments performed by the nineteen Mercedarians under me, as well as overseer of the construction of the single-naved church within the fortress of Santiago Atitlán. In the first quarter I was there, two thousand natives were baptized; in the second quarter, three thousand. My thoughts were of such kind: *The grace of God moves even through these savage people.* The first missionaries had arrived three years before, but it appeared that the Indians were just beginning to accept fully the teachings of Christ and that I had arrived to witness their complete transformation, to the glory of God and the workers of His faith.

I did not understand the error of this belief until the church had been completed and we began, for the first time, to instruct the Cakchiquel children in the catechism. I entered the church during the third meeting of the class and saw an Indian boy who was not listening to the lecture of Juan de Zumárraga. I approached him and saw that he was drawing a picture of a woman standing on the horns of the crescent moon. In her hands were stalks of maize. To make an example of him, I said, quite loudly, "Excuse me, Fray Zumárraga, we have a boy here who is not paying attention," and I took the drawing from him. "Who is this?" I asked him.

"The Virgin Mother," he answered.

"This boy is drawing pictures of the Blessed Virgin, Fray Zumárraga," I said to the entire class. "I suppose we can excuse that, can't we?"

Then I suggested the boy alter his picture to show the Virgin crushing the head of the Serpent, as in the painting hanging over our baptismal font. He refused: "No one can crush the head of Quetzalcoatl." I was so startled to hear the name of the Cakchiquels' pagan god that I stood dumbly over the boy for a moment before grabbing his arm and leading him hurriedly out of the church.

In the vestibule, I ordered him to tell me what he knew about Quetzalcoatl. He did not want to speak. I raised my hand to strike him. "He is the feathered serpent, the creator of all," he said, fearfully. My hand fell to my side. He continued, more bravely, "He created the sky and the earth, the four directions. He told the gods of the wind to blow and the gods of the rain to empty their gourds. He created the Obsidian Stone, then made man and woman, all the people of the earth."

I began to feel dizzy. "Is not the Serpent evil, did he not cause the Fall of Man?" I asked.

"Quetzalcoatl is immortal, like the quetzal, and wise, like the snake," he answered.

I thought: *If the children do not believe* . . . and, heartsick, decided to take the Cakchiquel boy into my especial care.

From Belehé Can (as the boy was named), I learned that pilgrimages were still made by many Indians to their holy city, Sololá, which was located on the northern shore of the lake. These pilgrimages were led by the tribal priests, who journeyed there to consult the calendar bequeathed them by their god. Of the sacred calendar, I was able to learn only that it contained eighteen months of twenty days and one month, at the close of the year, of five days. Each day and month had a sign; Belehé Can's birth-sign, of which he was proud, was the snake. The month of the five days, the month of the feathered serpent, was considered unlucky, and it was marked by religious sacrifices to Quetzalcoatl. I had heard many reports of the bloody acts of sacrificial violence committed at the Cakchiquel temple in the past and could not believe that the Indians, so many of whom we had converted, had not abandoned their pagan beliefs. Yet Belehé Can was only nine years old, and he had been taught the myths we had labored to dispel. I began to fear our Orders had accomplished nothing. The Cakchiquels were still coming to us in large numbers to be baptized, but I was no longer certain they had truly converted. Distributing the Holy Eucharist, I would often close my eyes, thinking, *Their god is a serpent.*

It was a difficult time to be prefect apostolic. The brothers under my jurisdiction had objected, even more fiercely than the Cakchiquel chieftains, to my taking Belehé Can into the monastery house. Perhaps they would not have objected had I told them my purpose, but I did not tell them and they continued to challenge my authority. I felt the need to restore both their faith in me and the Cakchiquels' faith in our teachings; I planned an act I believed would accomplish both desires.

Through the mediation of Belehé Can's father, the Indian priests were gathered in the church one evening. I instructed Juan de Zumárraga, Pedro de Gante, and Angel Palerm, three men of great strength, to remain in the vestry in case I should need their aid, then went out into the sanctuary. There I greeted the priests and surveyed their faces, my heart careening within my chest. On the altar I had placed a wooden cage covered with a purple vesture. I now removed the vesture and, with a gloved hand, took from the cage a quetzal we had captured that afternoon. I felt then the same feeling—of anticipation, of fear, of pride—that I felt in my first Mass before I consecrated the bread and wine. Holding the bird aloft, I said, "I will show you the folly of false worship," then

I took a stiletto out of my robe and lanced its heart on the stone altar. I did the act decisively, with conviction, but at the moment of the bird's death, I was seized with fear, thinking, *Now they will rise up and kill me,* and called out, in a voice that shook, for Brothers Zumárraga, de Gante, and Palerm. They came instantly from the vestry, but there was no danger: the Indians had fallen to their faces on the stone floor of the church in great fear. But my fear was not lessened by theirs; I was so strangely frightened, I began to feel ill. My fellow Mercedarians led me out the vestry door into the cool night air and walked me through the still courtyard. After we had walked several minutes, I began to feel well again, even confident that I had made an important step toward the Indians' conversion.

But two days later we discovered that the Indians had secretly left the fortress of Santiago Atitlán. Deputy Governor Jorge de Alvarado the following day led forty horsemen, ninety foot soldiers (including sixty crossbowmen and musketeers), and two cannons and limbers into the forest, hoping to quell an uprising before it began. Meanwhile, Pedro de Portocarero and Hernan Carrillo, Alvarado's captains, ordered that the fortress prepare itself for siege. Everything was readied, and we began to wait. That day we heard sounds of battle in the distance, and our fear intensified. But before nightfall the sounds ceased, and for two days there was silence—silence so heavy prayer was almost impossible. Then, on the morning of the third day, the Cakchiquels attacked the fortress. They scaled the walls with ladders, three living for every one killed on the battlement by our soldiers. One of the first over the wall brandished Alvarado's severed head on his lance. He raised it high, even as our arrows struck him. When a musketeer finally felled him, another Indian picked up the lance. We were truly afraid. Our soldiers were few, and the Indians were many and well armed. They carried lances, knives, and bows, and wore cotton corselets three fingers thick. Their breastplates and helmets were smeared with blood. Caught weaponless in the church when the fighting began, I watched helplessly as the Indians slaughtered my people. From the window of the vestry, I saw the savages slash the throats of soldiers, merchants, and clerks of government. I watched a vile Indian kill the pregnant wife of our proconsul, then plunge his knife deep into her belly. I prayed: *Hail Mary, full of grace, the Lord is with thee . . .*

When the Indians' shouts could be heard outside the church, I fell to my knees, as did the other missionaries who were there, to prepare myself for death. But when they entered, bloodstained, scowling, our prayers became pleas for mercy. I remember hearing myself say, in a voice that sounded strange to my ears, "Do not kill me, I am your brother, please do not kill me." I felt disgust at my weakness, but even more, I felt joy when they did not harm me. I said a prayer of gratitude to God as they led us outside, through the labyrinth of fallen soldiers and Indians, to the steps of Alvarado's court. There we were joined by the missionaries who had been in other buildings or in the battle. Of the sixty-four missionaries of the Mercedarian, Franciscan, Dominican, and Augustinian Orders, I alone was not bound with cords and led away toward Sololá behind the dancing head of Alvarado. I was detained by the Cakchiquel priests, now wearing breastplates emblazoned with snakes and quetzals. I felt a certain pride that I was the only one chosen. It was a feeling such as I felt the moment before I killed the quetzal, and like that feeling it became fear when I realized that I did not know why or for what I had been chosen. The youngest of the priests, a man who had been a regular communicant at my Sunday services, spoke, answering my thoughts: "You killed a quetzal and did not die." Another priest, an old man with deep-set eyes and a long hooked nose, raised his hand, silencing him. His breastplate bore the image of Quetzalcoatl, with lizard-like head and a hackle of feathers at the neck. He glared at me as he spoke: "We will know soon if you are god or demon. When the month of Payriché passes, the spirit of the feathered serpent will descend, demanding hearts. You will be tested, and we will know if we are to fall on our faces before you or offer your heart to Quetzalcoatl." I could not look into his fierce gaze, so I cast my eyes downward.

"And my fellow brothers?" I asked.

"They will die," he answered.

My head was light with the thought of so much death, so I was only dimly aware of the ceremony that took place before Alvarado's burning court. I remember the setting of the fire, the flutes and drums, the unceasing chant, the dancing savages, the quartered dogs, all with the confusion of someone just awakened from a deep sleep. It was not until I felt the prod of spears at my sides that I realized the ceremony was over and the journey to Sololá about to begin. The chief priest (as I knew the old man to be from his authority) and several of the elder priests mounted my dead countrymen's horses and led the way out of the courtyard. I followed, guarded by the rest, on foot.

During the first league of the journey to Sololá, I saw all about me the bodies of my countrymen strewn in the grotesque postures of death. The cannons, their limbers still half-piled with balls, were draped with bodies. Two men and a horse were impaled on stakes at the bottom of a pit we passed. Many were lying, some headless, on the road, and had to be stepped over.

Eventually, we passed beyond the scene of the great battle and entered the tangled forest of coyal, jícaro, and pacaya trees on the western ridge of the lake. Here, my mind no longer numbed by the sight of the dead, I realized that I should have told the other missionaries, our proconsul, even Alvarado himself, what I had learned from Belehé Can. The thought that this omission should be the cause of so many deaths made me fall to my knees between my guards and begin to pray aloud for God's forgiveness. Perhaps I knew, even then, for what I truly wanted his forgiveness, but I prefer to think I did not. That knowledge did not come fully, I believe, until my sin was made manifest in the deaths of my fellow brothers. But I was not able to think long about my sin, whichever sin it was, for two of my guards pulled me to my feet and, on the chief priest's orders, bound my wrists and blindfolded me. Then they tied a rope around my neck and led me like a horse through the thick forest.

After a time, I began to hear the rumbling of water over rocks and realized we were nearing the river Quicab, which rushes through a deep gorge into Lake Atitlán. When we reached the gorge, we abandoned the horses and crossed it on an unsteady rope bridge. Hundreds of feet below, the sulfurous Quicab roared. I thought one moment I would fall, then the next that I would jump. Finally, I reached the firm earth on the other side. When all had crossed the bridge, we turned east and began following the river plateau. I knew we had reached the outer limits of the Cakchiquel holy city when I heard voices mingling with the roaring water. Then I heard the groaning of huge stone doors, and we entered Sololá. As we walked through the mortared streets, the voices became louder and louder. Soon we reached a large square, and I heard the roar of Spanish and Cakchiquel voices. As I was led forward, I heard my countrymen calling me. I strained to hear what they were saying but could not.

Then, my foot struck stone and my captors explained that I was to ascend steps. Suddenly I understood, or thought I understood, the meaning of the blindfold: I was at the pyramid of Quetzalcoatl; the steps were the Avenue of the Dead; they led to the sacrificial altar; I was being tricked—afraid I was a god, a god they feared, the Indians were going to kill me, perhaps more hideously than the others. I wanted to twist away from my captors, try to escape, but I knew it was madness even to consider it, so I ascended the steps obediently, even placidly, though my mind was swirling with fear and despair. It was not until I reached the summit and felt my clothes being cut off me that I realized to what I was about to submit myself. I started to struggle, then stopped, afraid of the knife. Every instant I expected it to strike through my robe and into my heart, as I had struck the quetzal, but it did not touch my skin. Then I was naked. I thought, *They will cut off my genitals!* and offered up a prayer to God and the Virgin almost simultaneously. But no blow came; instead, my blindfold was cut away and I beheld, from the summit of the truncated pyramid of Quetzalcoatl, the mass of Cakchiquels and Spaniards so far below me in the square, surrounding the rows of obelisks, their faces upturned. A strange feeling came over me then, a kind of vertigo, and for a moment I was someone else, someone I had never known or dreamed. I knew, even then, that I could not appear any larger to the men below me than they did to me, but I felt immense, as if I were larger than the world and no longer a part of it. I spread my legs apart and stood firmly, powerfully, my fists clenched, and thought, *Do they know who I am thought to be?* The cry that rose from their throats assured me that they did.

Then I came back to myself and, my mind roiling, staggered away from the precipice. Two priests took me by the wrists then and led me to the ceremonial chamber of the temple. At that time I was too overwhelmed with fear and horror to notice the sacrificial altar or, beside it, the statue of the feathered serpent with its upturned head and gaping mouth. Nor did I notice the designs carved on the three tiers of the ceremonial chamber itself: the feathered serpent coiling around the sun, quetzals feeding on human hearts, a priest sowing a field with seed from his erect penis. All this, and more, I saw later, during my convalescence. But then, I saw nothing and heard only the chief priest's words: "You are to remain guarded in the chamber, without food or drink, until the sun has ascended and descended the temple seven times. Then the month of the feathered serpent, and the ceremony of blood, will begin, and we will learn if you are god or devil."

After I entered the chamber, the priests fastened a jaguar hide over the aperture, eliminating all light. The darkness frightened me, but I was more afraid of the sinful pleasure I had felt while standing on the summit of the pyramid. I told myself it was the giddy height of the pyramid and the relief of not being killed that had made me feel as I had, but I knew it was something else. I made myself think, *I am naked, and a man*, and turned my thoughts to God and prayed to Him, vowing to resist the ceremony and die a martyr.

I had no means of telling time save by my hunger and thirst, so I do not know how long I remained faithful to my vow. I believe, however, that it was four or five days. I would like to say that I kept my resolve longer, but I was a big man, bigger than I am now, and I was used to eating all I needed and more. As time passed, my hunger hollowed me, until I became so empty I was no one, only a body, a vessel waiting to be filled.

By the morning after the seventh day of fasting, I did not care whether I lived or died. When the guards removed the jaguar skin and let me out, I fell to my knees in the brilliant dawn and covered my eyes with trembling hands. A voice taunted me: "Do you hunger, Fray Hurtado?" Another voice: "Are you thirsty? Would you like a long drink?" I could not find the strength to tell them I no longer cared. I shook my head no. Then I heard the chief priest say, "He is ready. Bring him the holy liquid." A bowl was placed before me, and I was told to drink. Opening my eyes, I saw the bowl in a blur. I lifted it slowly to my lips and drank, long and deep. The liquid was bitter and could not satisfy the emptiness within me, but I drank it all. After I finished, I found my eyes had adjusted to the light. I stood shakily and saw, once again, the mass of my people gathered so far below me. I felt nothing for them, only wondered, *Do they know how I have suffered?*

The chief priest approached me then, a stiletto carved from obsidian in his hand. I thought he was going to kill me as I had killed the quetzal, but I could not run, so dead was my soul. But he did not try to kill me. Instead, he gave me the stiletto and instructed me in the rite to be performed with it: beginning before the sun had fully risen, and continuing throughout the five days at each sunrise and sunset, I was to cut my tongue, forearms, genitals, and thighs and offer the blood to Quetzalcoatl by burning it with copal gum. For this purpose, I was to be taken to the deepest chamber of the pyramid, a chamber far below ground. I heard his words distantly, as one hears music from another room. Only one half of me was listening to the priest; the other was watching the sun glint on his breastplate, making the feathered serpent seem almost alive.

The Cakchiquel holy liquid must have been a soporific, for I remember nothing until the chief priest awakened me as the sun began to set. I did not recognize the place in which I found myself.

In the half-light I could see that it was a cell with dark obsidian walls, but like a cave there was a large natural aperture through which I could see the Quicab and the steep wall of rock on the other side of the gorge. I was lying on a stone altar, and on both sides of me were braziers giving off a horrid burning odor. I did not know, nor do I now know, how I had made the cuts required of me that morning, but the incisions were there, and as the sun set, I traced the red lines with the black tip of the stiletto and bled once more. The blood throbbed from my thighs and coated my knees and shins; my genitals shone with blood; my arms oozed red; the blood from my cut tongue filled my mouth and had to be spat into the bowl. To see my blood fill the bowl exalted me strangely. It gave me a feeling of immense power to see my blood before me, though I knew it meant I was losing my strength, and I was fascinated by the fact that, as I hung my head over the bowl, I could see my image in the dark fluid. I thought, at the time, that it was the soporific that made me think such things, and I vowed to refuse it, even if it meant death.

I lay back on the altar then and watched the chief priest pour my blood from the bowl into the large braziers beside me. The horrid odor increased. When the priests finished bathing me, the chief priest offered me the soporific. But I shook my head and said no. I expected him to force it upon me, but he did not; he merely nodded, and left. I slept then, briefly, until the pain of the incisions awakened me. Again I did not know where I was, but this time I was anxious. I felt a guilt that was elusive, like a dream, and I began to think I had been dreaming, but I remembered nothing. I was sick, but it did not feel like the sickness hunger brings. I wished to have the power to atone, but for what, I did not know. Then I saw a face before me, illumined in the darkness by the braziers, and recognizing the chief priest, I asked for the soporific.

When I next awoke, the sun was rising, and I no longer felt the sickness of the night before. With a strange calm, I repeated the ritual incisions, then lay back and watched the black walls grow red with sunlight.

I did not think I knew, then, why I was submitting to the savage rite, but I must have, for I continued to make the incisions even though I believed that it was sinful to participate in pagan ceremonies and that my duty as a man of God was to submit to martyrdom. I continued in my sin without concern for damnation or death. And I did not consider myself a victim.

But after the morning rite on the fourth day, I was so weak from hunger and the loss of blood that I thought I was close to death, and I began once more to fear for my soul. Resolving to resist the ceremony and die in a state of grace, I refused the soporific and asked to be carried to the mouth of the cell, where I could look up at the heavens and prepare myself to meet God. The chief priest dismissed the guards after they moved me, then approached me with a bowl in his hands. I pushed it away, thinking he was offering me the soporific again, and turned my eyes to the river outside. Then he put the bowl to my lips, and I tasted my blood. I looked at his calm eyes, his nodding head, and drank several swallows. Then, dazed, I requested the soporific.

Before sleep encircled me, the chief priest spoke, telling me how in the beginning Quetzalcoatl created the Obsidian Stone in the depths of Xibalbay and how He made man, kneading maize-dough with the blood of the serpent and the blood of the quetzal, to give homage to the Stone. I remember being told that Quetzalcoatl became man once before, that His mother hung His umbilical cord on the temple door to signify the divine birth then threw herself into the gorge, that He promised to return again. I saw the old priest before me and, behind him, the altar and the braziers, as I heard through the roar of the Quicab the story of the highest god, Quetzalcoatl, the creator of all, and understood—or thought I understood, in my torpor—this god who disguised himself in the thought that is *bird* and the thought that is *serpent*.

When next I came into consciousness, expecting to see the chief priest before me, telling me of the wonder of the blood of man, I was holding the obsidian blade over the incision on my left forearm. I thought: *It is madness to kill myself slowly, I will strike out my life with one blow!* But I traced the reddened scar gently and watched the blood throb into the bowl. Then I finished my incisions and lay back as the priests added my blood to the copal gum and bathed me. My tongue had swollen; I could not make a fist for the pain in my arms; to urinate was to burn; I could not walk nor stand. I began to pray for my death but did not know to whom I was praying, so I stopped, confused, telling myself I would know the following day.

The next morning, after twelve days of fasting and five days of gradual self-sacrifice, the chief priest gave me a long staff on which a carved snake crawled toward a pair of wings. Then the other priests lifted me onto a litter and carried me through the labyrinthine passages of the pyramid and brought me before the people, who began to chant with one voice my new name. At the sound of the name, a thrill pierced my heart and rose, swelling, into my head. I felt that it was my name, that I had become what they had waited to name. It was a horrible thought, but I did not have the strength, nor the will, to resist it. Even now, after these many years, the mere memory of the name, its simple consonants and vowels, makes my sinful blood pulse as with a fever. I wish I could forget it, but I cannot. Though I have never spoken the name to anyone, it echoes always in my soul.

The Cakchiquels thronged about me, anxious, afraid, not daring to touch me or my staff, as I was paraded through the rows of obelisks and back, twice passing the closely guarded missionaries, whom I had, in my ordeal, forgotten. Their pleas for help reached my ears; they begged me to intercede on their behalf. I was gratified that my apotheosis had given me the power to save them, and I resolved to order their release at my first opportunity.

The Cakchiquels carried me to the summit of the pyramid and placed me on a throne behind the sacrificial altar. The ceremonial chamber of the temple was glowing with a huge fire and smoke was rising out of an aperture in the roof. On the altar was the chief priest's long obsidian knife. Then the chief priest appeared, wearing a mask with painted serpent's snout and fangs, and a cloak made of the iridescent blue and green tail plumes of quetzals. On his hands were bound the clawed forefeet of a jaguar. The incantation of my new name arose among the priests and was repeated by the Cakchiquel nation below. I beheld the missionaries as they were led up the Avenue of the Dead. The first to reach the top was a familiar face; I knew him to be one of my Order, either Roberto Ossage or Alejandro Marroquín or perhaps Carlos Macías, but I could not remember his name. I looked at his pale, bloodless face. He looked at me, then closed his eyes. My heart seemed to tilt on its axis, sending a shudder through my breast. It was not a shudder of sympathy or fear or even disgust. It was something worse. It is awful to say, but I felt then a passion like that I felt later, when I first lay with a woman.

I did not order his release. Instead, I watched as my countryman was bound on the altar, his face contorted into a berserk beauty, and the chief priest spoke ritual words of purification over him. Then the priest plunged the knife into his chest and cut out, and held in his hand, the still-quivering heart. He placed the heart in a large urn beside the altar, then turned to me and nodded. I looked away. The next missionary, perhaps Juan de Zumárraga or Juan de Herrera, was killed in the same manner and his heart placed with the first. The slaughter was immense; all of the missionaries were killed and carried into the chamber to be burned. After all were dead, I requested the soporific, wanting to sleep away the dizzy horror, but instead, the hearts, many still pumping absurdly, were offered to me. I rose from my throne then, wanting to throw myself on the fire with my countrymen, but before I could take a step, the world seemed to tilt, the bloody altar spun in front of me, and I fell onto the stone floor, unconscious.

For some time after that, my mind was not right, and I believed I was home in Spain, a boy again, eating the meals my mother prepared for me. My delusion must have lasted for several weeks, for when I finally realized who and where I was, my health was greatly improved, and I was no longer emaciated. And when I understood how I had been returned to health, the horror of my apotheosis became clear to me, and I knew I had to escape or go mad.

There were no guards set on me and my commands were met with the expediency deserving of a god, so when I thought I was strong enough to complete a journey to Santiago Atitlán, where I was certain Spanish forces would be gathering for an attack on the Indians, I ordered that a canoe be brought to me. The chief priest and several of the other priests watched me from the mouth of the cell where I had endured the ceremony of apotheosis, but only the chief priest spoke to me before I left. His words were spoken reverently, yet they were a recrimination and a warning: "You cannot escape your blood."

After overcoming the rapids of the Quicab and entering onto the smooth-surfaced lake, my mind broke with the horror I thought I had left behind. I imagined I saw a body floating in the distance, and I paddled toward it. And as I paddled, I saw another, then another. I paddled closer, then saw they were the dead bodies of my countrymen. They were floating on their backs, their charred visages staring at the sun, their gaping chests red with blood. As I stared at them, more corpses rose to the surface around my canoe until I was surrounded by them. They were everywhere. And the stench of my soul was great.

How I finished my journey to Santiago Atitlán I do not know. All I know is that when I arrived I was taken into the monastery house and cared for by the newly arrived missionaries. When my delirium subsided, I feigned a relapse and was excused, on that account, from resuming my duties as prefect apostolic of the new Mercedarians, as well as from explaining my wounds. When finally I chose to return to health but would not perform my duties as a priest or confess my sins and receive the Holy Eucharist, I became a disgrace, someone who is looked down upon by all. For solace I sought out a woman of the brothel, and got her with child. I became then more than a disgrace; I became an outcast, someone to be shunned like a leper. And now, unrepentant after twenty years, I am universally considered the lowest of human beings, less a man than a demon, and though I would spare my wife and son their shame, I bear happily the cross of that judgment, for it has provided me with what little comfort is possible in my life.

*Here Ends the History of Eusebio Daválos Hurtado*

There is no doubt in my mind, Your Eminence, that the tribunal, after hearing the story related here, will understand that my intentions in reading it to the novices and brothers were not heretical. I intended only to present the evil association of bloodlust with religion by pagans who reject the message of Christ. The Holy Office will see that the heresy lies in the madness of the story's author and will seek him out for Inquisition, if he is still alive. As for myself, I trust my dutiful appearance will be appreciated by the Inquisitors and rewarded, as the tribunal is most just, with a document of apology that I may present to my archpriest upon my return, as well as a document reprimanding Brother Vasco de Quiroga for his condemnation of me, as a proper recompense for the shame to which I have been subjected.

Written this twenty-eighth day of the month of January, year of the birth of our Savior Jesus Christ one thousand five hundred and fifty-six, by your faithful servant in Christ,

Fray Miguel Sabogal

# DELIVERANCE

**B**efore *we get started, I want to make sure you understand why I'm here. The court has appoint—*

Is this thing turned on?

*Yes. And you don't have to lean forward. Just speak in a normal voice and the mic will pick it up.*

What do you want me to do? Just tell everything that happened?

*Yes. But first I want you to understand that what you tell me is confidential; it can't be used in court. The tape is for my benefit only, to help me assess whether—*

My name hasn't always been Deliverance Egg, you know. I say that right at the first because I suppose you need to know my real name.

*I already know it. It's listed here in this folder, along with the arresting officer's report. But I want to hear your side of the story.*

But you need to know why I changed my name. That's an important part of the story. And "Egg" is my real name, so I didn't make it all up. My real name is Anna Louise Egg, my father's name was James R. Egg (the "R" is for Richmond, like the city in Virginia, though he never lived there a day in his life), and I was born in Sedalia, Missouri, the Queen City of the Prairie. No one called me "Scrambled" there, but that's what they call me here, so when I turned twenty-one I took the bus downtown to the courthouse to change my name from "Egg" to whatever popped into my head. But when I was sitting there in the Clerk of Court's filling out the change-of-name form, I don't know what happened to me, but I couldn't do it. I couldn't just get up and walk out like a fool either, though, so what I did was leave my last name "Egg" and change my first name to "Deliverance." You might think I chose "Deliverance" because I'm a Moonie or a Seventh Day Adventist or something like that, but I'm not. I haven't even gone to church since Mama died and Daddy married that teen-aged ticket vendor at the Avalon. Why I chose it was because my favorite movie star in the whole world is Burt Reynolds and my favorite movie of his is *Deliverance*. He wears a leather vest in that movie without a shirt under it, and when he paddles his canoe, his biceps ripple the way a horse's skin does when flies are bothering it. If you haven't seen that movie, you really ought to.

*We can talk about the movie some other time, Miss Egg. Right now, I'd like to hear what happened the night you were arrested.*

I'm getting to that. I just told you about my name so you'd know how I am about names. I love names. I really like to give people names that fit them. I'll see some joker strutting by the Country Kitchen, where I bus dishes, and I'll say to Rosy, "There goes Sylvester Gumball" or something like that, and Rosy, she'll just about fall off her stool from laughing. Or we'll be walking down the street and I'll see some guy and call him whatever comes into my head, like "Radar Ears" or "Hamster Cheeks." I'm crazy like that. That's why they called me "Scrambled," in part at least. But the reason I say this is so you'll know why I call Rosy "Rosy Blue" instead of "Jennifer Marie Kelsey," which is the name Old Guernsey gave her when she adopted her. I call her Rosy Blue because that's the color her lips are, rosy blue, because, you see, she's not American. She's from Bangladesh, but she's lived in Minneapolis since she was seven months old, which is why she talks English as good as I do.

*How long have you known Miss Kelsey?*

Her name's Rosy Blue, not "Miss Kelsey," and she was an orphan till she met me. Old Guernsey may be her legal mother, but I'm her real mama, so in a way I guess that means I've known her ever since she was born, though not really. Anyway, I'm her mama and her best friend, and when we wear our burgundy sweatshirts I'm her twin sister. We do just about everything together, even though she's just twelve and I'm—well, I'm not going to put my age on this tape for everyone to hear. You'll just have to guess, though if you already know my real name you probably know how old I am, too.

*Yes, I have that information. Please go on.*

But other people don't know. If anyone asks, I tell them they'll just have to guess. That's my way—keep people guessing. Ask anybody who hangs around Madison and Comstock and they'll tell you the same thing.

*How do you think Mrs. Kelsey would feel to hear you say Jennifer—Rosy Blue—isn't her daughter?*

She's not. Everyone knows that. All you have to do is look at them and you can see they're not even related. She looks like an old cow. That's why I call her "Old Guernsey," that and the fact that when she walks her rump hitches like a fat old cow's. The first time I called her Guernsey-Butt, Rosy had to sit down on the curb to keep from peeing in her pants. Of course, that was years ago, when she was just a little kid. I can still remember some of the things she used to say back then. One day, I remember, she was crying on her stoop. "What's the problem?" I said, the way I do. "My goldfish got sex and died," she answered back. I swear that's what she said: "got sex and died"! Riviera claimed he heard me laughing—

*Riviera?*

You know, Ronnie Rodeberg. The wannabe rapist. He said he heard me laughing three blocks away that day, and I don't doubt him, though everything else he's ever said is a lie. I've got this laugh that sounds like a seal bark, only higher. I bought Rosy two new goldfish that day, but Old Guernsey made her give them back. She hates me because Rosy likes me better than her. Anyway, it's definite that Rosy is no kid anymore. She's more grown up than I'll ever be. She's like Joan of Arc, who was a hero and a saint even though she was just a girl. I won't ever be a hero or a saint, but when I'm sweating in hell, at least I'll know that Rosy's in heaven because of me.

*Do you think the court should discount Mr. Rodeberg's testimony?*

Is a wild bear Catholic? Does the pope shit in the woods? Of course they should discount it. He's a natural-born liar. The way Riviera tells it, I'm to blame for everything, but no one with his hat screwed on frontways ever believed a word Riviera said. Even Coast-to-Coast—that's his father—once said that Riviera and the Truth had never met but once and that was in a dark alley. And the way he raised his eyebrows let you know he thought Riviera had got the best of that fight, though he lost every real fight he ever fought on account of being so spindly and "civilized." Coast-to-Coast used to joke about Riviera like that all the time, and it always made me feel bad because he was his father, after all. But it was true: Riviera has always been a liar, even before he took it up professionally, cooing to his customers ("clientele," he calls them) at the Minneapolis Academy of Hair Design. And he never lied in any usual way, either, just like he never dressed or talked in any usual way, which is why I call him Riviera. For example, he always drew a circle over his i's instead of a dot. Now I call that a lie, and I ought to know because I lie all the time.

*Are you lying now?*

No, I'm not, but would I tell you if I was? My point is, if I wasn't such a liar, I wouldn't be here talking into this dumb tape recorder and Riviera would be giving some pimply teenager the business in his apartment. But if Riviera thinks he can lie his way out of this, he doesn't know Deliverance Egg. Just because my lie started the whole thing doesn't mean he's innocent. After all, *I* didn't try to rape anybody.

*Do you think Mr. Rodeberg is guilty of attempted rape?*

Of course I do. And you will too, soon as I tell you what happened.

*Yes. Please tell me what happened.*

It was like this: it was just before dark, the time when the streetlights go on all up and down Madison and most everybody is home cooking supper, and everything is so quiet after the shops have closed that you want to shout. I was standing near the bus stop on the corner of Madison and Comstock, but I wasn't waiting for the bus, I was just talking to a guy who was waiting for the bus. I didn't know this guy, but I was talking to him because I like to talk. I like to be around people. I can't sit in my room above the tailor shop all by myself or I'll start bouncing off the walls like a pinball. I have to talk to someone or I can't even get to sleep at night. That's how I am. So I was down at the corner talking to this guy in a sharkskin coat with the collar turned up and matching hat. His ears were white from the cold. I'd named him Silva Thin because he looked like the kind of guy who would smoke Silva Thins, though he wasn't smoking anything then. He was just sitting on the bench, ignoring me, but I kept talking anyway.

"My favorite movie star is Burt Reynolds," I said to him. "Who's yours?" But he just looked up the street, then at his watch. "I've seen almost every picture he's ever been in," I added, "and I've got a poster of him tacked up on my wall, beside my bed, so he's the last thing I see when I go to bed at night and the first thing I see when I wake up in the morning. You know the poster I mean? The one where he seems almost like he's ready to wink at you?"

But this guy was like most guys, he didn't want to talk about Burt Reynolds. I don't suppose you care much for Burt Reynolds either, right?

*I'd rather we kept the focus on what happened that night.*

Just what I thought. Men are all alike. At any rate, when this guy didn't want to talk about Burt Reynolds, I changed the subject. "Want to see my ID cards?" I said. You see, I collect ID cards. Now and then someone will leave a purse at the Country Kitchen, and sometimes I'll take out the driver's license and charge cards. I know what you're thinking, but I don't *steal* them; I just collect them. If I used them, that'd be stealing, and I never use them, not ever. I just like to look at them and imagine what all these different people are like. You should see all the strange names they have. Dworkin. Schwartzengruber. Matsuguchi. Names like that.

Anyway, I took a pack of IDs out of my sweater pocket to show
Silva Thin, but he wasn't interested. He just looked away and said,
real quiet, though I could still hear it, "Shit."

I said, "What?"

Then he looked at me and said, "Aren't you freezing?"

You see, I didn't have my peacoat on, just a Hawaiian-style
muumuu and that pink cardigan Rosy was wearing when they
arrested us. I was in such a hurry to get out of my room I hadn't
put on my peacoat. Sometimes it feels like the walls are closing in
like in a Vincent Price movie and you just have to get out. So I
got out and left my peacoat hanging on its hook by the door. I *was*
freezing, but I wasn't going to let Silva Thin and his white ears
know it.

"I don't need a coat," I told him. Then I smiled, just a little,
and said, "There's other ways to keep warm, you know."

*Were you propositioning him?*

Don't you think that for a minute, Doctor Freud. I'm no whore.
In fact, I'm a virgin, and if it weren't for Tampax I could prove it.
I was just making a joke, but it wasn't the kind of joke you want
people to laugh at. But Silva Thin laughed. It was a sharp, short
laugh, a *ha!*, and it hung in the air between us, a little cloud of
breath, like after a tiny H-bomb.

"You?" he said. "That's rich! That's really rich." He was looking
around like he wished there was someone else there to see how
rich it was.

I didn't know what to do at first, but then I said, "What's the
matter? You got an ingrown cock?" As soon as I said it, his face
got this ugly, squashed look. It scared me, so I said, "I'll be seeing
you, Silva Thin," and started off down Madison like nothing had
happened. But I felt trembly all over.

I'd only gone a few steps when Silva Thin started cursing me
real loud. I mean *loud*. And it was the kind of cursing a businessman
does, the kind that makes your heart seize up, not like the swearing
of a cabby or construction worker. I don't know whether it was
mostly his cursing or the cold that made me start running, but I

took off then and didn't stop until I reached Rosy's house a few minutes later. I leaned against one of their elm trees and tried to catch my breath. Then all of a sudden I was crying to beat the band. Bawling worse than Rosy did when she skinned her knee skateboarding that time or even when Mr. Guernsey fell over dead on the sidewalk during the Aquatennial Parade two years ago. I'm like that sometimes. I just start crying. The dumbest things can set off. For instance, there's this commercial that always makes me cry. A little boy is lost in a huge department store and his father is looking frantically for him and finally he finds him and picks him up and hugs him like he'll never let go. And then the next second they're in McDonald's or someplace eating a hamburger. He's so happy he found his kid that he buys him a Big Mac. I can't help it, every time I see that commercial I start crying.

*Miss Egg, could you just tell me what happened that night?*

I *am* telling you what happened that night. If you want to understand what happened later, you got to know everything that happened before.

*Okay, okay. Please continue.*

Like I was saying, I stood there outside Rosy's house crying for a long time. Finally, the tears stopped coming and I wiped my eyes with my sleeve and went up on the front porch and peeked in the window to see if Rosy was in the living room. She wasn't, so I snuck around the side of the house and looked in the kitchen window. There she was, sitting across the table from Old Guernsey, eating something that was steaming. She was wearing that same plastic bib she was carrying when Officer Handcuffs—the one they call Bob—brought us in, even though, like I said, she's twelve years old and name me one twelve-year-old kid who needs a bib. Old Guernsey is just crazy. She can't stand stains or dirt. Rosy told me she even mops the basement rafters, if you can believe that. She told Rosy dust rises with the heat and brings spiders and roaches with it. She hates bugs worse than anything so once Rosy and I caught all sorts of them in the vacant lot next to the Christian Science Reading Room, then let the whole jarful loose in her bedroom while she was asleep. Rosy got strapped with a belt for that, but I was the one that really got the blame. "Don't ever let me catch you near my daughter again," Old Guernsey yelled at me across the street the next day. "She's not your daughter," I yelled back. She stood there, holding a bag of groceries, and glared at me for the longest time, and I glared back. Eventually she went on home. The old cow.

But this time I'm not taking the blame. I didn't do anything anybody wouldn't do. I was freezing cold, my teeth were jumping around so much I thought I'd bite my tongue off, and I was feeling sick inside from running and crying, so I snuck back around to the front and rang the doorbell, then quick ran around to the kitchen window again. Old Guernsey was already on her way to answer the bell. I waited till she was out of the room, then tapped on the window. When Rosy looked up, her lips made a big O and she put her spoon down. I pointed toward the back door, then dashed around to it. In a second, the door opened a little and there was Rosy's olive-brown face and blue-black hair peeking around it.

"What d'you want, D'liverance?" she said. "Mama's here, you know."

I said, real breathless-like, "Rosy, there's a *man* after me," then looked around like he could be anywhere.

*Did the man from the bus stop chase you?*

No. No. I was just saying that. Anyway, Rosy said right away, "Does he got a *knife?*" You could tell how much she looks up to me, her brown eyes were so wet and shiny. You see, the last time I told her someone had tried to rape me, I said he'd tried to stab me when I wouldn't give in, but I bit his wrist and made him drop the knife on the sidewalk.

*Were you telling the truth then? Or was that a lie too?*

Oh, it was a lie, but it wasn't a real lie, just a fake one. I wasn't trying to get anyone in trouble, the way Riviera did with his lies. I didn't say so-and-so did it or anything like that. It was just like TV—you know, drama. Some excitement to liven up the day. And I didn't point the finger at anyone, not even Silva Thin, that night. I just said, "Come with me, Rosy. He won't dare do anything if there's two of us. I'll wait till you can sneak out." You see, I needed to be with her. You have to understand that. I couldn't have just gone home alone, not after the way Silva Thin cursed me. But I could tell that Rosy was worried what Old Guernsey would do if she snuck out with me again. So I added, in a whisper, "He had his fly down and it was *out*." Rosy's eyes got big then, and I knew she'd come with me. In a few minutes, I thought, Rosy and I would be sitting in my warm room, talking or playing dominoes or looking at the models in the Sears catalog.

But just then Old Guernsey came back from the front door and saw me. She yelled my name—my Christian name, the name Mama and Daddy gave me—then started to run, if you want to call it running, towards me. "Sneak out later if you can," I said to Rosy in a hurry and then I took off. But the stoop was icy and I slipped and landed on my butt, hard. I was so embarrassed—I don't like for Rosy to see me looking unsophisticated—but I got up quick and ran off down the sidewalk, my rear end smarting. The old lady stopped at the door, of course, because she knew she could never catch up with me. "I'm calling the police on you, Anna Egg, and this time they'll put you away," she yelled, and then I heard her yell something I didn't understand but that sounded frantic, almost crazy. I turned down a side street, still running. It was heavy dark by then, and I didn't stop till I reached a streetlight, and that was when I understood what Old Guernsey had been yelling so frantic about: Rosy had followed me out the door. She came running up to me, breathing hard. She looked so funny, her face all serious-somber above that bib with the yellow duck on it, that I couldn't help but laugh. I leaned up against the streetlight like one of those ceramic drunks you see in gift shops and just laughed and laughed.

"*Shh*," Rosy said. "What if he hears you?" She meant the man who was after me.

"I didn't have any trouble with that guy who tried to knife me, did I?" I asked.

"No," she said, "but you never know what can happen. This one might have a *gun*."

I thought a moment, touching my chin the way people do in the movies when they're thinking hard, and then I said, "I bet you're right, Rosy Blue, I bet this guy *did* have a gun, because he kept one hand in his jacket pocket. So maybe we'd better high-tail it out of here."

*How did you feel, lying to Rosy like that?*

It wasn't a real lie, like I said, it was just for fun. At any rate, I didn't know where to go. We couldn't go to my room, like I'd planned, because the police would be looking for us there, thanks to Old Guernsey. I thought for a while and then it came to me: the depot. I'll go down there once in a while and spend a few hours talking to the people waiting for buses. You can meet people from most everywhere, but I've never met anyone from Sedalia, Missouri, even though it's the Queen City of the Prairie and the home of State Fair Community College. Wouldn't you like to go to a college named after a state fair? I bet that'd be a fun college. If I ever went back to school, that's where I'd want to go. Anyway, I asked Rosy if she wanted to hop a bus downtown and spend the night at the depot, and right away she nodded and said okay. I could tell she was nervous, though, because she kept on nodding.

"Old Guernsey'll skin you if you stay out all night," I warned.

But Rosy didn't care. "I can't let you face him all alone, can I?" she said. "What if something happened to you?"

I just about cried then, I was so proud. Here she was, getting herself in trouble with Old Guernsey and risking getting shot or raped, all to protect me. Rosy may be young enough to be my daughter, but in some ways she's old enough to be my mother, if you know what I mean.

*Yes, I think I do. Please go on.*

We were really getting cold. Rosy's lips were bluer than ever, and she was shivering. She gets cold very easy because she's so thin. I keep telling her to eat more, but she's real picky. When she comes to the Country Kitchen, I try to sneak her a milkshake, but she hardly ever drinks the whole thing, even if it's chocolate. She's not like most kids. Anyway, she was shivering so bad I gave her my cardigan. It hung way down to the patched knees of her jeans, and you could see the head of that goofy duck through the V above the buttons. She looked so cute I couldn't help giving her a hug. Then we rolled up her sleeves and took off for the bus stop.

Silva Thin was gone by then, of course, and we were all alone. No one likes to wait for buses after dark on Madison. Even the streetlights don't stop some people. Somebody is always getting mugged or raped. We waited about five minutes, hopping first on one foot, then the other to keep warm, and then the bus came down the street like a big red glowworm, all lit up inside. I dropped two quarters into the fare box, and we sat in the back, near the heaters, rubbing our legs and arms and faces. Everybody in the bus stared at us, and when people stare at me and Rosy, I go into my act.

"Rosalind," I said, just like I was Queen Elizabeth or something, "did you remind Butley to polish the silver while we're at the opera?"

This pimple-faced guy across the aisle began to laugh.

"What're you laughing at?" Rosy said.

"Her majesty here," he answered back. There was another guy with him who was chewing his gum to beat sixty, and he stopped chewing just long enough to laugh and say, "Where'd you get those clothes—the dumpster behind Goodwill?"

"Fuck you," Rosy said, and then they really laughed, their heads whipped back like wolves'.

"*Shh*," I said, but Rosy was mad. You should see her when she gets mad. She won't listen to me when she gets like that. "I wonder if the Archduke will visit us in Vienna again this spring," I said, and ahemed like royalty.

But Rosy was glaring at Acne and Wrigley. "Go blow yourselves," she said.

Acne laughed again, then said, "I bet you don't even know what *blow* means."

"Oh yeah?" Rosy said.

"My, how time flies when you're chewing gum," I said to Wrigley, but Rosy didn't laugh.

"I do too know," she said. But she didn't, really. You could tell.

"It's better than chewing your *cud*," Wrigley said, like a real wit.

"Don't you talk to D'liverance like that, shitface," Rosy warned.

About then a nurse who was sitting in front of us moved up towards the front. Everyone else was sneaking glances back at us, especially the driver. I could see his eyes in the rearview mirror. They looked worried instead of mad. I thought he was probably a nice man, the kind of guy who really cared about his wife and kids, and I felt sorry for him. How would you like to drive a bus at night in Minneapolis? You never know what kind of riffraff you're going to pick up. So you see I didn't want to give the driver any trouble, but when Acne leaned across the aisle and said to Rosy, "Look who's calling who *shitface*," meaning her dark skin, I hopped up and banged him on the jaw with my fist. That was all the driver needed to see. He slammed on the brakes, and I went flying face-first onto the floor. The next thing I knew, the driver was pulling Rosy off Acne's friend. "She bit me," he was screaming, "she bit me!" And Acne was saying, "That one hit me in the face. Look at my face." His cheek was already red and puffy. I stood up, wobbly-like.

"Who do you think you are?" I said to Acne. "Burt Reynolds?" He was touching his cheek like it was a big pimple about to pop.

"All right," said the bus driver, "that's enough. You two"—he meant me and Rosy—"will have to get off here. I won't have any more fighting on my line."

So that's how we ended up walking down Hennepin towards the bus depot. If it wouldn't have been for Acne, or Old Guernsey, or Silva Thin, none of this would have happened. So many little things lead up to one big thing that you can never tell what God's got up his sleeve.

*Do you think you're responsible for any of what happened?*

Not any more than God is, and I don't see you "assessing" him. He's getting off scot-free, just like he always does.

*So I take it you're not religious?*

I just said I believe in God, didn't I? Can you get more religious than that?

*All right. Please go on.*

Okay. Where was I? Oh yeah, walking down Hennepin. It was so cold we ducked into the Leamington and warmed up in the lobby for a while. Rosy said we should just sleep on one of the couches scattered there under the chandeliers, but I knew the hotel dick wouldn't let us catch even twenty winks before he threw us out. Besides, I had another reason for wanting to go to the depot. I hadn't said anything to Rosy yet, but I'd been thinking for quite a while about going back to Sedalia. I didn't have more than two dollars in change on me, but I knew I could use one of my credit cards to buy bus tickets. I know it's against the law to use someone else's card, and I didn't do it so the police can't accuse me of that, but I kept thinking how nice it would be if Rosy and I could live there all alone, without anybody to bother us. I saw us living in the same house where I'd lived with Mama and Daddy until Mama got sick and died. I've got some pictures of that house back in my room. It's a big white house with a wraparound porch and a huge front yard full of red oaks and willows. It was wonderful. In one of the pictures, Daddy is doing chin-ups on a branch in one of the red oaks. He was a good-looking man, the kind who always wore white T-shirts in the summer because he was so tan and had big biceps, and I can understand why that girl at the Avalon ran off with him, though I can't understand how he could do it. It was a rotten thing to do to Mama, even if she was dead, and it was a rotten thing to do to me, too. I mean, that girl wasn't much older than *Rosy*. If I had Daddy's address, I'd write him a letter and tell him just what I think of him—and in so many words, too. Anyway, I hadn't said anything to Rosy about going to Sedalia because I wasn't sure she'd go. She's only twelve, you know, and sometimes I think she only pretends she doesn't like Old Guernsey just to make me happy.

*That's an interesting perception, Miss Egg. Do you think Miss Kelsey— er, Rosy—pretends other things too?*

How would I know? I'm not her, though I wish I was. Anyway, do you want to hear about what Riviera did or not?

*Yes, yes. Of course.*

It was on our way down Hennepin that we met him. He was coming out of DiNapoli's, and as usual he was a sight. Shiny baby blue nylon zippered cap (cocked over his right ear, of course), matching prima jacket, white pants, and navy vinyl platforms at least three inches high. The guy's a walking fashion casualty. How he gets any customers at that hair saloon, I'll never know.

Anyway, he talks as weird as he looks. "Well, pinch my behind," he said when he saw me, "if it isn't Miss Ann of Green Eggs and Ham." That's what he's called me ever since I started calling him Riviera, back in school. He thinks he's pretty funny, and I guess maybe he is, but that doesn't make it all right to rape a twelve-year-old, does it? At any rate, the next thing he says to me is, "Imagine running into you twice in one day." It *was* quite a coincidence. Since the days when we were growing up in the same neighborhood and going to Madison High together, I hadn't seen him more than a dozen or so times a year. But I'd seen him just that morning, at his father's hardware store on Comstock, pretending he'd dropped by for a visit while he worked up the nerve to ask his old man for another "loan."

Anyway, he was talking to me, but he was looking at Rosy, and I didn't like the way he was looking at her. His eyes went up and down her like an elevator. He's famous for liking young girls, if you catch my drift. Back when he was a senior, in fact, he took this freshman girl named Mandy to the prom, and the next time I saw her she had a hickey the shape of Wisconsin on her neck. So I wanted to get Rosy away from him pronto. I turned to her and whispered, "Come on, Rosy, let's get out of here." Something about the way I said it must have scared her because her eyes suddenly got wide. "What's wrong?" she said, and this is where I made a mistake, and I admit it, it was a mistake, because before I could think I whispered back, "It's *him*. It's the one I was telling you about." I don't know why I said that, but I did. Anyway, Rosy's mouth dropped open and she stepped back. But she didn't run, she stayed right there with me. I don't think she even *thought* about leaving me alone with him. And she was plenty scared: when

Riviera stuck his right hand in his jacket pocket, where the gun would have been, her throat made a funny little sound, like a mouse-squeak.

*What do you mean, "him"? The man you call Silva Thin?*

No, no. The guy who pulled a gun on me.

*But there was no guy who pulled a gun on you, right?*

Right.

*You just imagined him.*

No. I made him up. That's a different thing.

*How is it different?*

If you imagine someone, you don't know if they exist or not—you can't be sure. But if you make someone up, well, you know that person isn't real.

*Do you imagine a lot, Miss Egg? Do you sometimes wonder if something really happened?*

Do you want me to tell the story or not?

*Yes, please.*

And I'll tell it the way it happened, not the way Riviera told it to Officer Handcuffs. According to that liar, we stopped him and asked him to loan us the money for a hotel room. He did rent us a room at the Montrose, that's true, but it was his idea, not ours. I wanted to go to the depot, remember? And he didn't really offer to rent us a room either. His exact words were, "You chicks look like you're freezing" (he was looking at Rosy's bib when he said that) "so why don't you come up to my room and warm your tail feathers by my radiator?" God, the way he talks. But did you notice he said *his* room? Like he already had one? Anyway, I was going to tell him to go sit on his radiator till his chestnuts were roasted, but before I could open my trap, Rosy said, "Okay." She was looking at his hand in his pocket, and she said it like it was her last word. It almost didn't get out of her throat. Like this: "Ok—ay." I had no intention of going to Riviera's room myself, much less letting Rosy go. Like I said, Rosy is awful pretty. And what's more, she's foreign, and guys like Riviera think it's "sophisticated" to you-know-what with foreigners. The more foreign and "exotic," the better. But the way

Rosy said "okay" choked me up so with pride and love and happiness
I couldn't say anything. She thought Riviera had a gun and still she
wasn't going to run away and leave me with him.

So we started back up Hennepin, listening to Riviera jabber
about this and that. He told us about this Panama hat he was
saving up for, and about these riding gloves he had his eye on.
Things like that. We'd gone about three blocks when he started to
tell us about this beehive hairdo he'd given some Amazon that
afternoon. He'd worked on it all afternoon and she'd hated it,
even though it was exactly what she asked for, so he had to undo
the whole thing. He took his hands out of his pockets to show us
just how high the beehive was, and the next thing I knew Rosy
had tackled his knees and knocked him to the sidewalk. I just
about shit a pickle.

"What the hallelujah?!" Riviera said.

"Go!" Rosy yelled at me. "Quick!"

But I didn't go anywhere. Riviera shoved Rosy off and spanked
her hard on the butt. "So you're loony, too," he said. He was flushed
in the face but more like he was surprised than he was mad.

"Don't you lay a hand on her," I said, and tried to kick him in
the middle leg, if you catch my drift. But he grabbed my foot and
twisted it till I fell flat on my can. That's another coincidence: I
landed on exactly the same spot I did when I slipped on Rosy's
steps. I have a big bruise there now, and it's not just black and
blue like people always say about bruises, it's green and yellow
too. A rainbow bruise. Anyway, after I fell down, Riviera jumped
up and grabbed Rosy's arm.

"*Run*, D'liverance," Rosy said. "Run before it's too late!"

"Will someone tell me what is going on here?" Riviera said.

Just then a red-faced man who was passing by stopped and
said, "What are you doing there, young fella?" and Riviera said,
"Just committing a murder, sir, nothing to worry about." The
man answered back, "That ain't funny," like he wasn't going to
take any guff, but he didn't do anything, he just walked on, glancing
back at us, like everybody else.

I stood up and tested my ankle. It was all right. Rosy looked at me, but I wasn't going anywhere. Then she looked at Riviera and said, real quiet, "You can take me. Just leave D'liverance alone." Riviera looked confused, but kind of pleased. And I was pleased, too, but for different reasons, of course.

"Let's continue our promenade, ladies," Riviera said then, and let go of Rosy's arm. And then we started walking on down toward the Montrose.

*Why didn't you just take Miss Kelsey and leave? Did Mr. Rodeberg threaten you in any way?*

No, he didn't make any threats, and if he had, he would've found himself flat on his back on the sidewalk. I'd've punched him out. I only went with him because I figured we'd get a free hotel room for the night. I had no intention of letting him rape Rosy. I was planning to wait till we were in his room and then knock him out with a vase or a lamp like they do in the movies or shove him into the bathroom, shimmy a chair under the doorknob so he couldn't get out, and then sleep with Rosy in his warm bed till morning, when I could bring up my idea about going to Sedalia. I wished I had a picture of the old house so I could show Rosy what it was like there, but I didn't. I knew I'd have to describe it as well as I could, so all the way to the Montrose I tried to think of the words I'd use. But I couldn't think of any that were right, everything I thought of sounded like a description of any old house right here in Minneapolis, so I finally decided to tell her that I knew where her *real* mother and father were and get her to go with me that way. I know that was a rotten trick to think up, but I figured she'd be happy once we got there and the good would outweigh the bad. It's like with Judas: if he'd never betrayed Jesus, no one could ever get into heaven. We'd all be screwed. That's the way things are sometimes, and there's nothing you or I can do about it.

At any rate, when we got to the Montrose, we found out that Riviera had lied, as usual. He had to go to the desk and pay for a room—$14.98, to be exact. The Montrose is no Leamington, let me tell you. While he wrote his Johnny Hancock in the registration book, I whispered Rosy my plan to lock him in the bathroom and sleep in the bed ourselves. Rosy relaxed a little then and gave me an almost-smile. But when we all went upstairs to the room, we found it didn't have any bathroom at all. The room was real small, just a bed, a sink, and a ratty chair. The bathroom was down the hallway, and everybody on the wing had to use it. And there were no vases or lamps to clock his skull with—just a dinky plastic ashtray and an overhead light. I didn't know what to do. I looked at Rosy, and she looked back at me as if to say, "Go on, run, I'll be all right, save yourself." But I didn't go, and I didn't have any intention of going.

Riviera sat down on the bed then, pulled a half pint of sloe gin out of his left jacket pocket, and took a smack. Then he stuck the bottle out toward Rosy. She looked at me, then took the bottle. She drank a little swallow and coughed. It was real cute. I could tell it stung behind her eyes because she started to tear up a little.

"Let her go now," she said to Riviera, after she got her breath back.

"*Let* her go!" he said, and shook his head. "You're a strange duo, let me say that." Then he looked at me. "Oh dear me," he said. "I forgot to pick up an afternoon paper." He took his wallet out of his hip pocket and pulled out a ten. "This should cover it. Would you run down to the lobby and buy me a copy," he said with a wink.

"Cover what?" I asked.

"The paper," he laughed. "And your trouble for fetching it for me."

I wasn't planning to go, like I said, but you should have seen Rosy. She was as noble as Joan of Arc and the rest of them. She was standing there beside the bed with my sweater hanging down to her knees, so scared her lips were quivering. But her eyes were telling me to go. She was going to offer herself, her innocence, for me. For *me*. I could have kissed her right then, I loved her so much. But what I did was say, "All right. I'll go." And I went.

*When you left, did you know what Mr. Rodeberg intended to do?*

Of course I did. That's why I didn't go any farther than the end of the hall, then came right back and listened at the door. It was one of those cheap hollow doors and I could hear everything they said clear as a summer day.

"Have another swallow and nestle up," Riviera said. "I won't bite, at least not right off." He laughed a little, and then I heard the bedsprings creak. "Mind if I take your bib off?" he said next. "Unless you're planning on eating something." But Rosy must not've gotten it because he added right away, "That was a joke, grumpy. Don't you ever smile? You afraid your face will crack in two or something?"

She must have smiled then, at least a little, because he said, "That's better." Then they were quiet for a while. I couldn't hear anything but I imagined him kissing her, unbuttoning my sweater, touching her tiny breasts with his big hands, and . . .

Then he said, "How old are you, anyway?" and she answered twelve. "Twelve," he repeated, and whistled through that gap in his teeth. "This will be a new Guinness record."

Then Rosy, her voice trembling: "You won't kill me, will you?"

"*Kill* you!" he said. "Seems to me you were the one trying to kill *me* a while back."

Then I heard the bedsprings again and Riviera said, "Where are you going, my little chickadee?"

"I'm just taking my jeans off," Rosy said.

*How did you feel when you heard her say that? Is that when you ran for help?*

No. I couldn't move. I was too overwhelmed by the way she said it. Her voice hadn't trembled at all! I imagined her standing there, not more than four and a half feet tall, taking her clothes off in front of Riviera, and I started to cry. I felt just like a mother must feel when her daughter takes her first step or says her first word. I put my hand over my mouth so they wouldn't hear me.

*Weren't you worried about Miss Kelsey?*

I was terrified, so terrified I couldn't move at first. I just stood there listening, and then I couldn't listen anymore, my brain was buzzing like flies against a screen, and that's when I ran down the

stairs to the lobby and yelled, "Rape!" as loud as I could. There
was one old man and two middle-aged couples sitting in the lobby
reading papers and magazines, and every one of them nearly fell
over when I shouted. "He's raping her!" I yelled. "She's only twelve.
You've got to stop him." The hotel clerk was the first to reach the
stairs. "Follow me," I said, and dashed on up the stairs to the
room. "Here it is," I said, and the hotel clerk pounded on the
door. "Open up!" he shouted. The three men and the two ladies
were behind him now, yelling, "Unlock this door!" and, "Open
up right this minute!" and I said, "Break down the door before
it's too late," but it wasn't necessary because Rosy opened it and
stood there calm as anything.

"You can come in," she said.

"For Christ's sake," the hotel clerk said, because Rosy was
naked. She was standing there, looking brown and small. Her
breasts were little bumps with nipples like chinaberries, and she
didn't have any hair down there at all. I looked at her face. She
seemed sort of dazed, like she didn't really know she was naked
or anything.

"Ohh," said the fat lady, as if she was about to faint.

"We ought to kill the son of a bitch right now," said the man
with the red tie.

Someone, I don't know who, said, "Call the cops. Somebody
call the goddamn cops," and the fat lady said she'd go.

Then I looked past Rosy and saw Riviera in the far corner by
the sink, trying to pull his pants on. It was the first time I ever saw
a real penis, except when I walked in on my father once when he
was going to the bathroom. Somehow seeing it made me mad,
almost as if he *was* that man with his fly down and cock out who'd
tried to rape me, and I started to curse him as loud as I could.
"You asshole!" I shouted, louder even than Silva Thin. "You
fucking asshole!" I had never hated anyone more. The clerk had
to hold me me against the wall so I wouldn't strangle him. I swear
if I could have gotten my hands on his scrawny neck I would
have killed him, and the funny thing about it is that I've always

liked Riviera. He's a lot like me, and we've always gotten along. But I would have killed him then, I'm not kidding. Really. I would have even killed Burt Reynolds then, I think, if it had been him.

By this time, people were coming out of their rooms to see what the commotion was, and some of them had gathered around the door. Rosy never said a word during all this, but Riviera was talking nonstop the way he always does, saying, "She said she was eighteen, I wasn't raping nobody. You can't believe Anna Egg, she's crazy as a loon, everybody knows she's nuts. She's responsible for all this. I swear I thought the girl was eighteen, she looks eighteen to me," and so forth. But the old man just told him to "tell it to the judge." He must've said that ninety times: "Tell it to the judge." And me, I stood there and watched Red Tie's wife help Rosy put on her jeans and my sweater.

"Are you all right?" I finally said to her. She was holding onto her bib like she wouldn't ever let go.

"He never touched me," she answered.

*Do you believe her?*

Oh, he may not have touched her, at least in *that* way, but it was attempted rape just the same. And if they don't get Riviera for that, they'll at least get him for contributing to the delinquency of a minor. The funny thing about that is she's not a delinquent at all. She never was, of course, though sometimes she'd cut school to go to the movies with me and such, but she's even less of a delinquent now than she ever was. Like I said, you should have seen her. It's not everybody that can stand naked in front of a bunch of people and still look noble and beautiful and triumphant, but Rosy did it. And she did it because she's my Rosy, my Rosy Blue, and when all this is over, I'm going to ask her if she'll go with me to Sedalia and I bet you ten dollars she will.

# CONSTELLATIONS

If Marly hadn't gotten sick, Angela wouldn't have been on the bus that morning. She had seemed fine at her first feeding, a little slower to take the breast than usual maybe, but otherwise normal. And she only cried a little when Angela put her down for her nap. But an hour later, when Angela went into the bedroom to see if she needed her diaper changed, she saw her scarlet skin, her limp, still body, and panicked. She picked her up and held her against her chest and started pacing beside the crib. Marly was so hot that Angela could feel her skin burning right through her clothes. She didn't know what to do. This was the first time Marly had ever been sick. There was baby aspirin in the medicine cabinet, but she'd heard somewhere that you shouldn't give aspirin to infants or they might get some disease, some syndrome she thought it was called, and they could even die. Then she remembered how her mother had put a cold washcloth on her forehead when she was little and running a fever, so she quickly laid Marly back down in the crib and ran into the bathroom, soaked a washcloth under the faucet, then hurried back to the crib and began to cool her daughter's hot face. Marly's eyes puckered and she whimpered a little, but otherwise she didn't even seem to know her mother was there. Angela had to do something; but what? She placed the washcloth on Marly's forehead, then ran over to the phone on the nightstand beside her bed and, her fingers trembling, dialed Dr. Garrick's office. He was with a patient, so she explained everything to his nurse, talking so fast the nurse had to ask her to slow down. The nurse told her it was probably just a normal fever but the best thing to do would be to bring Marly in right away. "Dr. Garrick will work her in as quickly as possible," she said.

As soon as Angela hung up, she lifted Marly out of the crib, grabbed her purse and the diaper bag, and started toward the door. Tony had taken the car to work, as usual, so the first thing she thought of was the bus. She was in the habit of taking the bus to the park with Marly in the afternoons. Only later, after it was all over, did she think that she could have called a cab, or asked Lisa, from across the hall, to drive her to Dr. Garrick's office. But that morning, she didn't stop to think; she just hurried out of the apartment and down the street to the bus stop on the corner.

It was unusually hot and humid, even for August in Louisiana, and by the time she reached the bus stop she was sweating and her brown bangs were sticking to her forehead. She wished Tony had been home to help her, and for a moment she felt anger swirl up inside her the way dust whirls up in wind. But even as she felt it, she knew it didn't have anything to do with his being at work instead of there with her and Marly. Two years ago, she'd woken up and found a note on the kitchen table, propped up against his empty juice glass. She had stared at the words *leaving* and *Julie* and *sorry* as if they were remnants from some long-dead language, and when she finally finished reading the note, she took his juice glass to the sink and rinsed out the pulp as if nothing else mattered in the world more than a clean glass. Only then had she started to cry. But she wouldn't let herself cry now. Tony had come back to her after only a week, and eventually she'd forgiven him. At least she'd *said* she'd forgiven him, but from time to time she realized, as she did now, that she hadn't and probably never would.

There was no one else at the bus stop. For a moment, she was worried the bus had already come, but she checked her watch and saw it was only 11:07: one was due in just three minutes. Marly's face looked even redder now. Angela didn't want to sit on the bus stop bench, where Marly would feel the full heat of the sun, so she stood in the shade of a live oak and watched for the bus. While she waited, she stroked Marly's soft, sweat-soaked blond hair and cooed at her, as she did whenever she tried to get her to stop crying. But now she wasn't crying. Her silence scared Angela more than any tears possibly could.

Finally, the bus appeared around the corner and stopped in front of her, brakes screeching. Angela hurried in, dropped two quarters in the box, and started down the aisle. Evidently the air conditioning had broken down again because the bus was stifling. All of the passengers, except for a few older women with freshly permed hair, had their windows open, and most were mopping their faces with handkerchiefs. Angela took the first empty seat, one toward the middle on the driver's side, then laid Marly gently beside her and slid the window back as far as it would go. She heard the brakes hiss when the driver released them, then the hot smell of exhaust stung her nostrils as the bus swung back out into traffic. The breeze that came through the window was too hot to cool Marly's burning skin, and Angela began composing in her head an angry letter to the bus company, complaining about the ancient, run-down buses and their unreliable air conditioning and torn vinyl seats.

The bus stopped several times to pick up passengers, but Angela paid no attention to them, only stroked her daughter's forehead and worried about how long it was taking to get to Dr. Garrick's office. But then a boy got on that Angela couldn't help but notice. His left eye and cheekbone were purplish black, his nose red and crusted with blood, and his upper lip puffy and split. He was tall and thin, gangly, with a big Adam's apple, and Angela thought he looked like Ichabod Crane from that old story, only younger. He walked slowly down the aisle while the driver waited for a chance to pull out into the heavy traffic. Then he stopped in front of the two boys who were sitting across from her and Marly. They were about his age, fourteen or fifteen, and they were wearing the same kind of baggy jeans and backwards ball cap he was wearing, so at first Angela thought they were friends and he wanted to sit with them. Then one of them said, "Look who's come back for more," and they both laughed. And suddenly, as if time were a movie that had lurched ahead a few frames, she saw that the boy was pointing a gun at them and they were holding up their palms and saying, "Wait, wait!" Then Angela heard a shot. She was so surprised that she didn't understand for a second what had happened. She sat there and watched a small arc of blood pulse out of one boy's shoulder. It looked like water bubbling out of a drinking fountain, only it was red. *What a strange thing to think*, she thought, and wondered why she wasn't screaming. And then the wounded boy howled and clasped his hand over his shoulder.

The next thing Angela knew she was on the sidewalk across the street in front of a Burger King, crouching behind a parked car. She didn't know how she'd gotten there, but as soon as she saw where she was, she felt a sudden spurt of joy. *I'm safe*, she thought. *I'm alive.* Then she noticed that her forehead was throbbing, and when she reached up to touch it, her bangs felt wet. She looked at her fingers and saw it was blood. For a second she thought she had been shot after all, but then she noticed her hands were scraped raw, and her forearms and elbows were bleeding too. And her shoulders, breasts, and ribs were hurting, as if she'd been beaten up. What had happened to her? Slowly, like a distant memory, it came to her: she had squeezed sideways through the bus window, dived headfirst onto the asphalt, scrambled to her feet, and run through the traffic to the other side of the street and safety.

Then it hit her. She stood up and leaned against the parked car, feeling dizzy and strangely light, as if she had to hold on to something or she'd float away. *My Marly. She's still in there.*

She looked at the bus. Half of the passengers had run to the back and the other half to the front, and for some reason she thought of her high school science class, the time they watched cells divide under a microscope. In the middle of the bus, all she could see was the boy, standing and waving his arms around. She could tell he was shouting something, but there was so much noise—people yelling and crying, cars passing, horns honking—that she couldn't hear what he was saying. But she heard the shots—how many, she didn't know, but there were several of them, all so close together they almost sounded like one long, echoing shot. After that, there was an immense silence for a moment, and then the passengers started screaming and yelling and crying again.

*I have to save her,* she thought, and saw herself running to the bus, climbing back in the window, and taking her daughter into her arms; she saw herself standing there in the aisle, holding Marly, comforting her, while the rest of the passengers fought their way out onto the street, screaming and calling for help. "Don't worry, sweetheart," she was saying. "Mommy's here."

But she hadn't moved. She was still standing on the sidewalk, leaning against the parked car. She looked down at her empty arms, then up at the bus, almost expecting to see another Angela in there. The boy turned then and walked slowly to the front of the bus, all the passengers cowering to each side to let him by. He stepped out the door and for a moment he stood there in the street looking dazed while drivers swerved and slammed on their brakes to avoid hitting him. Then he looked right at Angela and for a second she thought he was going to shoot her next. But he just turned and walked a few steps, then began running down the middle of the street, not fast, but the way people do in dreams, almost in slow-motion, barely a jog, and before he'd gone fifty feet, a skinny black man in a gray business suit came out of nowhere and tackled him from behind. He knelt on the boy's back and shoved his face into the asphalt. "Got you, you bastard," he said. The boy didn't say anything. Within seconds, the passengers poured out of the bus, shouting and crying and calling for a doctor, and several of the men ran to help the man restrain the boy. But he didn't need any help; the boy wasn't struggling at all. One of the men, a burly guy wearing a New Orleans Saints T-shirt, wrenched the gun out of the boy's hand and stepped away from the small crowd, shouting and holding the pistol above his head like a trophy.

Then Angela gradually became aware that a young woman in a blue waitress uniform was standing beside the bus, holding Marly and asking, over and over, "Has anyone seen this baby's mother?" Marly's face was scrunched up and red and she was crying now, crying so hard she had to gasp for breath. Angela closed her eyes, then opened them. But the woman was still there, holding her squalling daughter. Then an old man wearing a hat with a jaunty green feather pointed at her and said, "That's her." The waitress walked over to her, her eyes tight and her mouth set in a hard, thin line, and said, "Is this your daughter?" Angela made herself nod. The waitress looked as though she was going to say something then, but all she did was hand Marly to Angela and turn around, as if she couldn't bear to be in her presence another second. Angela hugged Marly and whispered, "Shh," but she kept crying, the sobs catching in her tiny throat. A moment later, the bus driver walked over. "You all right?" he said, looking at her face. Angela nodded. Some blood slid down to the bridge of her nose, but she didn't wipe it away. "The paramedics will take care of you when they get here," he said. Then he handed Angela her purse and Marly's blood-specked diaper bag. "Here," he said, his eyes shifting away. "You forgot these."

She stood there awhile longer, shivering despite the heat, and watched everyone stand around in clusters, some near the bus and others around the captured boy. There was a woman leaning against the bus and holding a cell phone, and a man was saying to her, "Call 911 again. Tell them to hurry." Then she heard a voice to her right say that one of the boys was dead and the other was "gut-shot." She repeated that word to herself several times, trying to take in its meaning. Then she made herself look inside the bus. There, across the aisle from where she had left her daughter, three men were hunched over the two boys, doing something. *Their poor mothers*, she thought, then remembered she was holding Marly and hugged her so hard her bruised ribs hurt. By now the passengers were surrounded by people who had come out of the stores and restaurants, and they were telling them what had happened. And when they looked at Angela, she knew what they were saying.

She didn't wait for the police or the ambulance. As soon as she heard the sirens, she ran, just as if she were the criminal. She didn't even decide to run; she just found herself running, and when she realized what she was doing, she didn't stop. She ran around the corner, then turned up an alleyway, Marly crying harder and harder as her face bounced against Angela's collarbone. She ran and ran and didn't stop until the pain in her side made her gasp and double over. She was blocks away from the stores and restaurants now, and she walked past the quiet old houses beneath the canopy of oaks, crying as fiercely as her daughter, the tears mixing with the sweat and blood running down her face. She wished she were home, lying on the old sagging couch in their living room, watching TV, Marly napping in her crib or playing in her playpen, just like every other morning. Then she remembered how she'd made Tony sleep on that couch the first month after he returned home, not letting him back into their bed until the night he knelt before her and cried so hard he almost couldn't breathe. But even then, it was another three months before she let him make love to her. And how much longer had it been before she even said his name? She'd withheld it, as if merely saying his name implied a kind of intimacy they'd never have again because of the unforgivable thing he'd done to her. As she walked aimlessly, hugging her daughter, she remembered the way his lip had trembled the first time she forgot and said his name.

As she passed by, a young woman in a halter top and gym shorts turned off her lawnmower and asked her if she needed help, but Angela just kept walking. She wondered what Tony would say when he saw her cuts and scrapes. She could make up some explanation—she tripped on a crack in the sidewalk, or a big dog knocked her down, or maybe she was mugged by a teenager wearing baggy jeans and a backwards ball cap—but what if he knew she was lying and demanded the truth? The truth. What was the truth? She looked up at the swaying leaves as if they might whisper the answer. Yesterday, she would have said the truth was that she was the perfect mother. She'd stopped drinking the day she learned she was pregnant, and she'd scolded anyone who smoked in her presence. She'd changed her diet also, eating all the right foods and forcing herself to drink milk, which she hated, and she gave birth naturally—eight hours of labor without so much as an aspirin so her baby wouldn't be harmed by drugs. She even quit her job at the Social Security office, a good-paying job, so Marly wouldn't have to go to daycare. Ever since Marly was born, she had devoted her life to her, putting her and her needs first. Yesterday, she would have said she'd give up her own life for her daughter.

Marly had finally stopped crying and fallen back asleep. Angela's back ached from carrying her, but she didn't want to shift her to her other shoulder for fear she'd wake her. Two little boys ran past her then, yelling something, and a yellow Lab came loping across the street after them just as a car turned the corner. The car stopped immediately, but Angela still imagined it hitting the dog, the tires crushing its rib cage and skull, blood everywhere. She stopped walking and stood there on the sidewalk, shaking. *I left her on the bus*, she thought. *I left her.* She would never do anything like that again, not ever. She would show her, and Tony, that she was a good mother. And then she remembered why they'd been on the bus in the first place. She looked at the street sign: Van Buren. She wasn't that far from Dr. Garrick's office, maybe just ten or twelve blocks. She turned down the street and walked away as fast as she could.

As she walked, she heard Tony interrogating her. "How could you do it?" he'd say, his face red, his lips set in the same thin, hard line as the waitress's. "How could you be so selfish?" She'd deserve those questions, especially after all the terrible questions she'd asked him those long days and nights after he came back to her. "What color is her hair?" "Is she prettier than me?" "Do you love her?" "How many times did you make love with her?" "What did you say to her afterwards?" She'd asked so many questions, and asked them over and over, in order to punish him, but asking them hurt her too. Still, she'd kept on asking them.

It was odd but in all that time she'd never thought to ask him the one question that now seemed the most important: she'd never asked him what he felt like the moment he left her. He'd told her how he couldn't sleep that night and how he finally got up and sat at the kitchen table, holding his head in his hands, staring at a blank piece of paper and waiting for the words to come. He was thinking about the early days, he said, about how he'd introduce her to his friends with the line "This is my angel Angela," and how sometimes he couldn't touch her without trembling because he loved her so much, and he was wondering how love that was once that strong could have disappeared. And he was thinking about Julie, how he'd met her at a bar one night after one of their arguments, and how she reminded him of Angela when they first met. And he thought too, he admitted, about killing himself. But he wanted to live. Yet what he had with her wasn't a life anymore, so leaving was his only hope, the only way he could save himself. He'd told her all of this, but he hadn't told her how he felt when he walked out the door and headed down the stairway to the parking lot and freedom from her and from who he was with her. Now she believed she knew how he'd felt, and how that feeling had changed almost immediately, and how he must have fought over the next week to get that feeling back, then returned home when he realized that he couldn't, that he'd never feel that way again, that it was never possible to feel that way in your life except for one horrible moment, the way she had felt when she looked across the street at the bus and thought, *I'm safe, I'm alive.*

She walked for a long time, it seemed, her mind so full it was empty, not a single thought remaining long enough for her to acknowledge it, and when she finally stopped and looked around, she didn't recognize where she was. She was no longer surrounded by houses; now she was on a street lined with small shops and cafes. She should have gotten to Dr. Garrick's office long ago; she must have gone the wrong way. She couldn't do anything right. What would Tony think of her if he knew what a bad mother she was? Her breaths started to come faster and faster, and for a moment she was afraid she'd hyperventilate. When she finally got her breath again, she whispered, "I'm so sorry," but she couldn't have said whether she was talking to Marly or to Tony.

Just then a thin, old man wearing Bermuda shorts and a V-neck undershirt put his hand on her arm, startling her. His frown was almost a scowl. "Did somebody hurt you, young lady?" he asked, peering at her bloody face. She backed away, saying "No." Her first instinct was to turn and run away, but she stopped herself and said, "Can you tell me where Dr. Garrick's office is?" It was a simple sentence but it made her feel proud, responsible, a good parent.

"Sure," the old man said. "It's just three-four blocks back thataway." He pointed down the street, the way she'd come. She must have passed the office and not even noticed it. She thanked him and then hurried back down the street, holding Marly to her chest, kissing the top of her head from time to time and whispering, "Everything will be all right, don't worry, there's nothing to worry about, I'll take care of you."

A few minutes later, she stood in front of Dr. Garrick's white clapboard office building with forest green shutters and stared at it as if she'd never seen it before. It looked unreal, almost as if it were a movie set. She imagined opening the door and stepping through to the nothing on the other side of the facade. Marly was still sleeping, little bubbles of spit at her lips. Her face was so flushed she looked like a movie Indian. Angela hurried up the brick sidewalk.

When she walked into the waiting room, the receptionist, a large woman with hennaed hair and hoop earrings, stood up behind the counter. "Oh my goodness," she said, "have you had an accident?" Without thinking, Angela answered, "Yes." So a few minutes later, when Dr. Garrick hurried into the examining room, Angela had to explain that no, she hadn't been in an accident, she was all right, it was Marly, her fever, that he needed to take care of. But even as she spoke, even as she looked at Dr. Garrick's frowning face, his bushy white eyebrows and the gray eyes squinting at her over his glasses, she was thinking that, yes, in a way it was all an accident. So many things had to happen to make it possible. If the bus's air conditioning had been working, she wouldn't have opened the window. If the bus hadn't been so full, she would have sat near the front, away from the boys who were shot. If Marly hadn't gotten sick, they wouldn't have been on the bus. If AT&T hadn't transferred Tony from Little Rock, they wouldn't live here. And if she'd never met Tony, if they'd never married, if he hadn't left Julie and come back to her, Marly would never even have been born. It was all a series of accidents. Even love was an accident, nothing more than the chance convergence of two people. And what about the boy who pulled out a gun and shot two other boys? What accidents led him to commit his crime at that place and at that time? And whose crime was worse, his or hers?

She stood there watching Dr. Garrick examine her daughter on the table covered with white paper—*like butcher paper,* she thought, and shivered—and saw Marly's tiny chest rise and fall beneath his stethoscope. *How small her heart must be, how tiny what keeps us alive.* Her own heart began to beat harder, and she suddenly felt dizzy again, the way she'd felt earlier, when she'd had to lean against the parked car to keep from floating into space. "Dr. Garrick," she said, stepping toward him, "I think I'm going to faint." And then the room rose up dark around her.

That night, while Tony made love to her gently, careful not to touch her bruises or the gauze bandages that Dr. Garrick had put on her wounds, Angela remembered the first time they'd ever made love. It was the year before they were married, and she and Tony had driven out into the Arkansas countryside, away from the city lights, to look at constellations. They stood in a meadow, under the huge sky, each holding a corner of a star chart that glowed phosphorescent in the dark. The heavens were mapped, the stars weren't random. She followed Tony's finger as he traced Virgo's glittering robe. That was the moment she felt love flare inside her, the moment all of this had started. She'd kissed him then, trying to tell him with her lips what she had just felt. He must have understood because a few minutes later he took a wool blanket out of the trunk of his father's old Impala and spread it across the matted grass, and they made love there, the star chart glowing beside them on the blanket like a miniature mirror of the sky above. She remembered how she had opened her eyes halfway and looked woozily over his shoulder at the stars. They were so far away, yet they seemed so close she could almost reach out and touch them. And they seemed to be a part of everything she was feeling right then, or rather she and Tony seemed a part of them, a part of everything that made the world beautiful. She was happier than she had ever been. This was the moment her entire life had been leading her toward. She closed her eyes then and saw her future mapped out before her like a beautiful constellation: she would marry Tony and bear his children and love them with all her heart and they would all be happy forever.

But now, warm tears slid down Angela's temples into her hair as her husband moved over her, loving her in his ignorance, feeling sad that his poor wife had been mugged that morning by a teenager, a random crime. His eyes had swelled with tears that afternoon when he saw her bandages and bruises and heard her story, but then he began to curse the boy who mugged her and promised to take the day off tomorrow to look for him himself—you couldn't trust the police to do anything, he'd said, clenching and unclenching his fists. She'd sat next to Marly on the couch where he had slept alone so long and watched him pace back and forth, his anger the only thing keeping him from weeping, then she closed her eyes and in that sudden darkness heard herself say, "I forgive you." She'd said it before, but this time she meant it. She opened her eyes, to see if the world had changed. Tony stopped pacing and looked at her, his lips slightly parted. "I really do," she added. He cleared his throat and swallowed. "Angela," he said, nothing more, then took her face in his hands and, bending over, kissed her.

And now she lay under him, staring up into darkness so complete she couldn't even see his face, and listened to him moan quietly. Whenever his moaning paused, she strained to hear if Marly was crying in her crib across the room. She didn't hear anything, not even the sound of her breathing. The room was so silent and dark, it seemed as if Marly wasn't even there, or was so far away she couldn't ever reach her.

# BEAUTIFUL OHIO

This couple came in and took a table in the far corner, where the shadows almost swallow up the candlelight. That's how I knew they were lovers, not father and daughter. That, and the way he held her hands and leaned over the table, his eyes never leaving her face all the while he talked to her. He was old enough to be her father, though: at least forty-five, maybe fifty. But his hair was that sort of premature gray that somehow makes a man seem younger instead of older, and he had the tan of a movie star or a doctor. He was wearing a white sport jacket and a navy knit shirt open at the neck, and he had two silver rings on his left hand. The girl was just a girl, blond, like they always are at that age, at least for a summer. She wasn't wearing any makeup that I could see, but then who needs it when you're that young? I'd seen the dress she was wearing—one with a lacy yoke and puffy sleeves—in the window of Cohn's, so I knew it was expensive. I wondered if he bought it for her, or if her daddy did.

Of course I thought right away about Roy and that high school dropout of his. How could I help it? I try not to think about him, but what can I do? Lenny tells me to forget Roy and marry him, but it's not that easy. We were married sixteen years. His new wife was still crawling around in diapers when we walked down the aisle.

Just thinking about Roy took the breath out of me. I can be going along, doing my job, happy, not thinking about anything,

and then all of a sudden I think about him. I should expect it by
now, I suppose, but I'm always surprised. That night, the thought
of him hit me so hard I wanted to go home, make myself a drink,
and climb into a tub full of soapy water. But I couldn't go home.
I had two more hours left on my shift, and besides, Lenny was
there, and he'd want to know what was wrong. I thought of asking
Tia to take their table for me, but she already had a full section
and I didn't want to have to explain. So I took two menus out of
the rack and started through the imitation arbor toward their table.

I don't know why, but somehow I just knew they were talking
about his wife. Maybe it was the way they were leaning over the
table, like conspirators, or maybe it was how they were smiling. I
don't know. But as I walked toward them, I could almost hear
him saying *the old bitch*, just like Roy did when he introduced me to
his dropout after the divorce: *I'd like you to meet the old bitch*. The old
bitch. *Me*. She didn't look a day over sixteen, but I didn't say
anything. I had something all planned, some comment about how
Roy had finally gotten the baby he'd always wanted, but when I
got my chance, I couldn't say it. I just waved my hand, like I was
dismissing two children. Then I watched Roy's green Pontiac speed
down the street. That was almost two years ago now, but
sometimes I still find myself imagining that old car driving up to
our house and Roy stepping out, a sheepish smile on his face, and
saying, "Honey, I'm home." I don't love him anymore—it isn't
that. If he asked me to marry him again, I'd say no. I just want
him to come home, to say he'd been wrong to leave.

Then I thought about Lenny, sitting home alone all these nights,
waiting for me to give him an answer, and I started to feel so trembly
I stopped at an empty table near theirs and pretended to straighten
the placemats and silverware while I got ahold of myself. I was
close enough then to hear what they were saying, and I almost had
to laugh, I'd been such a fool. They weren't talking about his wife,
or divorce, at all. They were talking about *clay-eaters*.

"What they do," the man was saying, "is they mix the clay with
tomato soup. They call it river beans."

The girl shook her head. "I can't believe it. I could understand it if they were starving or something, but why would anyone *want* to eat clay?"

"They crave it. No one knows why, but they do. If one of them moves away from the river, they crave it so bad their relatives have to mail them packages of it."

"Care packages full of dirt," the girl laughed.

I'd been a perfect fool and I knew it. Still, when I finally went up to their table, I felt my stomach turn over the way it would if I were waiting on Roy and his new wife. "Hello," I said, my voice wavering a little, and set the menus on the red and white checked tablecloth. "My name is Gloria, and I'll be serving you this evening."

The girl flicked a strand of blond away from her eyes and smiled at me. "Tell me, do you have river beans tonight?" Then she and the man laughed.

"You'll have to excuse us," the man said. "We've been talking about a TV special I saw, about these people in Kentucky who eat clay."

"Real clay," the girl added, like I didn't understand.

"That's right," the man went on. "They dig it up out of the banks of the Ohio River and eat it. Not just poor people either: bankers, doctors, you name it."

He smiled.

I can't explain why, but right then I decided I had to give Lenny his answer. I couldn't wait another night.

"I'll be back in a minute to take your orders," I said, then turned and went back to the kitchen. Edward, our cook, was spreading pepperoni slices on a pizza crust. He took one look at me and said, "Hey, Sunshine, what's the problem?"

"Nothing," I said.

"Sure," he said. "I can see that." Then he wiped his hands on his apron like he was going to give me a hug and make everything all right.

"Don't touch me," I said. "I'm fine."

When Lenny and I first met, I didn't know what to think of him. He wasn't anything like Roy. Roy was short, like me, and burly

with a coarse black beard, and Lenny's tall and lanky and he has a
dirty brown mustache that he chews whenever he's nervous, which
is almost always. Roy never said what he was thinking much, but
Lenny, he'll say whatever comes into his head. When I sat down
in the chair opposite him in Dr. Phelan's waiting room, he asked
me, "What's wrong with you?" At first I was going to snap back
something like "None of your business," but when I saw his face,
so shy and friendly, I couldn't help but tell him about my varicose
veins. "I'm on my feet a lot," I said. Then he said, "I'm here to
find out if I've got Agent Orange or just some dumb allergy,"
and he opened his top shirt buttons and showed me his red, raw
chest. "Horrible, isn't it?" he said. "I look like a napalmed gook.
Isn't that a joke?" I must have made a face because he said, "I'm
sorry. I've got to learn to shut up. I've got a big mouth, and I
don't think before I open it." Then he grinned and pointed at his
head. "Post-traumatic Stress Disorder," he said, rolling his eyes.
The way he said it made me laugh, but only for a second, and
then I was embarrassed. I felt like I had to say something, so I
said, "Have you been coming to Dr. Phelan long?" And he said,
"You know, you're really pretty. But you shouldn't wear green. I
think you'd look better in blue. A light blue, powder blue I think
they call it. It'd show off that frosting in your hair."

It wasn't long before we started going out, and when he lost
his job at Accurate Plastics and couldn't pay his rent, I took him
in. I felt sorry for him, I guess, and maybe I even thought I was in
love with him. I can't remember now. At any rate, he was only
going to stay until he found a new job. But when he started working
at the Remington plant, he asked if he could stay—just until he
got back on his feet again—and I said yes. Then he lost that job
too. For weeks, he looked for work, but then he started staying
home, sitting in the La-Z-Boy and watching reruns of *The
Honeymooners* and *I Love Lucy*. All he did was sit there and smoke
cigarettes and drink beer. When I came home, he'd tell me he'd
been out looking for work, but I knew better. Once I picked up
his ashtray and counted thirty-seven cigarette butts, then asked

him if he expected me to believe he'd been out looking for jobs all day. That was when he first asked me to marry him. "I love you, Gloria," he said. "I won't ever be any good without you. If you just say yes, I'll be a new man. You'll see." He'd caught me off guard, and I didn't know what to say. I just stood there a moment, looking at him, trying to think of something I could tell him. Then he turned and walked over to the picture window and looked out at the rain. "To hell with Roy," he said. "When are you gonna forget about him? Do you think he lays awake nights thinking about *you*?" Then I said we shouldn't discuss such an important thing when we were tense and angry. "Let's talk about this tomorrow," I said. And the next morning, at breakfast, I told him I needed more time to think about it. After that, he asked me every day for a couple of weeks, and I always said I didn't know yet. After a while, he stopped asking, at least in words. But every time I came home I could see the question in his eyes.

I was crying as I drove home that night, thinking one minute how sad Lenny would be when I told him my answer and then the next how that man leaned over the table and kissed that girl, like no one else was in the restaurant or the world. When I pulled into the driveway, I just sat there a minute, wiping mascara off my cheeks and trying to prepare myself. I didn't want to have to hurt Lenny, but even more I wanted everything settled; I wanted things simple, clear.

As soon as I opened the car door, I could hear that music again, and I knew Lenny was drunk. Whenever he drinks too much, he puts on Big Band music. It was the first thing he heard when he came home from Vietnam. As soon as he got his discharge at Fort Ord, he hitched a ride back to Little Rock with a buddy, and when he walked in the house, his mother was baking bread and listening to "Moonlight Serenade" on the hi-fi. She hadn't been expecting him for another week. After they hugged and kissed and cried, she gave him a slice of bread fresh from the oven and they sat in the kitchen and listened to Glenn Miller

together. He'd never liked that kind of music before, but now he
did, because sitting there, listening to those songs and eating that
bread, he couldn't believe in the war anymore. It was just gone, a
bad dream. He felt so happy he got up and danced right there in
the kitchen with his mother, danced his idea of a waltz, both of
them crying away.

I slammed the car door and started up the walk. Lenny was
playing "In the Mood" so loud I knew he was in bad shape. Mrs.
McDougal across the street had probably already called the police.
I walked up the steps and put the key in the lock. Then I just
stood there a moment, looking at the peeling siding Lenny had
promised to scrape and paint, the broken shutters, the overgrown
shrubs. Finally, I turned the key and stepped in. The living room
was warm, all the lights on. I didn't see Lenny anywhere.

"Turn that thing down," I yelled.

Lenny came out of the kitchen then, wearing a blue apron
that was dusty with flour. His hands were white too and he held
them out in front of him, like Frankenstein in the movies.

"Gloria," he said. "You're home."

"Lenny," I said. "You're drunk."

He wiped his hands on a corner of the apron, then turned
down the record player. "No, I'm not," he said. "I'm *plastered.*"
Then he went back into the kitchen. After a second, I heard him
kneading dough on the squeaky table. It was midnight, and he
was baking bread. I set my purse on the end table and sat down
on the old flowered loveseat. For a second, I thought of just
blurting it out: *I don't love you. I don't want to marry you.* But I decided
to wait, to build up to it so he wouldn't take it so hard.

In a few minutes, Lenny came out of the kitchen, still wearing
his apron, and sat down in the La-Z-Boy next to the loveseat. I
could hear the timer ticking away in the kitchen. He always lets
the bread rise three times, thirty minutes a time. That meant it'd
be at least an hour, maybe two, before he was done baking. I saw
him sitting in the La-Z-Boy, waiting to take his bread out of the
oven, while I slept in the bedroom alone, and I suddenly felt so

sorry for him I thought I'd wait until tomorrow to tell him. But I knew I couldn't. I couldn't wait even one more night.

Doris Day was singing "Sentimental Journey" now. "What music," Lenny said, nodding toward the record player. "You can just see all the people dancing. The whole country dancing." He looked at me, woozy, and blinked his eyelids hard. "I'm making bread," he said.

"I know," I answered, and tried to smile.

He looked away then and sighed. "I thought you'd never get home," he said. "The time, it's been moving so slow tonight."

I didn't say anything. Lenny sighed again, then tapped a Winston out of the pack on the end table and lit it. Taking a long drag, he leaned his head back and exhaled slowly. Lately, his rash had started up his neck, and I wondered if one day it'd cover his face. I imagined his face raw and burned-looking, and I shivered.

Without looking at me, he said, "Hear anything interesting at work?"

For some time now, all we talked about was other people's conversations. It was easier than having our own. Sometimes, when I hadn't overheard anything interesting, I made something up, just to have something to talk about. But that night I didn't have to make anything up. I told him about the clay-eaters, just like I heard it, only I said it was two businessmen from Memphis who told me about them. Somehow, telling the story exhausted me. I wanted to go to bed and sleep.

"Clay?" he said, blowing out a stream of smoke. "Actual *clay?*"

"That's right. River clay. They dig it up right out of the banks of the Ohio."

Lenny threw his head back like a wolf and laughed. Then he began to sing. "Drifting with the current down a moonlit stream, While above the Heavens in their glory gleam . . ." He laughed again, softer this time. "The beautiful Ohio," he said, shaking his head. Then, his voice suddenly quiet, almost a whisper, he added, "Gloria, you're killing me. Don't you know that?"

I got up.

"Where are you going?" Lenny asked.

"I need a drink. I'll be right back."

Switching on the kitchen light, I saw the crockery bowl on the table, a dishtowel over it and, beside it, the timer, ticking hard and fast like my heart. I opened the cupboard where we kept the liquor and took down a bottle of Evan Williams and poured myself half a tumbler, then filled it with cold water from the tap. I took a couple of long swallows there at the sink, and felt my insides burn.

"Gloria," Lenny called.

"Just a minute," I yelled back. I took a long, deep drink, then started back out to tell him it was all over.

Lenny's head was slumped down over his chest and his eyes were closed, so for a second I thought he'd passed out and I could go to sleep in peace. But then he lifted his head and, eyes still closed, said, "Blue Moon." He pointed to the stereo. "People fell in love dancing to that song."

I had to say something, but I didn't know what. For weeks I'd been trying to decide what I'd say—I wanted it to be something gentle but firm, affectionate but cool—but I could never concentrate enough to get the words right. My mind always slipped ahead to the morning after, when I'd wake up alone and sit at the kitchen table drinking coffee and watching the sparrows play at the feeder outside the window. I saw myself sitting there, the room warm with sunlight, the birds making their quiet music, and I knew I wanted that moment more than anything.

I sat back on the loveseat and took another burning swallow of bourbon.

"Lenny," I finally said. But then I found I didn't have any other words.

"What?" Lenny turned to look at me. He was chewing on his mustache.

I took another drink. "Nothing," I said.

"No," he said. "You were going to say something."

"I've forgotten," I said. "It'll come to me later."

Lenny stood up then, swaying a little. He looked at me a moment, like he was about to say something, but he bit his lip and sat back down.

"Gloria," he whispered. "Tell me."

I looked down at my lap. Finally, I said, "I want to have a talk with you." It was a simple sentence, but after I said it, I was out of breath.

Lenny looked up at the ceiling and sighed. "I'd like us to have a baby," he said. "I want us to be a family. I want to do all the things families do. I want to push our baby down the aisles of Safeway in a shopping cart. Get Christmas cards made from a photograph. Sit in the barbershop while he gets his hair cut. And every year on his birthday draw a line on the doorjamb to show how much he's grown." He looked back at me. "After we die, there'll be nothing left of either of us."

That was the one way Lenny was like Roy—he wanted a baby too. I'd told him time and again that I was too old but he never listened. It wasn't that I didn't want a baby. I'd wanted to have one with Roy, but he had something wrong with him. His sperm count was okay, Dr. Phelan said, but for some reason they moved too slow. Dr. Phelan even removed a varicose vein from his testicle, figuring it was making his sperm too hot to move fast enough. But that didn't do anything either. Every now and then I wonder if he ever got that dropout pregnant. Sometimes I hope he did, and sometimes I don't.

I looked at Lenny, his sad face. "We talked about this before," I said.

Lenny stubbed out his cigarette in the ashtray. "No, we haven't. Not really. I've talked, but you haven't."

"What's that supposed to mean?"

Lenny looked at me. "Just what are you so scared of?"

I started to get up. "Maybe we should talk about this when you're not drunk."

"I'm not drunk," he said, taking my arm.

"Yes, you are."

"Okay, so I'm drunk. What's your excuse?"

"*Please*," I said, but I wasn't sure what I was begging for.

"Okay," Lenny said and let go of my arm. "Just sit down. I won't say anything more about a baby."

I sat down. The stereo was playing "Chattanooga Choo-Choo."

"Can we turn that thing off?" I said. "Can't we just sit here in quiet?"

Lenny got up and switched it off. Then he turned to face me. "I was hoping," he said, then closed his eyes and swallowed hard, "I was hoping we'd do some dancing tonight. I was hoping this would be the night. I even bought some champagne and"—he gestured toward the kitchen—"I'm baking bread."

He looked so sad standing there that I closed my eyes, and for some reason I found myself thinking back to a day years ago when I was still in high school, long before I'd even met Roy. I was sitting in a dark classroom staring at the slides Mr. Moffett had taken that summer in Spain. There were castles on high cliffs, cathedrals, goatherds leading their flocks beside mountain roads, white houses with red tile roofs, markets full of tapestries, sheep's heads, fish, and pots, and dancers in red and black whirling under colored lights—so many amazing and beautiful things. I remembered imagining myself standing on a castle parapet, looking out over hills of olive trees, the wind whipping my hair off my forehead. Someday, I vowed, I'd go there. Even the names Mr. Moffett recited in the darkness made me ache to be there: Salamanca. Jaen. Torremolinos.

I opened my eyes and looked at Lenny. "I don't know what to say to you," I said. "I really don't."

"I'm going to get a job," Lenny said. "Really, I am. I've decided to go into refrigeration. Appliance work. I could take a couple of courses. There're lots of jobs. Small engine repair. Things are breaking down everywhere and I could fix them."

"It doesn't matter," I said. "That's not what I'm talking about."

"What are you talking about?"

I took another swallow of the bourbon. "Don't make me say it," I said.

"Okay," he answered. "Let's talk about something else. Let's talk about Roy and his little sweetheart, okay? What do you think they're doing right now?"

"Lenny," I said. "Stop."

"Do you think maybe they're dancing and drinking champagne and—"

"Please stop," I said.

"Stop what?" he said, swaying before me. "Breathing?"

"Don't you talk to me like that," I said, and shook my finger at him. Then I felt foolish, like a schoolteacher scolding a little child.

Lenny hung his head. "Gloria," he said. Just my name, nothing else.

"It's late," I started to say.

Lenny looked up then. His face was wet. "Don't leave me," he said.

The day Roy left, I was already late for work but I went into the kitchen where he was packing and reminded him to take some silverware or some of the beer glasses he liked. He was just piling things into a Jack Daniels box. I remember telling him he should wrap the glasses with some newspaper; that way they wouldn't break. And all the time I'd wanted to say, *Please don't go.*

I said yes. He held me against him, and I said, "Your apron . . . the flour," but he said, "It doesn't matter" and kissed me. Then he said, "Let's take the champagne to bed." I said, "But the bread . . ." and he said, "Let it keep rising."

In bed, he started to touch me. I wanted to say no, but I couldn't. I had already said yes. Such a simple word, almost a hiss. I wanted to say I was too tired, too . . . something, but I didn't dare, not now. I let him take my panties off, and I let him enter me bare, without a rubber, for the first time.

"I love you," he was saying, as he rocked on top of me. I thought about all those nights Roy and I tried to make a child, all those nights he came in me again and again. And I thought of the bread rising in the kitchen, rising over the lip of the crockery bowl, huge, and then Lenny kissed me and I tasted smoke and

beer in his mustache and I thought, *The smell of coffee and sunlight.
The quiet music of the sparrows. Torremolinos.*

And suddenly I felt bloated, not with child, but with *clay*, and I
saw myself lying there, on the banks of the beautiful Ohio, my
mouth and hands smeared with clay. I shut my eyes on that vision,
and Lenny arched over me, holding himself at arms' length above
me, and moved in me faster and faster until finally he came. "Oh,"
he said then, and it could have been a word in a foreign language:
I didn't know what it meant, whether happiness or discovery or
pain or surprise. And then he lowered his weight down on me.

# BROTHERS

When my mother called to tell me how little time my brother had left, I decided to risk a run-in with Frances and go home to see him. This was about a year ago, towards the end of autumn, and all while I drove down the highway, I watched the leaves in the farmers' groves fall, red and gold and yellow and brown, and thought about what I'd say when I got there. "Marty," I saw myself saying, "we're brothers. If you can forgive Frances, you can forgive me. And I forgive both of you. So let's let bygones be bygones, OK?" The way I imagined it, he'd just look at me for a few seconds, his jaw set, then his face would slowly thaw and there'd be that smile I remembered from when we were kids. It sounds stupid now, but that's what I expected, more or less.

Even though I live less than an hour away, I hadn't been home to see Marty or Frances since the summer we last spoke to each other, nearly eleven years before. I'd driven over to see Mom at the retirement center every month or two, but I always made sure to visit on a weekday, when Marty and Frances would be at work. And I'd never stopped by their place, though I always thought about it. Once, we passed on the street, Marty in that shiny new pickup of his and me in my ramshackle Escort, and though I'm sure he recognized me, he didn't wave and neither did I.

I was nervous about seeing Marty again, and even more nervous about seeing Frances. But when I got to their house—the house we'd both grown up in, the one Mom sold to him for less than a song after Dad died—the nervousness disappeared and anger took its place. The house was damn near dilapidated. The paint was peeling off, big flakes of dingy white everywhere, like sunburned skin, and one of the shutters beside the upstairs window—the bedroom we'd shared as kids—was missing. Marty hadn't been sick long enough for the house to get this bad, so that was no excuse. It was laziness, pure and simple. And Frances was no better. It griped me the way they'd just let the place go to pieces. Even after Caroline and the boys left me, I kept my house up. I was out there mowing the yard and clipping the hedges the same day they left. And even though my arthritis has gotten a lot worse lately, I still keep everything in tiptop shape.

The sidewalk was drifted thick with leaves—here it was October and no one had done any raking—and I kicked at them as I walked up to the house. That was a mistake, one of many I made that day, because I stubbed my toe hard on something buried under them. And I mean *hard*. My toe hurt so bad my eyes watered. I was ticked off already, but then I saw what had injured me: it was a chunk of the sidewalk that'd heaved up and cracked off during the winter. I couldn't believe Marty had just left it lay there all this time. If he weren't my brother, I would have sued him in a minute.

So I was mad even before Marty and Frances said the things they did. I was mad as I limped up the steps and I got madder as I stood there looking at the faded rust-colored door, remembering how bright red it was the summer my dad painted it and the shutters. I was mad but I was determined not to show it. I raised my hand to knock on the door. But then I hesitated. I wasn't sure if I should knock or ring the doorbell. The idea of doing either one made me feel odd, like I was a salesman or Jehovah's Witness, not someone who used to live here, someone who was *family*. Eventually, I rang the doorbell. Then I stood there, hoping my brother would open the door, not Frances. If I could get through all this without seeing her, it would be a lot easier.

But I wasn't that lucky. When the door opened, there she was.

Even though she was in her mid-fifties now, Frances still wore her
hair long, but it wasn't the same honey color it used to be. I suspect she
would have described the new color as "platinum blonde," but it was a
bright, unnatural white. I suppose she thought it made her look like
Madonna or something. I always used to like the way Frances dressed
and acted younger than her age, but now it kind of turned my stomach.

I don't know what she thought of the way I looked now, but
clearly she didn't like seeing me. She put her hands on the hips of
her blue jeans. "Jesus," she said. "What are you doing here?"

My stupid toe was throbbing like crazy now. I didn't say anything
to her about it, though. "I've come to see Marty," I said. But she
didn't let me in; she just stood there, the door half open, and looked
at me, her nose wrinkled up like she was smelling something foul.

"Aren't you a little late?" she said, and for a second, I thought
she meant he'd already died. But then I realized what she'd meant.

"Maybe," I answered. "But I want to see him."

"He's not here. He's down at Len's, like always."

I couldn't believe it. I'd expected him to be home in bed, or
maybe even in the hospital already, but he was at a *bar*. And it
wasn't even three o'clock yet. I started to wonder if Mom had
lied to me, if this whole cancer story was just a way to trick Marty
and me into making up. Lord knows, she'd been trying long
enough. But I knew Mom wasn't a good enough actress to fake
all those tears or make up all that stuff about lumbar punctures,
cerebrospinal fluid, and blast cells.

"He's at *Len's*?"

Frances just sighed. "Where did you expect him to be, sitting
here at home waiting for his dear brother to drop by and make
what's left of his life even worse?"

"It doesn't have to be like this," I said. "Why don't we sit down
a minute and talk?" I glanced over her shoulder toward the living
room. They still had that same sagging green couch. Frances and
I had made love on it a few times the summer before everything
went to hell, and seeing it brought back all of the guilt and worry
and excitement of those days.

She glared at me. "If you think I'm going to let you, of all people, into our house, you're crazier than I think."

And then she closed the door.

Mad as that made me, I couldn't help but laugh a little. I mean, here I was, shut out of my own house, the house I thought I'd inherit one day, since I was the oldest. And the person shutting me out was the woman that cost me my family. I thought about getting back in my car, turning around, and heading home right then and there. I'd stop to visit Mom on the way, of course, but I'd make it a quick one, then get back on the road. I couldn't wait to get away. I saw myself driving down the highway, the fallen leaves skittering across the road in the wind, some oldies rock 'n' roll on the radio, and I started to feel better already.

But I didn't go home, like I should have. Instead I did something dumb: I drove down to Len's. I decided I wasn't going to leave town until I did what I came there to do, and that was to talk to Marty. I was planning to tell him I was sorry about everything. I was going to take the blame, put it all on myself. I *wasn't* to blame, not completely anyway, but I was going to say so just the same, to make him feel better. I figured it was the least I could do for my only brother before he died.

When we were growing up, Marty and I were more like friends than brothers. Everyone was always amazed when they found out otherwise, because we did everything together and never fought, the way brothers usually do. We both had other friends but we preferred each other's company. We went to movies and ball games together, and we almost always double-dated. Our dates used to complain that we spent more time talking to each other than to them. And we did. But after he married Frances, the double-dating stopped. He'd met her while working construction in Arizona one winter, and when they came back home to Minnesota to live, she and Marty and Caroline and I went out a couple of times together. But Frances put an end to that pretty quick. Marty said she told him, "I want to go on a date with *you*, not Caroline. And that's who I feel like I'm out with, because all you do is talk and tell jokes with Ted all night." So after that, Marty and I didn't get together the way we used to, because he was always out doing something with Frances. The last time Marty and I were together, the night before everything blew up, we'd gone to Len's for a couple of drinks. I hadn't been back since.

Len's is your typical small-town bar—a handful of tables and booths, neon Bud and Miller Light signs on the paneled walls, a couple of pool tables in the back room—except for one thing. Along the wall opposite the bar, there's this fireplace, a sort of old-timey hearth-like thing that looks like it's made of fieldstone but it's actually some lightweight synthetic material. And the fireplace is fake, too. There's no chimney, or even a place to put logs. Instead, there's just some wallpaper with a picture of burning logs on it. On the mantel are all the trophies the bar's softball and bowling teams have won over the years, and hanging above it is this painting of a cozy-looking log cabin with yellow, fire-lit windows and smoke curling out of its chimney.

I didn't see Marty when I walked in. The bartender was someone I didn't recognize, a tall gangly guy with mutton-chop sideburns and a bulging Adam's apple. I stepped gingerly up to the bar—my toe was still killing me—and asked him if he'd seen Marty. "He's in the back," he said, and nodded toward the pool room. I was a little nervous about talking to Marty, especially after the way Frances had treated me, so I bought a beer, drained half of it, and stood there at the bar a minute, watching the boxing match on the TV with the bartender and two rumpled-looking customers sitting on stools. The fight was more than twenty years old, a rerun on one of those cable sports channels, and they must have known who won it, but they cheered and waved their fists when Ken Norton knocked Muhammad Ali to the canvas. "That'll teach the nigger," one of them said, as if Norton were the Great White Hope or something. That was Ali's great talent, I realized: he turned everyone he fought into a honky, even if he was the same color as him. That gave both the

white folks and the black folks someone to cheer for. Who'd
pay top dollar to watch one black man fight another otherwise?

I finished my beer, ordered another, and then took a deep
breath and went back to the pool room. I found Marty sitting at a
corner booth, watching two red-faced farmers in overalls play a
game of eight-ball. There was no one else in the room, otherwise
I might not have known the man sitting there was my brother. He
was wearing one of his old work shirts—*Marty* stitched in blue
above the pocket, and below it, in gold, *Goodyear*—and it just hung
on him. His arms were thin and pale, except for the bruises—
Mom had said you couldn't so barely touch him without causing
a bruise, his platelet count was so low. His face, too, looked pale
and gaunt. He just plain looked *old*. He looked like Dad did, in his
last days. And he hadn't shaved for at least a week. The only thing
that was the way I'd imagined it was his baseball cap: I knew he'd
be wearing one, to hide the effects of the chemo and radiation.
He'd always been vain about that hair of his, combing it every
time he passed a mirror. I used to think he did that just to needle
me about how bald I was getting. But now, even with the hat, I
could tell he was balder than I was.

"Marty," I said, and he turned to look at me.

"Well, shit," he said, scowling. "Looks like the vultures are
already starting to circle."

I decided to let that go and sat down across from him. When
I set my beer on the table, he picked his up, like he didn't want
even his beer to share a table with me.

"Frances told me you were here," I started.

"That's what I figured," he said, and took a swig from his
longneck.

Then we were silent for a moment. One of the pool players
let out a groan and the other one did a little dance as he chalked
his cue. The jukebox was playing some country song with sad,
nasally lyrics and a cheerful, up-tempo beat.

"How're you feeling?" I asked him.

"I'm not dead yet, if that's what you mean," he said. Then he shook his head like he regretted his words and added, "It's a motherfucker, Ted. I wouldn't wish it on my worst enemy."

I knew what he was trying to say: he wouldn't wish it on *me*. That was just like Marty. He'd say something nice, like he didn't want you to suffer the way he was, and at the same time call you his worst enemy. Everything he said cut two ways. Still, that was the closest he ever came to saying he was sorry that Frances had pushed us apart, and I tried to feel grateful.

"Look," I said. "I'm here to make things right between us. There's been too much bad blood for too long. It's time we put a stop to it."

"Bad blood," he repeated, and shook his head again. He started to peel the label off his bottle of Bud. "That's almost funny, since that's exactly what I'm dying from." He smiled a little, then looked at me. "All those damn white blood cells. A regular blizzard's worth of 'em."

His face scared me, those gaunt cheeks and his eyes so big and glistening. "What are you doing here then?" I said. "Shouldn't you be home in bed, taking care of yourself? It can't be good for you to be drinking this shit"—I nodded at the Bud—"or breathing all this smoke." I don't know why I said that about the smoke: no one was even smoking, though the place did smell like damp cigarette ashes, the way bars always do.

"The concerned brother," he said then, and took a long draw on his beer. When he finished, he said, "Fuck you."

"What's wrong with you?" I said. "I *am* concerned. You're my brother, goddamn it."

"Congratulations, Ted. You've saved your soul. Too bad you can't save mine."

I sat back and tried not to say anything I'd regret later. "I came here to say I'm sorry. I came to tell you everything was my fault."

"Well, you've done it, so now you can go on home. Mom'll call you when it's over, and then you can come to the funeral and beat your fucking breast in front of everybody."

I leaned forward. My face was heating up. "That's not fair," I said, gritting my teeth. And it wasn't. And I proved it that December, when Mom and I went to his funeral. I didn't cry once, though my throat ached with tears the whole time. I didn't cry until afterwards, when I was back home and alone, and then I cried so hard I could barely stop.

"I suppose not," he answered, "but I don't much feel like being fair right now."

"So you want me to leave."

"Not yet," he said. "There's something I've been wanting to tell you. Something I think you should know."

"What?" I said. I figured he was going to say something nasty about me and Frances, but he didn't.

"Caroline was here last week," he said. "We've kept in touch all these years."

"So?" I said, trying to sound blasé. My heart was starting to beat hard. I was picturing her in Marty's house, sitting there on that couch, Frances and Marty stoking her hatred of me with their lies. I could see her beautiful, porcelain-white face go red with the heat of her anger, see her eyes shrink as Frances blamed it all on me once again. She'd always told them I was the one who kissed her first that Christmas Eve, but that's not true, and she knows it.

"When she was here," Marty went on, "she told me something you'd said to her once, back when you were first married."

I looked at him, but I was still seeing Caroline's face, those eyes.

"She told me you once said there was a bond between brothers that she couldn't understand, since she was an only child. She said you told her it was a love unlike any other."

I didn't remember saying that, but I believed it was true. I still do, despite how he treated me that day. Hardly a day goes by that I don't remember something he said or did when we were young that makes me miss him so much I can hardly stand it. It can be anything, even something small and stupid, like the time he woke me up one morning by tickling my nose with a feather, then said, "Want to play checkers?" I remember something like that and I just choke up.

"What's your point?" I said.

He leaned toward me. There was sweat on his upper lip, and he looked tired, as if just sitting there talking to me had exhausted him. "I always thought the same," he said, then laughed this laugh that sounded more like a cough.

I just sat there.

He leaned back. "Now you can go," he said, waving the back of his hand at me. "Take your sorry ass back to your empty house."

I wanted to say that at least it *was* my house, a house I'd paid for with honest work, not a house that was just given to me. But I didn't. I stood up.

"Marty," I said, "I drove all this way to make things right between us. But if you—"

"Look," he said. "I'm the one who's dying. Feel sorry for me, not yourself."

I turned then, and left. On my way out, I heard the bartender saying to one of the customers, "I still say Foreman threw that fight over there in Africa." There were three men sitting at the bar now, and all of them nodded.

When I got in my car, I took off my shoe and sock and looked at my toe. My nail was cracked damn near in half and blood was oozing out from under it. I was getting more and more sure I'd broken a bone, too. But I didn't blame Marty for it, even though it was his neglect of his property that caused me to break it. I blamed myself, because none of this would have happened if I'd been smart and stayed home.

I should have gone right back home that minute, but I didn't. Instead, I went back over to Marty's house. I didn't know what I was going to say to Frances, but I knew I had to talk to her. I couldn't leave things the way they were. I had to do something.

As I limped up to the house, careful not to stub my toe on anything under all those leaves, I remembered how one fall, when we were kids, Marty and I made parachutes out of old sheets and jumped out of the oak tree into a pile of leaves Dad had raked up for us. We did it over and over and never even sprained an ankle. We were immortal in those days. Nothing could hurt us then. Somehow, remembering that made me even madder.

I didn't ring the doorbell this time. I knocked on the door and waited a while, but Frances didn't answer. I knew she was in there—her car was parked in the driveway—so I knocked again. Still no answer.

"Frances," I called out. "Open the door." But she didn't. So I pounded on the door with my fist. I didn't pound very hard but still little flecks of paint fell to my feet like rusty snowflakes.

"Go away," I heard her say then. She must have been standing on the other side of the door all that time. That of course just made me madder.

"You have no right to tell me to go away," I said. "Let me in!"

"I'll call Marty," she said.

I felt my face heat up again. "You bitch," I said. "You ruined my life."

"I'll call the cops," she said.

I remembered that night in the kitchen, when she kissed me. It was the first Christmas Eve we'd celebrated in the house after Mom had given it to Marty, and we'd all been sitting around in the living room after opening presents, Mom and Marty and Frances and Caroline and the boys, and she'd suddenly gotten up and gone into the kitchen. A minute or two later, I went in there to fill up my glass of wine and found her standing at the sink, looking out the window at the dark and crying. "What's wrong, Frances?" I'd said and put my arm around her shoulders. They were shaking. She'd turned to me then, tears in her eyes, and said, "I don't think Marty loves me anymore."

I pounded on the door so hard my hand began to sting. "You'd better let me in," I said.

"Go away!"

I remembered the dress she was wearing that night. It was rayon or something like that, something silky, and it was the bright clear blue you see in those ads for Caribbean vacations, and her eyes were blue, too, and her hair then was the color of honey with sunlight shining through it. Even though I'd always thought Frances wasn't nearly as pretty as Caroline, at that moment she seemed beautiful to me. She struck me as everything a man would ever want, and it angered me that Marty had made her feel so bad, and on Christmas Eve, too. I thought maybe I'd been wrong all these years to think she didn't deserve a man like Marty. Maybe it was Marty who didn't deserve a woman like her. But I didn't say any of that, of course. What I did was hug her and tell her she was being silly, of course Marty loved her, she was worrying for nothing. When she finally stopped crying, I let her go. That's when she kissed me. It was just a quick peck on the lips, the way a woman might kiss her brother. And I kissed her back, an innocent little kiss. I don't think either of us could have guessed, then, what we'd started, or how it'd end the next summer, all the turmoil of confessions and threats and tears.

I pounded on the door again. "I said, *Let—me—in!*"

Then I heard her running down the hall. I knew she was running into the kitchen—the same kitchen where she'd ruined my life—and I knew she was going to call the police. But I also knew there was nothing they could do. I hadn't done anything wrong. I could just stay there on the steps and wait for them to arrive and explain everything. But I was too angry to stay a minute longer. So I turned around and started to leave.

But before I got into my car and drove home, I picked up that chunk of concrete I'd stubbed my toe on and hurled it with both hands at the door. Then I stood there, breathing hard, and looked at the long, deep gash it left, the naked wood that'd been hidden by the paint. It felt good to think about Frances standing there on the porch, sometime after Marty was dead and buried, painting that scar over, trying to erase every last memory she had of me. I was angry, sure, but it was an exhilarating, happy kind of anger, one that made me feel as alive as I did back when we were together and making love in every room of the house.

I couldn't make that feeling last, though. By the time I turned onto the highway, I was bawling so hard I couldn't even stop to see Mom.

God, how I loved my brother.

# MISERY

*after Chekhov*

On the 17th of January in 1885, Alexei Dymov, an assistant editor of a Petersburg weekly, went to dinner at a restaurant near the Vyborgskaya with Nikolai Leikin, the newspaper's editor-in-chief, and Victor Kovalenko, a young law student from Moscow. For the past two years, Kovalenko had been writing a column for the newspaper, and Leikin had invited him to the capital for a fortnight's visit. Dymov was enlisted for the evening's entertainment, which would include dinner and—though this information was kept from him—a visit to a brothel.

Dymov was a short man, barely taller than a dwarf, and extremely hunchbacked. He was also afflicted with a form of palsy that left one side of his face rigid, so that when he smiled, which he rarely did, only one corner of his mouth would rise, making his rather squashed face appear lopsided as well. Despite these peculiarities, or perhaps because of them, Leikin often invited him to dine with him and his friends. On such occasions, Dymov rarely failed to entertain Leikin's guests with both his quaint conversation and his odd appearance.

However, on this particular occasion, Dymov had more to drink than was typical of him, and he began an argument that continued, off and on, for most of the evening and eventually became so loud that the owner of the restaurant came out of the kitchen and threatened to call for the police. Leikin had mentioned a business associate of theirs who had recently died of consumption, and somehow the conversation turned to the question of life after death. Leikin scoffed at the notion, calling it "a story to keep the serfs in line." At that moment, Dymov, whose grandfather had been a serf, rose in his seat and, swaying drunkenly, said, "I demand an apology."

"For what?" Leikin asked.

"For insulting my God," he answered.

"Your God!" Leikin howled.

"Yes, my God, and your God as well, were you not too blind to acknowledge Him."

Since Dymov had previously kept his religious faith from Leikin, knowing he would mock him for it, this outburst surprised Leikin as much as it did Kovalenko, who in his embarrassment proceeded to cut his sausage as if it were a task that required the utmost concentration. For a moment, Leikin sat there stock-still examining Dymov with his eyebrows elevated. Then he began to ridicule his little friend and his ludicrous faith. Before long, Kovalenko recovered from his embarrassment and joined his editor-in-chief in attacking Dymov. Jabbing his unlit cigar at the hunchback, he said that, in his opinion, religion was nothing more than "a tit for perpetual infants to suckle." Leikin laughed so hard at this that tears streamed down his ruddy cheeks into his bushy black beard, and Kovalenko could not keep from grinning at the triumph of his phrase.

Dymov recognized that "perpetual infants" was an attack on his dwarfish stature, but he tried not to let the personal affront interfere with the logic of his argument. Still, the longer the quarrel continued, the more he realized, to his shame, that he was less upset about their assault on God than he was about their mockery of him. He was particularly hurt by Leikin's mockery because for some time he had entertained an interest in Leikin's younger sister, Masha, a sickly girl given to blushing and stammering, and he had hoped that her brother would one day aid him in his efforts to secure her hand in marriage.

Although the cursing and quarrelling eventually subsided, the evening had been ruined for Dymov, and he was anxious for it to be over. However, Leikin had told them that they would be stopping after dinner for an hour's entertainment at the home of an acquaintance who lived near the Police Bridge—a certain Madame Vasilyevna who, Leikin informed him with a smile, was "a great patron of the arts." Dymov resolved to put in a dutiful appearance, then proceed to his lodgings and do his best to forget whatever hopes he had once held for the hand of Marya Aleksandrovna.

By the time the men finished their after-dinner cigars and brandy, paid their bill, and left the restaurant, it was nearly ten o'clock. It had been snowing since twilight, and now the snow was lying thick and wet on the streets. The men stamped their galoshes on the pavement, and Kovalenko and Leikin cursed the snow as roundly as they had earlier cursed Dymov. Then Dymov spotted a sleigh parked beneath the streetlamp at the corner. The sleigh-driver was sitting in the box, his body bent nearly double, and his cap and overcoat were so covered with snow that he looked like a ghost. His little horse, too, was white, save for her dappled flanks and slender legs and fetlocks. The cabman had evidently been sitting there a long time, waiting for a fare, and Dymov knew they would be able to purchase his services cheaply. He had already wasted more of his money than he'd cared to on a perfectly horrible evening, and he didn't wish to spend a kopeck more than necessary.

"Cabby!" he called, his voice so hoarse from choking back angry tears all night that it cracked. "To the Police Bridge. The three of us . . . twenty kopecks!"

The sleigh-driver slowly shrugged off the mantle of snow, but otherwise made no response. The three men, all of them stumbling from the effects of wine and brandy, made their way to the sleigh, cursing and grumbling all the while. Then they proceeded to argue about who would sit and who would stand.

"Nikolai and I are long of legs," said Kovalenko, swaying as he

looked down on Dymov, "so it is impossible for us to stand." Then
he tried to climb into the sleigh, but his foot missed the step and he
fell onto his back in the snow. He lay there, slack-jawed with surprise,
and Leikin and Dymov burst out laughing. For a moment Dymov
felt the warmth of shared laughter and believed that Leikin was
still his friend. But then he remembered how Leikin had laughed
when Kovalenko called him a "perpetual infant," and he realized
that he would undoubtedly repeat the story to Masha, making him
appear foolish in her eyes. Abruptly, he stopped laughing. "I won't
be made to stand," he said resolutely. "I won't, I tell you."

But after Leikin helped Kovalenko to his feet, they each took
one of Dymov's stubby arms and unceremoniously tossed him
up into the sleigh, then climbed in behind him and sat down
laughing.

Dymov was so incensed by this, the worst of the evening's
humiliations, that his face contorted into a snarl and he balled his
tiny hands into fists. He was about to attack his companions with
a flurry of curses and blows, but then he thought of Masha, her
pallid skin and frost-blue eyes, and he knew that if he lost his
friendship with her brother he would also lose any chance he had
for happiness with her. So, choking back his fury, he merely turned
to the cabman and grumbled, "What are you waiting for? Drive!"

The driver had not said anything during their quarrel, nor even
turned around. When the hunchback told him to drive on, he
simply clicked to his horse and tugged at the reins, causing cakes
of snow to fly off the little mare's back and shoulders. Slowly the
sleigh started off down the nearly deserted street.

Dymov leaned over then and breathed down the driver's neck.
"Faster!" he said. "We haven't got all night."

The driver nodded and gave the reins a shake. The sleigh began
to move past the dark shops and kiosks a little faster, and Dymov
hung on to the railing to keep from being jolted to the floor each
time the sleigh struck a hole in the cobblestone street.

Meanwhile, Kovalenko was beginning to see the humor of his
fall in the snow, and he and Leikin were laughing together. Dymov

felt his face flush and his scalp sting. He wanted to turn to his companions and tell them he hated them, but instead he began to taunt the driver.

"What a cap you've got, my friend!" he said. "You wouldn't find a worse one in all of Petersburg . . ."

The driver laughed, a brittle sound in the cold quiet air. "It's nothing to boast of!" he said.

"And neither is that nag of yours! Can't you make her go faster?"

The cabman said nothing, and they drove on in silence for a while. Dymov shuddered in the wind that tore at his collar. "Damn this cold," he said. "We shall all catch our deaths."

Then the sleigh struck a rut in the road and Kovalenko groaned. "Damn you," he said to the driver. "Be careful!" Then he moaned, "How my head aches . . ."

"My head aches also," Leikin said. "At the Dukmasovs' yesterday Vaska and I drank four bottles of brandy between us."

"*Four* bottles?" said Kovalenko, holding his head. "I swear, you lie like a serf. Why, I drank three times as much as you tonight, and here you are, drunk as a fishwife."

"Strike me dead, it's the truth! . . ."

"It's about as true as that a louse coughs."

The driver laughed again, thinly. "What merry gentlemen!" he said.

"The devil take you!" cried Dymov. "Will you get on, you old plague, or won't you? Is that the way to drive? Give her one with the whip. Damn it all, give her a good one."

But the cabman didn't take his whip out of its holster or even give the reins a shake. He simply cleared his throat and said, in a quiet voice, "This week . . . uh . . . my . . . uh . . ."

"Out with it!" Dymov said.

"My son died," the cabman said.

The old man's words startled Dymov, and for a moment he didn't know what to say. Then he said, "We shall all die," but his embarrassment made his words, which were meant both to comfort the old man and to apologize for his treatment of him, sound too terse. He sighed, then shivered, remembering how Kovalenko had smiled at him across the table in the restaurant, the candlelight glinting off his spectacles, and said, "So you think the dead shall rise up and sprout wings on the last day, do you?" And he recalled how Leikin guffawed when he answered indignantly, "No, but they shall rise up nonetheless, and no matter how imperfect they were in body and mind, on the last day they shall be perfect—perfect as their souls, which were made in God's image." And how, later, the waiter, an effeminate flaxen-haired boy in a white apron, had laughed confusedly when Leikin told him that their little friend couldn't wait to die so he could be as tall and straight-backed as his soul.

How Dymov envied the cabman's dead son! He was lucky to be out of this miserable world, lucky not to be his grief-stricken father, driving drunks through the cold streets for a mere twenty kopecks, lucky not to be a despised hunchback. Yes, Dymov believed in God, believed in Him enough to assert it no matter how much Leikin and Kovalenko mocked him, but tonight he could not love God, who made His creatures pay for eternal life with such horrible mortal ones.

"Come on!" he said abruptly. "Hurry up!" He was angry at the cabman for making him think such awful thoughts. He should not have to console this stranger. What did the old man's grief have to do with him anyway? Nothing! Absolutely nothing! Turning to his companions, he exclaimed, "My friends, I simply cannot stand crawling along like this! At this rate, we'll freeze to death before we get there."

Then Leikin leaned toward Dymov, his eyes half closed, and woozily said, "Why don't you give the old fellow a little encouragement . . . smack him one in the neck!"

At that moment, Dymov wanted once again to strike his employer, to split his thick lips with one artful blow, but he turned back to the driver and said, "Do you hear what he said? If you don't get a move on, I'll teach you a lesson with my fist."

But the old man didn't answer, or even turn to look at him; instead, he just drove slowly on, staring straight ahead as if he were thinking about his dead son and hadn't heard a word Dymov had said. Then, before he even knew he was going to do it, Dymov had slapped him so hard on the back of his neck, the snow rose like dust from his coat and cap. He felt his throat constrict, as if he were about to cry, and he wanted more than ever to be dead and lying in a casket, his hands crossed over his chest like wings. Oh, if only he were the cabman's son, so dead and so loved!

The driver laughed his thin laugh. "What merry gentlemen," he said. "God give you health!"

Then Kovalenko belched and said, "Cabman, are you married?"

"I? No, not I, gentlemen. The only wife for me now is the damp earth." He paused a moment, then added, "Here my son's dead and I am alive. It's a strange thing, death has come in at the wrong door. Instead of coming for me it went for my son . . ."

Then the old man turned around, as if to tell them the circumstances of his son's death, and when Dymov saw his sorrowful face he knew that, after all he had suffered that night, he could not hear the driver's story without deciding that his companions were right, that we are as perfect now as we will ever be, and after death we will rot in the earth and be no more than food for worms and fertilizer for weeds.

But just then he saw that, thank God, they had arrived at the Police Bridge. "Here we are!" he called with relief. When the sleigh stopped, they clambered out, paid the cabman, and staggered off across the street. The snow was still coming down, whirling in the light cast by the streetlamp, and the three men shivered in the cold. "Here is Madame Vasilyevna's," Leikin said with a nod, and he led them into the dark entry of an old but well-kept building.

As soon as they entered, Dymov heard raucous laughter and piano music. The music was not the Chopin or Tchaikovsky he was accustomed to hearing in the homes of other patrons of the arts; rather, it sounded like dance-hall music. He was puzzled by this fact. Still, he stamped the snow from his galoshes and hung his coat on the already burdened coat rack just as his companions did.

Kovalenko's spectacles had fogged up, so he took them off and wiped them on the sleeve of his dinner jacket. When he finished, he put them on and looked at Leikin intently, as if seeing him for the first time. "Perhaps we should have given the man more for his trouble," he said then. "Only twenty kopecks for such a long ride and his son so recently dead . . ."

"Oh, you mustn't believe that old story," Leikin said with a wave of his hand. "He was only trying to sigh and moan a larger fare out of us. I doubt if the sly old dog ever had a son—at least one that he knew of!"

At that, Kovalenko said, "Well, if the Petersburg cabbies are anything like the Moscow cabbies, I suppose you are right. But what if he were telling the truth?"

Before Dymov could say he had seen a look in the cabman's face that no actor could have imitated, the door to the drawing room opened, spilling loud music and laughter, and Madame Vasilyevna stepped out into the entryway. An ancient woman, she was wearing a mask of makeup and a decrepit fur-trimmed housecoat. According to a legend known by all who frequented her establishment, the housecoat had been given to her by Pushkin shortly before the great poet died, but if anyone were to ask her about this story, she would neither affirm nor deny it. She would merely say, "I pity you, for you will never know the kind of love I knew with the great man who gave me this coat," then she'd clasp its musty, moth-eaten collar about her turkey wattle of a neck and promptly vacate the room. But the three visitors bowing to her now had not asked about her coat, so she did not feel the need to treat them with her usual disdain.

"Welcome, gentlemen," she said, and offered Leikin her hand. He kissed it, then said, "Madame, I have brought a visitor from Moscow, a young law student who wishes to—how shall we say?—*cross-examine* a young lady in your employ?"

At that, Kovalenko nearly choked with laughter. But Dymov did not hear either Leikin's joke or Kovalenko's response, for he was staring through the open door into the drawing room, where there were a dozen or so women in various stages of undress. Some were sitting on the laps of men in overstuffed armchairs and settees, and others were dancing with sailors and merchants amidst the Chinese parasols, cheap plaster busts of philosophers, and colored prints of French landscapes that decorated the room. Beside the heavy red and gold brocaded drapes, a skinny, pock-faced piano player yawned as he pecked out a jaunty tune. With a sudden spasm, Dymov realized where he was.

"You devil!" he said to Leikin. "May you burn in hell, you and all these—these *strumpets!*" Then he stepped in front of the gasping Madame Vasilyevna, yanked his greatcoat from the rack, and hastily began to stuff his short arms into it.

Leikin said, "Now, now, Alexei! We did it for your own good. How old are you now anyway? Twenty-four, twenty-five? It's time you became a man."

"Yes," Kovalenko added. "Stay with us. In an hour or two, you will wonder what you were so upset about."

But Dymov was already at the door. He tried to open it, but his hand was trembling so violently he couldn't turn the glass knob. "Damn you!" he said, as much to himself as to Leikin and Kovalenko, then the door finally opened and he dashed outside and down the steps without so much as a glance back at the men who had betrayed his trust.

Once he had reached the street, he looked anxiously up and down it for the cabman, but his sleigh was nowhere to be seen. There was nothing to do but walk until he came upon it or another cab, so he set off down the street in the direction of his lodgings. He walked with his chin buried in his collar and his hands shoved deep in his pockets, but still the gusting wind made his teeth chatter and his eyes burn with the tears he had been suppressing all evening. How wrong he had been about Leikin! The man was nothing more than a pimp. Instead of helping him gain the love of his sister, he had tried to set him up with a prostitute!

Walking along, thinking such thoughts, Dymov eventually came upon a sleigh parked in front of a teahouse. As soon as he saw it, he called out, "Cabby, cabby!" but the man who turned and said, "At your service, sir" was not the one who had brought him to

Madame Vasilyevna's. Still, without a ride he would freeze to death, so he climbed aboard and gave the driver directions to his lodgings.

A few minutes later, the sleigh reached its destination, and Dymov disembarked and paid the driver. "Bless you, sir!" the driver exclaimed when he saw how much he'd been given. "Bless you!" And then he whipped his horse and drove off pell-mell, evidently afraid the hunchback had made a mistake and would ask for the ruble back.

Dymov watched the sleigh until it rounded a corner, then went into the building where he lived and climbed the rickety stairs toward his apartment. Passing the doors of his fellow lodgers, he heard bits of conversations, the clink of silverware against plates, the scratching of a bow on a poorly tuned violin, and he wished he knew even one of his neighbors well enough to knock on his door and invite himself in. He wanted to tell someone how his companions had humiliated him, mocking him and his God, and he wanted to confess the harsh words he had said to the cabman, the blow he'd delivered to his neck. If only there were someone, anyone, to comfort him in his sorrow, console him in his guilt! But there was no one. Perhaps this is what death is like, he thought as he unlocked his door: a terrible anguish, and no one to tell it to.

He had not been able to warm himself since the ride to Madame Vasilyevna's, so as soon as he entered his apartment, he lit a fire and stood beside it, hugging himself. Watching the flames flicker yellow and orange, he thought about the cabman, sitting in the cold somewhere, his body bent double with sorrow, and the snow falling steadily on his hunched back. Then, against his will, he saw Marya's pale body lying in the stillness of death, her open eyes aimed toward the ceiling, and he turned away from the fire. If only he could sleep, and wake in the morning with no memory of this terrible evening! But he knew he could not. He sat down on the edge of his divan and closed his eyes, but still he saw Marya's dead face.

Then he put his frostbitten face into his hands, and for a few moments his small chest shook and tears warmed his cold fingers.

When he finished, he sat there, his throat raw with the ache of crying, and stared at the door. Through the wall, he could hear bedsprings squeaking in the next room and its occupants, a teacher and his wife, grunting. Down the hallway, someone—the medical student perhaps, or maybe the postal clerk—was singing a folk song about a young girl and the moon, and out on the landing, a woman with a Georgian accent was saying goodnight to a man who kept clearing his throat. In all of these sounds Dymov heard the somber fact of death, and knew that it would be as unrequited as love.

He sat there listening a long time, until the only sounds he heard were the wind and, now and then, a sleigh passing in the snow.

# HOOK

I'm no saint. I know that. I've got some sort of problem, I don't know, my heart's rabid or something. I'm always in trouble. And I've got the scars to prove it, more than meet the eye. You know what they call scar tissue? Proud flesh. A doctor that sewed me up one night in West Memphis told me that. He said I must've had a full pound of proud flesh on me. An exaggeration, of course, like most things that're true. But I'm not proud of the scars—in fact, I'm ashamed of them. Still I told him, "You ought to see the other guy" and held up my hook so he'd get the picture. He nodded, and when he finished wrapping my shoulder with gauze, there was sweat on his upper lip and he couldn't look at me. "No charge," he said, casual-like. "It's on me."

I do that to people, and I hate it. It's not just the hook, though that gets to most everybody, especially when they see how I've filed the two tips—what a little boy once called my "lobster pinchers"—right down to a razor point. It's something else. If I knew what it was, I might just change it. Whatever it is, it's made me the world's biggest loser in love. Three times I've been married, and three times divorced. Three for fucking three, I'm batting a thousand. And the third marriage didn't last but the Fourth of July weekend. I don't know, I loved all three of them—still do, in fact—but they all left me for one reason or other. Leann, for "mental cruelty," which is a joke, considering how cruel it was for her to leave me. Charlotte, for throwing her new Sears hi-fi out the apartment window. And Jenelle, for the policeman who arrested me at our wedding dance. If I could only stay bitter, I'd be happy, but I swear some days I can't even work up the heart to take a walk in the exercise yard, I just lay around in my cell and think about the three of them shucking their panties in other guys' bedrooms. It just about makes me want to die, it really does.

And now I've lost Carina. Nobody can tell me love is a beautiful thing.

My old man would've whipped me if he'd ever seen me with Carina. But he's long dead and Carina isn't really a Negro. She's what they call a quadroon, though to the racists that live in this state she's pure Negro. And that means pure worthless to them. From the moment Carina's daddy bought the old Egan place west of Beasley, everybody in Crittenden County slandered him around the clock because he was white and his wife was black. Some folks even claimed he had a daughter—not Carina, another one— that had been born retarded from the marrying between the races, but I never believed it. I thought it was just racist talk. If there's one thing I can't stand, it's a racist. There are guys I knew in Nam who'd get all high and mighty about sleeping with a Negro but they didn't think twice about screwing slopes. The funny thing about it is that those slopes weren't even one-fourth American, much less three-fourths like Carina.

As for me, I never touched one of those women. If you don't believe me, you can ask the rest of Company B, 7th Cavalry Regiment. It was a regular joke with them.

War stories turn women on, so the night I met Carina at Snap's Bar, I danced her into a corner, sat her down at a booth, and told her my Purple Heart story. The candlelight made her face look a little yellow and slant-eyed, so I blew it out and we talked in the almost-dark.

"How it happened," I said, holding up the hook, "was we were on a mission in the rice paddies above Bong Son. Up to our asses in muck and no cover for thirty yards. We couldn't move, you understand, like in a dream where you're trying to run, you're straining every muscle, but you just can't do it. And then it happened, mortar and rifle fire from the tree-line. My pal Rudy, right in front of me, falls face-first into the paddy, and the water starts turning red. I raise my M-16 and aim and then I don't have it. I've dropped it. Right in the paddy. I look down and watch it sink, slow-motion-like, out of sight. I stand there staring at my rifle and can't imagine what made me drop it."

I took out a pack of Camels and lit one up. I kept expecting Carina to make some excuse and vanish, she was so young and everything—younger even than Leann—but she stayed there, looking at my hook, her brown eyes big.

"Shrapnel," I said, exhaling. "Ripped half my arm clean off and I never even felt it. It was the strangest thing."

"That's really sad," Carina said, and I could tell she meant it by the way she looked down at her own, whole hands. Then she looked up and said, "You mind if I touch it?"

I was surprised as hell, but I acted like it was a question I heard every day. "Sure," I said. "Go right ahead."

And she touched the hook, ever so gently, tracing it from stump to shank to tip. I swear it made me shiver, just like she'd touched my soul. If only she hadn't touched my hook like that, I probably would've been able to forget her, and I probably wouldn't be doing three to five here now. But she did touch it, and every time I close my eyes I can still see her touching it.

The worst thing about all this is that I was lying to her, just like I lied to all of them, except Leann. I didn't lose my arm in Nam, though the rest of that story is true: I did drop my rifle when the shooting started and Rudy did die, right there in front of me, in the rice. To this day, I can't eat rice. The truth about the arm is that I lost it when I was living in Memphis and working for the Cotton Belt railroad. It'd been drizzling one night and when I hopped up onto the step of one of the cars we'd just uncoupled from the Blue Streak, I slipped on the slick metal and fell. I never even felt the wheel pass over my arm. All I remember is my knee hurting like sin from hitting the step as I fell. The next thing I knew, I was in the hospital and the doctors had already sewn my forearm back on. But it didn't take, and the arm died. It's a strange thing to watch part of yourself die. The only thing like it is a divorce. At first the arm was white, so white there almost seemed to be a light somewhere under the skin, but then it got blue-black, blacker even than Carina's mama. When my fingers started to curl into a fist, the doctors gave up and sawed the arm off clean, just below the elbow. A week later, after the swelling had gone down, a doctor came and wheeled me through a tunnel to a building connected to the hospital where they had the prosthesis shop. Drill press, belt sander, grinder, band saw, lathe, vise: it looked like a high school industrial arts shop, except for the plastic arms hanging on the wall and legs standing on tables. All the while they made a cast of my stump, I just sat there, staring at all those shiny limbs. I tell you, it was spooky knowing that pretty soon my new arm would be hanging on the wall with the others, the flesh-colored paint drying.

Now everybody calls me Hook. Whenever I meet someone, I stick out my left hand to shake and say, "The name's Hook, bet you can't guess why." After that, they always smile like someone just cracked an egg in their pants. I hate doing that to them, but I keep on just the same.

But when I introduced myself to Carina that night, she didn't give me that sick smile like everybody else. "Oh, what happened to your hand?" she asked, just as sweet and innocent as you could imagine, and *I* was the one who smiled like a gut-shot gook. "Never mind for now," I said back. "There's nothing wrong with my legs. Want to see them dance?"

So we danced. You should have seen her: *everything* was moving. She was wiggling like her dress-tail was on fire. And when she'd turn around and shake her ass at me, it was enough to make you believe in God. I'm still amazed that she danced with me that way. I mean, she'd still be in high school if she hadn't quit and here I am, on the downhill side of thirty with a beer gut, scars, and a hook.

And she let me take her home. We sang every Hank Williams song we could remember all the way down the dirt road to her house, that ramshackle old place near the river bottom. Carina's daddy had tried to make a go of farming, but he never had a farmer's head on him. And twice the river flooded and he wasn't able to get a tractor out into the fields until it was already too late to plant. So it'd been almost a mercy when he dropped dead earlier that summer from baling cotton in the heat. But he hadn't had much insurance, so now things were even harder for Carina's family. Her mama had put the farm up for sale but so far nobody stupid enough to buy it had come along. Everybody knew the FHA would foreclose on the mortgage soon, and then the farm would be auctioned off for less than the nothing it was worth.

I asked Carina what they were going to do when the FHA foreclosed. "Ain't nothing for us to do," she said. "Only way out, far as I can see, is if Mama or me gets married." She was looking away from me and yet at me when she said that, if you know what I mean. If I hadn't been shit-faced drunk, I don't know, maybe I might have figured it all out then.

When we reached the house, we had to help each other up the steps, we were swaying about so. We weren't singing anymore. We'd reached that quiet that comes just before you fall in love. We were out there in the middle of nothing, just fields of withered cotton all around, and everything was silent except the shushing of the river. I felt like we were all alone in the world, and I hadn't felt like that since the time Leann and I holed up in a Holiday Inn, never going out, even once, for an entire weekend. We never even turned on the TV or the radio, we were that far gone.

But inside, Carina's mama was sitting up. Like I said, Carina's a quadroon, meaning one-fourth Negro. But her mama's half Negro, and she looked it. She was sitting on a splint chair by a kerosene lamp, her skinny legs propped up on a short stool, reading a *Woman's Day*. Despite the heat, she was wearing two ragged robes—a red one on top, and the other, which stuck out underneath, blue-and-white-checked. As soon as she saw me, she took her slippers off and started to put on these dusty oxblood-colored shoes.

"Mama," Carina said, swaying a little, "this here's—"

"I'll be taking a walk," her mama said back, without looking up from her shoes. She tied the knots so tight I thought she'd break the laces.

Then she was gone and before I could say anything, Carina gave me this kiss. It felt good, real good. Even Charlotte, my second wife, couldn't kiss like that, and she studied kissing like it was an art. She went to all the movies that hit town, and when she came home she'd try out the techniques the movie stars used, her mouth working on mine like she was trying to swallow my tonsils. We kissed damn near all the time. If we weren't kissing, she figured she wasn't having a good time. I'm sure she's going at it this very instant with some poor guy with chapped lips.

I heard Carina's sister before I saw her. Carina and I were still kissing, and my hand was slipping down the curve of her back when I heard this funny sound, half a hiccup and half a snort. I looked up. There she was, the famous sister I'd heard so much about but never believed in, standing in the doorway, half-hidden in shadow. The way she stared at us, with her tongue out and her hair bristly and black like a singed broom, she looked like a scarecrow.

"What the hell," I said.

"Oh, never mind her," Carina said, her eyes half-closed. "She don't know what she's seeing anyhow."

That was her name, far as I could tell: *She*. Carina never called her anything else. I watched her scratching herself and listened to her snorts.

"Why's she scratching herself like that?" I asked. I tell you, it was indecent.

"Let's go in here," Carina said, and pulled me into a bedroom. She closed the door and locked it. "Now she won't bother us," she said, and started to unzip her dress.

Outside the door, I could hear her sister snorting.

"Don't pay no attention to her," Carina said. She stepped out of her dress, slipped off her bra, then put my hand on her breast. The sister started snorting louder and pulling on the doorknob. I touched one, then the other breast, until the nipples stood out like rosebuds. Her breasts were beautiful. They weren't big, like Jenelle's, but they were beautiful just the same.

"You can use your hook," Carina said then, woozy-like. "I don't mind."

"Huh?" I said. I'd heard her, but I hadn't, if you know what I mean.

She showed me what she meant, raising my hook to her nipple. I had never touched a woman with the hook before, not even Leann. I touched Carina's breast for a minute, so careful not to prick her with the tips that I was trembling, then we laid down on the bed and did what men and women do. *She* stood outside the door all the while, snorting and scratching, but even so, it was something.

Every time after that, it was something too. And it was always the same: no sooner would I get there than her mama would put on her walking shoes and her sister would start snorting and scratching herself. When we wanted to be private, we'd go to my room over Slaughter's Grocery or drive down the river road till it stopped, spread a blanket in the high grass, and make love there. Once, Carina complained about some rocks under the blanket digging into her back, so I laid on my back and let her come on top. That drove her crazy, nobody had ever let her do that before, and afterward she cried a little, a happy cry.

"There, there," I said, and stroked her thick black hair with my hand. I knew she straightened her hair because I'd seen a bottle of Curl-Free on the shelf in their bathroom. I thought about how she'd look if she let her hair go kinky like her mama's and sister's and got herself a good tan. I imagined us walking down Main Street in Beasley, arm in arm, and all the people staring. In a way I liked the idea of making them stare like that and in a way I didn't.

Another time, Carina fell asleep afterward and I laid there on the blanket watching the fireflies flickering all around and smelling the dogfennel and bitterweed. I pretty well decided that night that I'd get my hair done up in an Afro and my skin dyed, if it came to that. I tell you, I was crazy with love.

I would have proposed to Carina that night except that when I walked her up the steps, she swayed a little, sleepy-like, and it made me think of Leann and the way she walked when she knew I was behind her, watching. Loose in the hips, almost like she was drunk. Leann was no great looker, no one would say she was, but when she walked like that, my heart wanted to bust out of its cage.

I tried not to think about Leann, but I couldn't help it. Before I knew what I was doing, I was remembering the funny way she had of washing her toes first when she took a bath, then soaping her legs and so on up to her face, rather than the other way around, which is normal. She had red hair except for a dime-sized circle of white on the side of her head where her daddy hit her with a gravy ladle when she was young and acting up at suppertime. I knew I shouldn't be thinking about Leann, but I kept reasoning that if I'd been better to her, we might still be married now. We might even have a couple of little girls. I could just see them, red-haired and freckled like Leann, in lacy white dresses and ponytails. I'd even go to church, just to show them off.

Leann, Leann. If it wasn't for you, I might have proposed to Carina right then and I'd be at peace now.

That's my trouble: I never stop loving anybody. Even now, after all that's happened, I'd marry Charlotte and Jenelle again, too. In fact, I'd marry all three of them at the same time and work day and night to keep them all in pantyhose if only that was how it worked in this blessed world. But it isn't. Even if they'd all agree to it, I'd wind up doing something to hurt them and they'd leave me again. Like I say, there's something wrong with me, something screwed up in my genes. How else can you explain some of the things I've done, like breaking Jenelle's brother's jaw at our wedding dance? I knew he was joking when he made that toast, but I hit him anyway. Sure, I was drunk, but that's no excuse. There's been lots of time I've been drunker and never hit anybody. It's a mystery to me why I act the way I do.

All I know for sure is that if Leann hadn't ever left me, I'd be a different person today. Her leaving shook me up worse than Nam.

Anyway, after I took Carina home that night, I couldn't sleep. I kept thinking about Leann. She's remarried now, her husband owns this cafe over in Culver. Albie Hendricks is his name—a big guy, six foot three, 230, a scrabble of black beard, and a Bowie knife tattooed on one hairy forearm. The story is that he flew Hueys out of Phu Bai during Tet, and he might have. He looks tough enough. But he was wearing an apron and flipping cheeseburgers the day of our fight. You couldn't get an apron on me. If they'd let me out of this goddamn place, I'd go ask her who wears the pants in the family, him or her.

The more I thought about Leann and Albie, the worse it got. There was this feeling, like something itching at the back of my brain, that I always get before I do something bad. I get this feeling and then there's nothing I can do but go ahead and do whatever it is I have to do. It was the middle of the night, but I couldn't stay in my room, so I dressed and went down to Snap's. It was locked up, of course, so I went around back and broke out the men's room window with my hook and climbed in.

By the time Snap came to open up, I'd already downed damn near a bottle of Beam. I'd intended to pay for it and for the window too—I'd even kept a tab on one of the bar napkins—but that didn't stop Snap from running down to the sheriff's office and reporting me for breaking and entering, theft of merchandise, and disorderly conduct. I wasn't guilty of any of the charges, really, except the last, and I wasn't guilty of that one until after they charged me with it. Half my trouble I don't cause. I take full responsibility for my half of the trouble, but that's as far as I go. I'm no saint, as I say, but I'm no devil either.

What happened was, they locked me up in the town jail. "Have a little mercy on a man in love," I told Sheriff Lowry, but he only cleared his throat like an animal snarling. One thing the law doesn't understand is love. When it comes to love, sheriffs are nothing but Nazis.

Since I was only part guilty, I refused to pay the whole fine, so
they kept me locked up the full thirty days. By the time they let
me out, I'd pretty much gotten over Leann. I'm good at getting
over her—I do it at least once a week. But even though I was over
her, I didn't go see Carina right away. One reason was that I had
to find a new job, thanks to that chicken-shit Clint I used to pump
gas for down at the Texaco station. He'd sent me a registered
letter saying that if it was up to him etc. but the company had a
policy about common criminals on the payroll etc. I didn't really
need a job—I still had a few thousand left from the insurance
settlement with the Cotton Belt—but just the same I spent the
next week checking around town until I found work at the hatchery
crating chickens. But the real reason I didn't go see Carina sooner
was her sister. The more I thought about Carina, the more I kept
thinking about her sister and figuring that if we ever had a kid, it
might turn out retarded like her. I even had a sweat dream about
it one night: I dreamed a nurse brought me this baby with black
singed-looking hair and a tongue stuck out the side of its mouth.
It looked like Carina's sister shrunk to doll size. And its skin was
as dark as her mama's—like coffee with just a touch of cream in
it. I woke up that night breathing like I was back in Nam humping
a heavy pack through the jungle.

But love got the better of me, like it always does, and I decided
to marry Carina no matter what our kids would turn out like. I
put on my blue suit, the one I'd married Leann and Charlotte and
Jenelle in, and drove out to her place. I was wearing the same suit,
but I was determined this marriage was going to turn out different
than the others. This time, I'd be the perfect husband. If Carina
wanted to watch one TV show and I wanted to watch another,
we'd watch hers. And I wouldn't drink anymore, except on
weekends, or get into fights. And I wouldn't even so much as
*think* about Leann or Charlotte or Jenelle. I imagined myself on
bended knee, telling Carina all this, and her starting to cry from
being so happy.

But when I got there, nothing went according to plan. First

off, Carina didn't kiss me or even say hello when she opened the door. And when her mama started to get her walking shoes on, Carina told her to stay put. Her mama sat back down at the kitchen table next to Carina's sister, who was eating an orange like it was the last one left in the world. "Carina," her mama said. The way she said it, it was half a question and half a warning.

Carina didn't answer. She just stood there and said, "What do you want from me, Hook?" She must not have used her Curl-Free for a while because her hair was as curly as private hair.

"I know I haven't seen you for some time," I started, but she interrupted.

"I know where you been, and why, so why don't you just—"

That's when I interrupted her back. "I came to ask you to marry me," I said. I said it like I was mad, and I guess I was. I mean, there I was, ready to give up everything—Leann, the respect of my neighbors, kids that could think—just to marry her, and she didn't seem to care.

Without saying one word about my proposal, Carina turned on her sister and said, "Don't suck that orange like a pig." Her sister just looked at her a second, juice all over her cheeks, then went back to the orange as fierce as before.

I didn't know what to say, so I went ahead with the speech I'd thought up during the drive. "I love you, Carina," I said, "and I'd like to take care of you. I got a new job that pays more than my old one, if you count in overtime, and with my insurance money and all we could maybe swing a down payment on a house and start a family, if you'd like."

Then Carina's mama said, "Daughter, you got to listen to the man."

"Goddamn it, Mama," Carina said, then started to cry. But when I stepped toward her, she stopped real sudden. "Why don't you just leave right now, Hook Tompkins."

"Carina!" her mama said. "You got to think about *us*, too."

"Shut up, Mama," Carina said back, and then the old lady's chin started to wobble.

"You don't love me," she said to Carina.

I was just standing there, trying to figure out what was going on.

Carina sat down at the table then and held her mama's hand. Her cheek muscles were working and there were tears stuck in her eyelashes.

"What the hell's going on here?" I finally said.

But Carina just kept looking down at the table like the wood grain spelled out a message she had to decode.

"I don't have all day," I said, and started to put on my hat.

Carina's mama started crying harder then, and her sister stopped sucking the orange peel. Her face puckered up and she started crying too, a sort of sobbing snort. All three of them were crying then. I'd never seen anything to beat it.

"I'm sorry," Carina finally said, still looking down. "Really, I am."

And suddenly I knew. What a fool I'd been.

"Who is it?" I asked her. "Tell me who he is."

But she didn't say anything. I lifted her chin and looked her in the eye. "I just want to know his name," I said, calm as a Sunday afternoon.

She looked away and closed her lips into a tight, thin line. She knew what I would do to him, whoever he was, and she wasn't going to tell me his name.

Her mama was crying softer now. She was going to be poor a long, long time. Whoever it was Carina loved, he was as poor as they were. And then it hit me.

"He's a Negro, isn't he," I said. "You picked a dirt-poor Negro over me, didn't you."

Carina looked at me, but still she didn't say anything.

"Shit," I said. That's all. I was so mad I couldn't think of anything else to say. I just stood there a second, clenching and unclenching my fist, then I turned and left. For a second, I wanted to burn their house down, the way we zippoed huts in Nam, but I just got back in my truck and drove on down the dirt road so fast I damn near fishtailed into the ditch on the first curve. I thought about the way she looked when I asked her what his name was and it made me so mad I slammed my hook into the dashboard and ripped a scar in the vinyl. I tell you, I was gut-shot with love.

Once I hit the blacktop, I turned toward Culver instead of Beasley. I didn't know why, didn't even stop to think why, until I drove up to Albie's Cafe. Then I knew. I kicked open the door, jangling the bells, and stepped in shouting, "Where's the sonofabitch that stole my wife?" There wasn't any need to shout, because the place is so small and Albie was right there in front of me, flipping burgers behind the counter. But I shouted anyway, so everyone would know why I was there.

"What the hell do you think you're doing?" the wife-stealer said to me. "I'm trying to run a business here."

"I'm gonna kill you," I answered back. "I'm gonna rip your goddamn heart out and feed it to the rats in your kitchen."

There was a moment then, when everything was dead quiet, except the ceiling fans whirring and clicking. Then I heard some chairs slide across the linoleum and some of the customers stand up slowly and start to ease toward the back door.

That's when Albie picked up the knife. It was just a paring knife, it wasn't even half as big as the Bowie tattooed on his forearm, but it sent all the customers running for the door.

In answer to his knife, I held up my hook.

"You're nuts," he said to me. "The marriage wasn't even legal, and you know it. She was drunk during the whole ceremony, she didn't even know what she was doing."

"You're lying," I said.

"She only stayed with you because she was scared to leave," he went on, sneering all the while.

"Come out from behind that counter," I dared him.

I didn't think he would, but he did. He stood sideways, like a fencer, and stuck his little knife out toward me. "It's time we settled all this," he said.

I tried to imagine him in Nam, flying wounded grunts out of the paddies, but he looked so stupid standing there in his greasy apron with that little knife in his big fist that I couldn't. I decided all the stories I'd heard were lies. The tattoo didn't prove anything except that he'd been drunk in Saigon once.

"You're gonna *bleed*," I said, and started to circle to the right, away from his knife, stepping between the tables and chairs to get to where I could lunge at him.

By this time, there was a small crowd gathered at the front window. I didn't look over there, but I could feel them pressing against the glass, trying to see through the reflected sun-glare into the cafe. I don't know why, but for some reason I was certain Carina's lover was out there, watching, some young Negro without a buck in his pocket. Somebody no better than a gook, and she was going to marry him instead of me. I imagined his hands on her breasts, thumbs stroking her nipples, and I kicked over a table. Albie's cheap melmac plates and silverware clattered to the floor and two glasses busted, ice tea everywhere. The second Albie looked down, I leapt toward him.

He jerked away just in time to make me miss his face, but I ripped his ear good. "You bastard," he said, and before I could get out of the way, he stuck me one in the ribs.

Outside, someone shouted, "They're killing each other!" He sounded almost happy about it. An old man's voice said, "Where the hell's that damn sheriff we elected?"

Albie touched his ear, then scowled at the blood on his fingertips. "You bastard," he said again, then threw the knife against the wall and leapt at me, grabbing my hook arm. I gouged his shoulder good, but he held on and knocked me to the floor. My hook was stuck in his shoulder. I tried to jerk it out but it wouldn't come and my stump was throbbing something awful. I kept hitting at Albie with my good hand, but he bashed my face pretty good before I finally worked my hook free. Then he rolled off me and scrambled behind the counter, holding his shoulder. Before I could even get to my feet, the sheriff had fired a warning shot into the ceiling. A chunk of plaster plopped onto a tabletop.

Then it was all gone—all the anger and the hate and even the love. "Shit," I said, and pulled myself up and sat down on one of the chairs. Then, without any warning or anything, I began to cry. Really cry. The funny thing is, I wasn't even sad. In a way, I wasn't even there anymore. I was somewhere else, watching this person who looked like me sitting there bawling. It was the strangest thing. I wondered if this was what Carina's sister felt like when she cried, or maybe even why she cried.

The sheriff and his deputy stood a good ten feet off with their revolvers pointed at my brains. I halfways hoped they'd shoot.

"This sure beats all," the red-faced sheriff finally said over his shoulder to Albie. He was breathing hard but trying to sound calm.

"I need a doctor," Albie said back. He was leaning against the counter and he looked pale and woozy. His hand was red where he was holding his shoulder, and blood was trickling from his ear down his cheek. I couldn't believe I'd wanted to hurt him.

"I'm sorry," I said, as the deputy helped him toward the door. "I mean it."

"Fuck you," Albie said back. Then he turned to the deputy. "He's nuts," he said. "He oughta be locked up for good, the sonofabitch."

I'm not nuts, but maybe Albie was right, maybe they ought to keep me locked up for good. Like I said, there's something wrong with my heart, some birth defect or something, that makes me always get in trouble. The fight with Albie wasn't much, I've been in a lot worse, but nothing ever got me so down. After they hauled me off to jail, I felt so low I vowed that when I got out I'd stay away from women the rest of my life. I'd be like a priest. They could walk right up to me and wiggle their tits in my face, and it wouldn't mean a thing to me.

But that was two months ago, and after a few days of looking at bars and gray walls and eating off tin plates, it's hard to think like that anymore. Even a priest would get mad, I think—even a saint—if they had to be locked up like this. But in here, there's nothing you can do about it except imagine, unless you want to get shivved in the shower room or shot for trying to go over the wall. So lately I've been thinking about what I'd do if I was out and could go to Carina's wedding. I've got it all figured out. The way I imagine it, I play it smart—I make my point but I don't do anything that'll send me back here. What I do is this: I come in the church late and take a seat in the back pew. Then I sit there quietly and watch her walk up the aisle in her white dress and take that bastard's arm. I don't get up and start a fight or anything. I just sit there, all through the vows and the songs, not saying a word, and when the wedding's over, I wait politely in the reception line, holding my hat in my hand, until I reach Carina and her husband. Then, when she finally sees me, she says my name like it's a prayer for mercy, but I don't even look at her, I turn away and look at her husband.

"Congratulations," I say to him. And then I stick out my hook and stare at that nigger till he shakes it.

# THE SACRED DRUM

People ask am I Chinese, Japanese, sometimes Korean? When I say *Hmong*, they look question at me. No one know Hmong. I tell them about home, the Annamite mountains, peaks like chimneys, the bamboo thickets where I play as boy. Laos, the other side of the world. Then they nod, question is answered. But still no one know Hmong, or me.

This is what I wish to tell them, that *Hmong* mean "free people." Fifteen years I fight the Communists. I am only rifleman at first, in battalion of five hundred, but when I am a boy in Lat Houang school I learn the tracks of Lao words, like clawmarks a bird leave in dust. So the great general Vang Pao, who is just colonel then, he order me to measure map coordinates for mortar. And later, I do such good job I am promoted officer, and ride in helicopter with American soldiers, treetop level, very dangerous, looking for pilots crash or shoot down in jungle near Vietnam border. We find one and down I go tied to rope sling, to carry up pilots, alive or could be dead. They are so heavy and me so small, I drop one sometimes. Sometimes too Pathet Lao or Viet Cong shoot at me, tracer bullets zip past like bees on fire. I am young then. And proud to be Hmong, fighting to protect our land, our freedom. And Yang Lia, only seventeen, she look down shy and smile when someone call me Lieutenant. When I come home from mission then, she wash my feet. No more. Now she is American woman, and American woman think freedom is not washing husband's feet.

I am American too, since 1976, but always Hmong, even when we leave our country to live in refugee camp like prisoners, seven in each tent, sick, eating grass, all we own taken by Thai soldiers. All this happen because we leave our sacred drum when we flee our home. We vow to build a new one soon as when we have a cow to slaughter and stretch its hide for the head. But we do not build this drum. Our sponsor, Pastor Young of Saint John Lutheran Church, he warn us it is a crime to kill cows in the city, even for sacrifice, and to live in the country mean farm loans, federal grants, and that mean application forms who can read? The sacred drum is part of all Hmong ceremony, especially funeral. Without it, how can you free the soul so it will not rot like the body and die?

Chue, our son, is American, born in Little Rock, where we live now since all these years. Chuck, he call himself. To him, a drum is for the rock and roll. Hmong tradition say when baby is born, bury umbilical cord under ghost pole, the center post which hold up the hut, so he will live in both worlds, this one we see and the other we only feel. But in America we live in apartment with carpet for floor, not dirt, and baby is born at hospital, not home. The doctor throw away our son's umbilical cord. There are no ghosts here, Chue say, only electricity. He is twenty-one—so young and so old. Why you talk so much about damn drum, he say. And don't bow when you shake hands, or call me Chue in front of friend. Lia nod her head when he talk like this. She talk the same way. When I say do something, sometimes she answer Yes sir, Mister Lieutenant Boss, and laugh.

A long time now, I am sick. Two heart attacks, I lie on the couch all day and look at the ceiling, this water spot the shape of Laos on a map. Lia tell me if I die she won't marry my brother, also American now, whose wife die in camp. At home, clan come first, even in name. Here I am Yao Feng, not Feng Yao. Everything turned around, backward. No one here care about clan, or me. Not even Lia. She work at Maybelline, making eyeshadow. Sometimes she stand at the mirror and try it on. How you like this shade? she say. She say it in American. I miss Hmong, each vowel have eight different tones and meanings, like music. I miss Lia too.

And sometimes I miss even the war. Like last night, when I dream a helicopter whir above me in the dark, loud, like a thousand birds flapping their wings. It lower me spinning down to rescue American soldier who is wounded so bad he is near dead. I am dizzy, bullets fly everywhere, so I hold on to the rope so tight. But then somehow the rope is not a rope, it is wood. I stop spinning then and stand there on the ground and look at it, and I see it is the ghost pole of our old hut. And I wake up then so happy, thinking *I'm home, home, and young,* and my heart is beating like a drum.

# RAINIER

When Barbara called to tell me about Chuck, I was so drunk I said, "Chuck who?" Then she knew I'd started back drinking again.

"Damn it, Alec," she said. "You're *drunk*."

I said no, I hadn't been drinking, only a small glass of champagne with dinner. Then she started to cry.

"Don't cry," I said. "I won't drink anymore, I promise." I was feeling awful. Only a month before, I'd mailed her a Xerox copy of my diploma from Intercept, the alcoholic treatment center in Missoula. I sent it to her because she spent half our marriage trying to get me to go there and I wanted to show her I'd finally done it. Maybe I wanted to make her feel a little sorry for me too, like if she'd stayed with me a few more years everything would have worked out. But now she knew I was drinking again. "Please don't cry," I said.

"You stupid drunk," she answered. "I'm not crying about *you*." Then she hung up.

It wasn't until then, I think, that I understood what she'd said about Chuck. I don't know why it took so long to sink in. I mean, I was drunk, but not that drunk.

I sat there in the kitchen holding the phone for a minute, then went into the living room and turned on the TV. I wasn't going to watch; I just wanted the noise. I sat down in the La-Z-Boy and picked up the bottle of Cold Duck from the coffee table and took a slug. It was warm and flat. I took another slug and laid my head back and closed my eyes. But that didn't work, so I got up and started walking around the apartment. I thought about getting out my tool box and planing down the closet door that stuck. I thought about calling Betty, my new girl. I even thought about trying to sew up the old tear in the bedroom drapes. But I just stood there by the window and watched the snow fall. It was coming down in such big soft flakes it almost looked fake. Down the street, the Greyhound sign flickered, slowly shorting out. I knocked back the last of the Cold Duck, then sat on the edge of the bed, staring out the window.

After a while, I went back into the kitchen. There was no more champagne in the fridge but I had some Early Times in the cupboard. When I took it down, I noticed the blender on the shelf above it. It was avocado-colored, the same as the fridge and stove Barbara and I used to have. I'd bought it for her on one of our wedding anniversaries, but she forgot to take it when she cleaned me out after the divorce. I'd never used it, even once, so I took it down and turned it on, trying all the buttons. Chop. Purée. Blend. It worked like new.

Later, I called Barbara back. Her new husband answered the phone, his voice hoarse, like he'd been crying or had just woken up. I'd never met him. All I knew about him was the little Barbara had told me: that he was a geologist at the oil camp outside of Rose Creek, and that he was a good father to Chuck. When Chuck graduated from Officers' Training School, Barbara sent me a picture of him in his dress blues, standing between two men in civilian clothes. One of them was lanky and stoop-shouldered; the other, squat and red-faced. On the back of the picture, Barbara had written "Ensign Charles F. Denton, with Gale and Uncle Zack." I knew Gale was her new husband's name, but I didn't know which one was him. I tried to imagine each of them making love to Barbara, but I couldn't. I couldn't imagine them tousling

Chuck's hair or taking him trout fishing either. So I didn't know
who I was talking to. "Hello," I said to him, whichever one he
was. "This is Alec."

Then he said, "Yeah? Alec *who*?" and I knew Barbara had told
him what I'd said. I didn't blame him for hating me. I would've
felt the same way if I was him.

"Listen," I said, "I'm sorry. I was drunk when Barbara called.
I was out of my mind. She threw me for a loop. But I'm not
drunk now and I want to say I feel awful and I want to be there
with you and Barbara now. Maybe I don't deserve to be there, but
I need to." I stopped, but he didn't say anything. I was afraid he
was going to hang up on me. "Mr. Denton?" I said. "Are you still
there?" He didn't answer. I closed my eyes and listened to the
three hundred miles of silence between us. "I just need to see
him," I said.

When he finally answered, I decided he was the lanky stoop-
shouldered man who was standing on Chuck's left. "All right," he
said. "Of course you can come. After all, you were his father too."

There's not much you can do in a car except think. During the long
drive from Bozeman to Rose Creek, I kept a twelve-pack beside
me, and every now and then I drank a can. I listened to the radio
too, when I could stand the sort of music they play on it these days,
and watched the wipers clean the snow from the windshield until I
was half-hypnotized. I even kept track of the gas I bought and the
distance I drove, so I could figure out how many miles per gallon
the old Nova was getting. But no matter what I did, I kept thinking
about Chuck. I remembered the strangest things. Like those
Hawaiian swim trunks he had—"jams" he called them—with yellow
and maroon flowers. The time he fell off his skateboard and broke
his collarbone. The way he once did a drumroll with his fork and
knife when Barbara set supper on the table.

But mostly I kept remembering the lie I told Chuck about
Mount Rainier. I hadn't thought about it for years. Chuck had just
turned twelve, but I hadn't been home for his birthday. I'd been

gone for four days, drinking, and when I came home he wouldn't even talk to me. I said, "Your dad's home," and he looked away; I said, "Are you mad at me?" and he ran back to his room. I'd been gone on binges before, but never that long, and never over his birthday. I felt so miserable I went back to his room and told him I'd take him out to Mount Blackmore the next day. He'd been begging me for weeks to take him there so he could earn his mountain climbing merit badge, but when I told him I'd take him, he didn't look happy or anything. And the next day, when we hiked up the mountain, I couldn't get him to talk. I'd say something about the trees or rocks—ask him what kind he thought they were and things like that—and he'd just answer with a word or two. So by the time we were halfway up the trail, I was getting scared that he wasn't going to forgive me.

So I told him the lie. We were taking a breather, sitting on a big slate ledge in the sun, looking down at the creek at the base of the bluff and the pine woods beyond, and I told him I had once climbed Mount Rainier. Chuck looked at me then, but he didn't say anything.

"This was a long time ago," I said. "Long before you were born. Even before I met your mother." Then I told him a friend and I had gone up the mountain in the winter of '51. "Everything went fine," I said, "until we got halfway up the mountain. Then the wind kicked up and snow began to fall and pretty soon we were caught in a first-class blizzard. We couldn't see anything, the snow was so thick, and the air was so cold it burned our lungs just to breathe. Before long the wind was blowing to beat Billy Hell and we could barely hang on to the side of the mountain, even with our spiked boots dug in." I went on to tell him we knew we'd freeze to death if we didn't get up to the next ledge and dig a snow cave, so we kept climbing, feeling our way up the mountain inch by inch like blind men.

The story was a true one, but it hadn't happened to me—I'd read about it in *Reader's Digest*. But I told it like it was my story, not somebody else's, and Chuck sat there looking out toward the horizon, his forehead creased like he was thinking hard. And as I told the story, I got excited and started to make up things that weren't even in *Reader's Digest*. I told him my friend fell and broke his leg so I had to strap him onto my back and lug him up the ridge with me, and I told him we were trapped there for three days before the weather cleared enough for me to carry him back down the mountain. I even told him my name had been in all the papers and the governor of Washington himself came to the hospital where I was recuperating to shake my hand and congratulate me for saving my friend's life.

I'd hoped my story would make Chuck proud of me, make him forgive me for being a drunk and a bad father. But he didn't say anything. He just sat there, looking down at his boots. I figured he knew I was lying, and was even madder than before. But then I saw that his lower lip was trembling.

"What's wrong?" I said.

"You could have died," he answered.

When he said that, I thought maybe I had won him back after all. "That's right," I said. "I could've died. But I didn't." And I tousled his curly blond hair.

But he kept looking at his boots. "But what if you *had* died?"

I tried to laugh it off. "Then I would've died," I said, and punched him lightly on the shoulder.

He reached down then and picked up a small stone and flicked it off the cliff. We watched it hit a ledge below and bounce off out of sight.

"Then I wouldn't have been born," he said.

I was wrong about Barbara's new husband. He wasn't the tall stoop-shouldered guy after all. He was the squat meaty-faced fellow with thick glasses. He didn't look at all like the type Barbara would marry, but then again neither did the tall lanky guy. And, I suppose, neither did I.

"You must be Alec," he said, when he opened the door. "I'm Gale. Come on in. It must be freezing out there."

I'd never met a man named Gale before. "Gale" seemed like a woman's name to me, even though it was spelled different, and I'd never liked the fact that Barbara had married someone with a name like that. I shook his hand. "Pleased to meet you, Mr. Denton," I said, and stepped in the house.

It was a nice house, a lot nicer than any house Barbara and I ever lived in. To the right of the entryway was a living room with a red brick fireplace and a blue and gold Oriental rug, and straight down the hall there was a dining room with a chandelier tiered like an upside-down wedding cake. To my left, there was a short flight of stairs that led up to a hallway of rooms. Everywhere you looked there were plants and fancy paintings. I felt like I was stepping into a copy of *Better Homes and Gardens* and I said so. Gale laughed. It was a host's laugh, high and cut short like a cough.

"Let me have your coat," he said. "Barbara's in the den. She'll be right up."

I shrugged off my parka and watched Gale hang it at the far end of the closet, away from his and Barbara's coats. Then Barbara came up some stairs near the dining room and walked stiff-legged down the hall toward me, her face tight like she was afraid something bad was going to happen. "Hello," I said. Then, before she could say anything, I leaned over and gave her a peck on the cheek. I glanced at Gale to see if he'd minded. If he had, he didn't show it. I didn't look at Barbara to see what she thought.

"Well, how was your trip?" Barbara said. She spoke like she had to force the words out, like they hurt her throat.

"It was good," I said. "Good as could be. Under the circumstances." Somehow the word *circumstances* made me look away from her. "I like your house," I added quickly. "I didn't think they had houses like this out in the middle of Wyoming."

Gale smiled. "The company takes good care of their people. They may make us live out here with the jackrabbits, but they provide us with good housing."

"That's good," I said. Then we all just stood there a moment. Finally Barbara said, "Gale, don't you think we ought to let Alec freshen up before dinner?" Then she turned to me, only she didn't look right at me. "Come on. I'll show you to your room."

"And I'll get us something to drink. What would you like?" Gale said, putting his fingers together the way servants do in movies.

"Nothing for me," I answered. "Thanks anyway. You go ahead."

Barbara looked at me, squinting just a little, like she was sizing me up. "Your room's just up the hall," she said, and led the way. I followed her, noticing how she'd spread out over the past six years. She'd always been a bit hippy, but now she was big. Still, I must admit I didn't mind watching her walk.

At the end of the hallway, she opened a door and switched on the light. "This is your room," she said.

I looked in and saw pale blue wallpaper and a bed with a wheat-colored comforter and dust ruffle. There was a reading light on the headboard, and it made me remember how Chuck used to lay in bed at night reading Hardy Boys books. "Was this—" I started.

"This is the guest room," Barbara said quickly. She nodded toward a door just up the hall. "That was his room." Then she looked at me, her face hard. "I don't want you in there," she said. "I don't want anyone in there. Do you understand?"

I didn't say anything. Then she continued, "I've put some towels on the dresser for you. The bathroom's right next door. If there's anything else you—"

"It's good to see you again, Barbara," I interrupted. "I only wish to God there was another reason for it."

She looked at me. "Don't think you're fooling anybody with your 'Nothing for me, thanks,'" she said. "I smelled that Binaca on your breath. I know you've been drinking. Now, I don't mind you coming in here and invading our home, but I don't want you getting drunk and embarrassing us at the funeral. If you can't stay sober out of consideration for me and Gale, I hope you can do it for Chuck. Is that clear?"

I set my bag inside the door. "I'm still crazy about you too," I said. For a second, Barbara looked like she was going to slap me, but then she just turned and strode off down the hall.

"I loved him as much as you did," I called after her.

During dinner, Barbara barely looked at me, and she didn't say anything to either of us, except when she asked Gale to pass the roast or the potatoes. As soon as we finished eating, she excused herself, saying she had a headache, and went to bed. Gale apologized for her. "This has been awfully hard on her," he said. I didn't know whether "this" meant Chuck, or me.

Later that night, Gale and I were watching TV in the den. Gale was on his fourth Scotch, but I still hadn't had anything but club soda. I was worried I'd get the shakes, like I did at Intercept, but I didn't want to drink in front of Gale. I wanted him to think that Barbara had exaggerated about me, maybe even made some of it up.

Gale was talking about the TV. The oil company had paid for cable TV hook-ups; that's why he could get so many channels. Twenty-three in all. "Imagine that," he said, "twenty-three channels right here in the middle of nowhere." He gestured toward the walls with his drink, like nowhere was everywhere around us.

"That's something," I said. On the TV a young blonde was stepping out of one of those antique clawfooted bathtubs and wrapping a white towel around herself. There were tiny soapbubbles on her shoulders and thighs. From the music, I could tell she was going to get murdered soon.

"There's still nothing to watch, though," Gale said, and he took off his glasses and rubbed his eyes with the heels of his hands.

"You tired?" I said. "Don't let me keep you up if you are." I was hoping he'd call it a night so I could sneak myself some bourbon. I knew I wouldn't be able to sleep unless I had at least a couple of drinks—the last two nights I'd had to drink the better part of a fifth before I could even close my eyes.

"No, I'm not tired," he said. "How about you?"

"I'm fine," I said.

Gale nodded like he was glad I was fine, then walked over to the bar and poured himself another drink. I was thinking about Barbara's luck with men. For someone who hated drinking so much, she'd picked a couple of winners.

"He was on his way to see his girlfriend," Gale said then. "Tammy Winthrop. When they found him, they called me at the camp. Told me there'd been an accident. That's all they said." He came back over to the easy chair and sat down heavily. A little of the Scotch spilled on his cardigan sweater but he didn't seem to notice. He set his drink down on the end table and sighed. "Hardest thing I ever had to do was identify him." He leaned forward and looked at me. "I mean, I thought they'd have him cleaned up and everything. But they didn't. They hadn't done a thing to him. All the blood and everything—" He stopped and sat back, shaking his head.

I was getting angry at him. I didn't want him to tell me this. But all I said was, "I'm sorry."

Gale sat forward in his chair again. "You had him when he was a boy. I'll always envy you that. But I saw him grow into a man. And he was a fine man. He would've made one hell of a fine officer, I can tell you that." Then he started to cry. He covered his face with his hands and his shoulders heaved.

I couldn't think of anything to say, so I just sat there, looking at the TV. A man in a ski mask had stalked the blonde to her bedroom and she was crouching in the corner of her closet, trembling. The man had a barber's razor in his gloved hand, and the music was going crazy. I watched for a minute, then turned away. I wasn't scared—that kind of movie never scares me much—but I kept thinking about that girl's father watching the movie and seeing her crouched there like that, naked and afraid. Even though I knew it was all fake, I couldn't bear to watch it anymore.

I had to say something to Gale. "Are you all right?" I finally said.

"I'm sorry," Gale answered, and wiped his eyes with his handkerchief. "Please forgive me."

"There's nothing to forgive," I said. "I feel the same way you do."

Then Gale finished his drink and stood up. "Well, I guess it's about that time," he said, looking at his watch. "We'll have to get up early tomorrow." And then his face fell apart again.

"It'll be all right," I said, but I didn't get up, pat him on the shoulder, or anything like that.

"Yeah," he said, getting a hold of himself. "I guess it will." He shook his head. "Sorry."

"No problem," I said. "I understand."

"Well, goodnight then," he said, and started toward the door. But before he got there, he stopped and said, "Listen, Alec, if you're going to stay up a while, why don't you go ahead and help yourself to anything you want?" And he waved his hand toward the bar.

I sat there, looking at him.

"I just want you to know I understand," he added. "And I'm sure Chuck would understand too."

I said, "Thanks, Gale. I appreciate that." But I decided that minute not to take a drop of liquor as long as I was in his house. And I wouldn't do it for him or Barbara or even myself; I'd do it for Chuck.

"I hope she's asleep," Gale said then.

"I do too," I answered.

He nodded, said goodnight again, and left.

I waited until I heard him climbing the stairs, then I got up and turned off the TV.

A few hours later, when I went up to my room, I stopped in the hallway outside Chuck's door and thought about opening it. I wasn't thinking about going in or anything—I just wanted to take a look. I wanted to see what his life had been like since he and Barbara left me. But I just stood there in the dim glow of the bathroom's night light and stared at the whorled pattern of the wood grain. Then I went to bed.

I couldn't sleep, so I laid there awake. The longer I laid there, the more I started to wish I'd drunk some of Gale's liquor after all.

But I couldn't take a drink, not until the funeral was over. Even if I had to stay awake all night, even if I had to get the shakes, I wasn't going to drink anything. I wanted to show Chuck I could do it; I wanted to prove to him I wasn't a drunk or a bad father.

So I laid there, trying not to think about drinking or Chuck. I thought about Betty and my new job at the Swift plant, and I wondered how long it'd be before I lost both. But thinking about Betty and my job only made me think of Barbara and the fights we had the winter I was laid off. I saw Chuck sitting on the old flowered couch, watching TV, pretending he didn't hear us fighting, and I remembered how I turned on him and shouted, "Don't just sit there like you're deaf and dumb," and how he swallowed like he was afraid I'd hit him and said, "Okay, Dad." And I remembered my lie about Mount Rainier again, I saw Chuck's lips trembling as he looked down at his boots and tried not to cry, and I felt like something inside me was falling off that cliff with the pebble he flicked over the edge. Then I tried to think about something else, it didn't matter what. I made myself remember my home town, the neighborhood I grew up in, and who lived in each of the houses on our street. I went down the block: the white two-story with the wraparound porch was the Petersons'; the squat brick house was the Randalls'; the rust-brown house was Old Man Roenicke's. But I couldn't remember who lived in the stucco house at the end of the block. Somehow it seemed so important that I remember. But there was nothing. The whole family was gone, as if it had never existed.

I made myself think of something else. I tried to remember all the houses and apartments I'd lived in since I was a boy and their addresses and phone numbers. I tried to remember the names of my classmates in high school and some of the dates I learned back in history class. But it was no use. Everything kept getting confused in my mind—places, addresses, numbers, names. I sat up and put my head in my hands.

Then I remembered Sheila, the red-haired waitress I was seeing when I first met Barbara. I hadn't thought of her in years. If I'd married her, everything would've been different. We would've been living somewhere far away, maybe on a farm, a quiet place in the country, and we'd probably have a child, a daughter maybe, a tomboy just starting to wear dresses. She would be slim and freckled, like Sheila, and when she laughed she'd toss her head back and hold her sides. Sheila and I would sit on the porch steps and watch her do cartwheels on the lawn. We'd be happy, nothing bad would have happened. Chuck would not even have been born.

I stood up then. I couldn't lay there anymore; I had to have a drink. I'd only have one, or at the most two—just enough to help me sleep. If I didn't get some sleep, I'd be worse at the funeral. And if I didn't drink something soon, I'd get the shakes.

But as I crept down the dark hallway, I heard something that stopped me. At first, I thought it was Barbara and Gale whispering, then I was sure it was the sound of them making love. I could've sworn I heard the small gasp Barbara used to make when I entered her. I'd forgotten that sound, and it cut through me like a cold wind. I stood outside their door and strained to hear. After a moment, I heard the sound again, and this time I knew what it was. It was Barbara, trying to cry quietly, so she wouldn't wake Gale.

I leaned my head against the wall then, and wondered if she had ever cried like that when I was sleeping beside her. And whether Chuck had ever stood outside our room in the dark, listening.

The next morning, when I went into the kitchen, Barbara was already there. She was wearing a yellow robe and drinking coffee from a blue enameled mug.

"Good morning," I said. I hadn't slept all night, and I felt worse than if I'd had a hangover.

"Gale's not up yet," she said, without looking at me. "I thought it best to let him sleep as long as he could."

I went to the counter and poured myself a cup of coffee. "That was good of you," I said. There was a Cuisinart on the counter next to the Mr. Coffee. I glanced at her fridge and stove. Harvest Gold.

I sat down at the table across from her. My head was throbbing and my eyes burned. I looked out the window. It was snowing, an easy snow, the kind that comes down peacefully and covers everything. The birdfeeder on the railing of the patio was already mounded over with snow. There weren't any birds around.

"Gale's a good man," I said. "I like him." I wasn't lying; I did like Gale, though I wished I didn't.

"I'd rather not talk right now," she said then, and pushed her fingers through her gray-blond hair. "If there's something you'd like for breakfast, just go ahead and help yourself."

"I'm not hungry," I said.

She shrugged. "Suit yourself."

Then we drank our coffee for a while without saying anything. Finally I put my cup down and said, "It's going to be a long day. It's going to be tough. Can't we be friends for just this one day?"

She didn't answer. She just sat there with her hands cradled around her cup for warmth.

"Damn it," I said. "I want to make this easier for you. Can't you see that?"

She kept looking at the coffee in her mug. "You could have made it easier for me by not coming," she said. "You've brought back a lot of bad memories."

I looked out the window, watched the snow drift down. "I haven't had a drink since yesterday afternoon."

"A half a day," she said.

"I know," I answered. "But it was rough. Especially last night. You don't know how bad I wanted a drink."

"Why?" she said then, tilting her head toward me. "So you wouldn't remember your son's name? So if someone said, 'Chuck is dead,' you'd just scratch your head and say, 'Chuck who?'" She picked up her mug. Her hand was trembling.

"That's not fair," I said.

"What you did to Chuck and me wasn't fair either," she said back.

I dipped my spoon in my coffee and stirred it, though it was already cool.

"I wasn't myself," I said. "I was drinking too much."

She didn't say anything.

Then I said, "I heard you last night. I was walking down the hall and I heard you. It made me wonder if you ever laid awake crying like that when we were married."

She looked up from her coffee. "Don't make this day any harder than it has to be."

"I'm sorry," I said.

She picked up the coffee cup again. "Just remember that Gale invited you here, not me. If you had to come, you could have at least stayed at a motel."

"If I *had* to come?" I said. "Chuck is my *son*. I have just as much right to go to his funeral as you do."

"Maybe so," she said. "But what makes you think Chuck would want you at his funeral? Did you ever think that maybe he wouldn't have wanted you here any more than I do?"

I wanted to say that Chuck had never blamed me for any of it, that he always knew it was the booze, not me, that was responsible. I wanted to tell her that he had always loved me, despite everything she'd done to turn him against me. But I didn't say anything. I looked out the window and watched the evergreens grow slowly more white.

After a while, Barbara said, "I'm sorry. I was just trying to hurt you. I didn't mean it." She still had her hands cradled around her cup, though it must have been cold by now. "Can we please stop talking now?"

I nodded. "If you want."

Neither of us said anything after that until Gale came into the kitchen a few minutes later. He was wearing a navy blue robe and slippers. "Morning," he said. His face was splotchy and his eyes were red behind his thick glasses. I wondered if his head was hurting as much as mine.

"Are you all right?" I asked.

"I'm fine," he said, trying to smile. "How are you?"

"I'm fine, too," I said.

"Good. Good." Then he put his hands on Barbara's shoulders and leaned over and kissed the top of her head. "Did you sleep all right, dear?" he asked.

"Just fine," she said, looking at me.

At the funeral, Gale asked me to sit in the front pew with him and Barbara, but I said no and took a seat alone in the back of the church. I didn't listen to the minister's eulogy or sing any of the hymns. I just sat there and tried not to look at the flag-covered coffin, or at Barbara. I could hear her crying, that same quiet sobbing I'd heard the night before, but I wouldn't let myself look at her.

I didn't look at Chuck either. Even though I came all that way to see him, when we filed into the church past his open casket, I couldn't look at him. I bent over to look at him, but before I could see his face, my eyes closed. All I saw were the gold buttons of his dress blues and the white gloves on his crossed hands.

I didn't see him, but in a way I saw him wherever I looked. The small brick church was filled with his classmates from Officers' Training School, all wearing their dress blues too. They sat stiff, at attention, hands unmoving on their laps. It occurred to me then that it was just some strange accident that one of them was not my son. I could have sat beside any of their highchairs, feeding them applesauce. I could have helped any of them with their homework. I could have romped around the kitchen with any of them riding on my shoulders. But Chuck had been my son. Somehow, it seemed such a random thing.

It wasn't until after the funeral that I started to get the shakes. The snow had turned to sleet during the service and everyone was standing in the vestibule, bundling up before going outside. Barbara and Gale stood by the Crying Room, waiting for the funeral director to bring the limousine around. The members of Chuck's graduating class filed past then, shaking hands and saying how sorry they were to lose such a good friend and fellow officer. Barbara and Gale's friends comforted them too. The women cried and wiped their eyes with Kleenexes or handkerchiefs. Their husbands stood beside them, said a few words, then put on their hats like it was the only thing they could do to keep from crying themselves.

I turned away and looked outside. The cars were lining up in the parking lot, their lights already on. Their windshield wipers were barely keeping up with the sleet.

Just then, a tall, skinny girl with sand-colored hair came up to me and looked at my face, her forehead pursed. "You're Chuck's father, aren't you?" she asked.

"Yes," I said. "How did you know?" Barbara had introduced me to the minister and the funeral director as her former husband, but she hadn't mentioned anything about Chuck being my son, and I hadn't said anything. Gale had looked away, embarrassed, but he hadn't said anything either.

"I've seen pictures of you," she answered. I must have looked surprised because she added, "I'm Tammy. I was Chuck's girlfriend." Then she looked down at her folded hands. Her fingernails were bitten down and the skin around them was red and cracked. "He was on his way to see me when he had the accident," she said. "Sometimes I blame myself for it happening." Then her eyes started to swell with tears.

I started to say "I'm sorry," but she took my arm suddenly.

"I want you to know," she said, "that Chuck forgave you before he died. He didn't hate you anymore. He even talked about the two of us driving up to Montana to see you, to set things right between you."

I couldn't believe what she was saying. "You're wrong," I said, pulling my arm away. "You're terribly wrong." I meant that Chuck had never hated me, that he'd always loved me in spite of everything, but Tammy didn't understand.

"No," she insisted. "It's true. He did forgive you." She took my arm again. "You have to believe that."

I stood there looking at her earnest face. For a second, it crossed my mind that I'd like to slap her. But I just said, "Thank you. I appreciate you telling me that."

"He really did love you," Tammy went on. "You have to remember that."

I was beginning to feel dizzy, almost sick. "I'm sure he did," I said, and tried to smile. "He always said he did."

Tammy looked down a second. When she looked back up, her face was working. "Oh, Mr. Falk," she said, gulping back a sob, "I'm so sorry!" And then she gave me a quick hug and turned and hurried outside. I watched her run carefully down the slick sidewalk to a blue Oldsmobile waiting in the parking lot.

That was when the shaking started. It was almost as bad as that time at Intercept, when I couldn't lift my own fork or spoon and a nurse had to feed me like a baby. But it was a different kind of shaking, a scarier kind. I was shaking so much I thought I'd have to sit down right there on the floor. I put my hands in my pockets so no one could see them shake.

A minute later, Gale called across the vestibule to me. "It's time," he said, and nodded toward the limousine idling behind the hearse. But I couldn't move. I was trembling so bad I just stood there. Gale came over and said again that it was time to go.

"That's all right," I managed to say. "I'll catch a ride with someone else a little later."

"What are you talking about?" Gale said. "You don't even know anybody else here."

Barbara came over then. "What's wrong?" she asked. "Mr. Gilmer is waiting."

"Nothing's wrong," I said. "You two go on ahead. I'll catch up in a little while."

Barbara looked at me. "Are you all right?"

I couldn't look at her. "I'll be okay in a few minutes," I said. "I'll catch up with you then."

Gale put his hand on my arm. "I know how you feel," he said. "I'll ask Pastor Davis if he can take you with him."

"Fine," I nodded. My teeth were chattering and I could hardly talk.

"Maybe you should sit down for a while," Barbara said.

"I'll do that," I answered. But I couldn't move.

"We've got to go," Gale said. "Are you sure you aren't coming with us?"

I nodded.

Gale took Barbara's arm then. "Come on, dear, everyone's waiting."

Barbara looked at me. "You won't try to go back to Bozeman before we get home, will you? I don't think you ought to drive right now. Not the way you're—" She didn't finish.

"I won't," I said.

Then she gave me her house key. "You can get a taxi to take you to the house," she said. "Maybe you can get some sleep. Or at least rest."

"You mean, maybe I can get a drink."

She looked like I had struck her. "No," she said, "I didn't mean that."

"You're sure you'll be all right?" Gale asked. I nodded yes. "Then we'd better go, dear," he said to Barbara.

The funeral director was standing beside the limousine under an umbrella, waiting to open the door for them. Barbara took a deep breath. "Okay," she said, still looking at me, then turned and went out into the sleet with Gale.


After the procession wound its way out of the church parking lot, I went out into the storm and began walking back to Barbara and Gale's house. I didn't know, then, why I wanted to walk instead of taking a taxi; after I reached the house I understood, but then, I just felt I had to do it, that somehow it would be wrong not to.

The house was on the other end of town, near the oil camp and the black pumping units rising out of the snow like giant grasshoppers, but Rose Creek was just a hospital, a post office, a community hall, a school, and a couple dozen blocks of stores and houses, so I didn't have far to walk. But it was awfully cold, and I didn't have any overshoes or gloves. After a few minutes, my hands and feet were numb, and the wind was blowing the sleet into my face so hard it stung. I felt exhausted, like I'd been walking for hours, even days. My breaths came out short and fast, little clouds the wind blew into nothing.

My shaking was getting worse. I had to have a drink, I couldn't wait any longer, so I walked as fast as I could. I walked past the silent houses with smoke rising from their chimneys, past the schoolyard where some children in snowmobile suits were playing King of the Hill on a mound of snow, past the turnoff that led to the highway where Chuck had died. I walked faster and faster until I was almost running. My face and hands burned from the cold, and I could tell without looking that they were white with frostbite.

When I finally reached the house, I stood on the front steps, the sleet pelting my back, and tried to open the door, but my hand was shaking so bad I couldn't get the key into the lock. I stood there a moment, trying to get ahold of myself. But it was no use. I couldn't even breathe right—I had to strain for every breath, as if the air was too thin—and I felt so empty and dizzy I had to hold onto the doorframe to keep from falling.

And then I saw myself climbing Rainier, inching my way up the sheer cliff, a terrible weight on my back, and it wasn't a lie anymore, I had really done it. And I hung onto Barbara's door, bracing myself against the rising wind.

I remember sitting in Gale's easy chair, drinking his bourbon and staring out his window at the ice-laden trees, but I don't remember going to Chuck's room. I don't even remember thinking about going there. I just remember finding myself swaying drunk in front of his door. And I remember deciding, as soon as I realized where I was and what I was about to do, that it'd been a mistake to come, that I should never have left Bozeman. Standing there, I saw myself driving across that empty state under the huge black sky, driving away from Barbara and Gale and what was left of my son, heading home, toward Betty and lovemaking and sleep. And I turned to leave.

But I turned back. I couldn't leave, not yet. I stood there a second, then took a deep breath and opened the door.

I'm not sure what exactly I expected—maybe I thought his room would give him back to me, if only for a moment, let me be with him for that last minute before he drove off to the accident that waited for him—but whatever it was, I didn't get what I wanted. The room was just a room. The bed was just a bed, the desk just a desk. Even the shirts that hung in his closet were just shirts. I stood there a while, looking at everything, then opened the top drawer of the desk: blank paper, some pens, a ruler, and a calculator. In one corner there were some pencil shavings. I picked them up and they fell apart in my hands.

I sat down at the desk then and put my hot face against the cool wood. It felt good against my cheek, and it made me think of when I was in grade school and the teacher wanted to find out who had done something wrong. She'd tell everyone to put their heads down on their desks and close their eyes, then raise their hands if they were the one. Closing my eyes, I remembered how I felt those times when I hadn't done anything, how I liked sitting there, innocent, imagining someone else's guilty hand rising into the air.

At first I thought the storm had woken me. Sleet was striking the window, sounding like flung pellets of rice. But then I heard Barbara, her voice wavering. "What are you doing in here?" I lifted my head from the desk and tried to see through the darkness. But I saw only a shadow, haloed by the hall light, and I heard it say, "Why did you have to come in *here*?" Then she flicked on the overhead light. I shielded my eyes. Through the bright blur, I saw Gale standing behind her in the hall, his coat still in his hand.

"I knew we shouldn't have stayed so long at Muriel's," he was saying. "I knew something would happen."

Barbara came toward me. "I asked you not to come in here," she said. She looked around and bit her quivering lip. "Why did you have to—" she started, but couldn't finish.

I realized then that I'd taken away her last comfort, that from now on when she came into this room I'd be here with him. "I'm sorry," I said, and stood up. My forehead swelled and throbbed, and I almost lost my balance.

"You're drunk," Barbara said then, and she stepped toward me, her hands clenched at her sides.

I wasn't drunk, not anymore, but it didn't matter. And it didn't matter that Barbara and Gale were angry at me. Nothing mattered now. It was all over. And suddenly I felt numb, almost peaceful, even though I knew it couldn't last, that any minute now all the pain and sorrow would come back, maybe even worse than before.

Barbara said something to me then, but I didn't hear. I just looked at her. Then I reached out and put my arms around her. She stayed stiff in my arms and kept her hands at her sides, but she didn't back away from me. I held her tight. "Chuck is dead," I told her. I said it like I'd only just found out about it and thought she ought to know.

# WHAT THEY DIDN'T NOTICE

FRANK

When Frank stepped out of the doctor's office, he didn't notice the sky. If he had been sixty years younger, perhaps he would have noticed that one of the clouds scudding up from the southwest looked like an enormous white horse. Its long neck was outstretched, as if straining toward a finish line, but it had no legs. Still, its mane and tail were flying.

Nor did he notice the ground. The soil in the flowerbeds that flanked the sidewalk was unnaturally black for this part of the country—imported, no doubt, from some northern state. Had he noticed the dirt, he might have thought about the clay that lay beneath it, damp and tinged with red, as if so many animals had died here for so many centuries that their blood could not be completely rained away.

In a nearby tulip poplar, a gray-green bird with a yellow breast sang over and over a deep-throated song, fracturing its melody each time with four or five abrupt, awkward pauses, but Frank did not see or hear it. If it had been another day, or another place, he probably would have noticed the mask around its eyes—like a raccoon's, only yellow—and recognized the bird as a yellow-throated vireo. Though he'd been an ardent birdwatcher since the year before he retired, it was a species he had never seen before, one he could have added to his Life List. But he did not see it, so it would have to remain on that larger list of things that were part of the world's life but not his own.

And when he reached the parking lot, he didn't notice how long he stood there beside his car, holding the key in his hand. He did not notice his hand either, how it looked like his father's— liver-spotted, the knuckles gnarled with arthritis. It had been thirty years since he'd seen his father's hands, crossed upon the black lapels of his last suit. If he had noticed, perhaps his hand would have started to tremble. But it didn't. It was still, like a small animal that freezes where it stands, hoping it hasn't been seen.

He stood there for nearly two minutes, a full minute longer than it took for the doctor to change his life.

### Ellie

When Frank left the house that morning, Ellie didn't notice how his voice quavered when he told her he was going to meet a couple of his friends for coffee.

And when he came home, she did not notice how quietly he closed the door, as if he didn't want to wake someone who was sleeping.

### The Doctor

The doctor did not notice:

(1) The way the carotid artery in Frank's throat pulsed while he listened to the biopsy results.
(2) The squeak of his nurse's shoes as she walked past the closed door.
(3) The way he kept clearing his throat, as if hinting that Frank should say something now, anything, whatever he was thinking or feeling.
(4) The fact that he nodded as he spoke, as if he were secretly agreeing with Frank's silence.
(5) The fact that he kept repeating the word *options*.
(6) A bird's song outside the window.
(7) The telephone ringing at the nurse's station and Loretta's bored voice saying, "I'm sorry, he's with a patient right now."

(8) His hand lightly shaking Frank's shoulder, as if to wake him.

(9) The coppery taste of fear on the back of his tongue.

### THE VIREO

The vireo did not notice the man passing below him on the sidewalk. It was also unaware of the obsessive repetition of its song, or even of the fact that it was singing. Least of all was it aware that this day could be unlike any other, or even that there were such things as days, as time, as death.

### ELLIE

That night, after they made love for the first time in weeks, Ellie did not notice Frank sobbing silently. And when, finally, his voice shaking, he told her what the doctor had said, she was not aware that the fingers of her left hand curled up slowly, like an animal dying, while her right hand stroked the back of his neck, the stubble left there by the barber.

### FRANK

After he told her, Frank looked at his wife's face in the dim light the moon cast through their window, but he did not see it, not really. He was seeing her face as it was forty-five years before, when they first met, and he was wondering where that young girl had gone, and where he had gone, the young man he was then, tall and thin and so strong from lifting hay bales that she couldn't stop touching his arms, his shoulders. Because he was thinking these thoughts, he did not notice the anger that tinged her voice when she asked him why he hadn't told her about his symptoms or his trips to the doctor. Nor did he dare notice that he was angry too, offended even, that she would go on living without him.

### THE VIREO

By the time first Frank and then Ellie finally fell asleep, the vireo had been sleeping for hours, its feathers fluffed against the cold and its head tucked under its wing. Torn clouds were streaking overhead, scarring the moon, and a wind was stirring the leaves that surrounded its nest, but the bird was oblivious. It noticed nothing, nothing at all. And in the morning, when it would wake, it would begin to live once again the one day of its life, singing its beautiful, broken song.

# TELL ME SOMETHING

She had been dying for nearly two months now, and each day he sat beside her bed in the nursing home and told her how much he loved her. At first she had liked hearing him say that, after all these years of silence on the subject, but now she didn't think she could bear to hear him say it one more time. And she dreaded almost as much hearing the daily gossip—what the waitress at Tubby's Cafe told him about that new minister over at the Presbyterian church, the one who quoted movies during his sermons; what everybody was saying about the city council's plan to put a second stoplight on the highway going through town; what that swindler Harlan Jensen was asking for his worthless farm. She'd even stopped looking forward to the latest news from the children—they still called them "the children" though Susie and Ralph had children and even grandchildren of their own now. One or the other called him almost every night, after he came home from the nursing home, to see how she was doing. They called her too, from time to time, but for some reason she couldn't think of anything to say to them and so there were long, uncomfortable silences. She knew it was only a matter of weeks, maybe days, before she would be moved across the street to the hospital and they would leave their homes in Atlanta and Pittsburgh and fly to her bedside to say their final goodbyes. She looked forward to seeing them, as she looked forward to seeing her husband each morning, when he entered her room with his rumpled out-of-date fedora in his big hands and that sad thin smile on his face, but she also dreaded their visit. The last time they came to see her—in April, right after they found the cancer in her pancreas—they'd started talking about soccer, of all things, this foreign sport her great-grandchildren were playing, and she'd instantly felt as though she were already dead and gone out of their lives. They went on and on until she decided to pretend she'd fallen asleep. It was a relief when they tiptoed out of the room and went down the hall to the community room to talk.

She hated to admit it, but the worst thing about dying wasn't the pain—though every time it reared up it seared her insides with a throbbing fire—but the boredom. She almost had to laugh when she thought of the phrase "bored to death." How many times had she said that? But only now did she have any idea how true it was. She loved her husband—always had, even after he betrayed her with that terrible woman who used to hang around at the bowling alley and drink with the men who were too old or lame to go to the war. But she was more bored with him than with anyone or anything. Each night she prayed to die without him finding out how tired she was of him and his face and his voice and all of his irritating habits.

So this morning, before he had even finished hanging his hat on the end of her bed, before he could kiss her forehead, before he could start in with his "How did you sleep?" or his "How's my sweetheart this morning?" she said. "Tell me something, Henry. Tell me something you've never told me before."

He clicked his dentures then, as he often did when he was nervous or worried. The sound made her grit her own teeth.

"What do you mean?"

She shifted in her bed, trying to take the pressure off the bedsore that was starting on her hip. "I mean, something you've kept from me. Something secret. Something that matters."

He sat down in the plaid armchair next to her bed. He was wearing the same wrinkled brown suit he'd been wearing all week, only this morning he'd forgotten to put on his tie. His dingy white shirt was buttoned to the collar, and she knew he'd be surprised, later that night, when he went to take off his tie and found it wasn't there. He leaned toward her, his forehead furrowed. "Are you feeling all right, Emma? Do you want me to call a nurse?"

She sighed. "I'm feeling fine." In fact, though, she was feeling light-headed and had been ever since she woke up. Even eating her oatmeal hadn't helped, as it usually did; it only made her nauseated. She looked down at the floor to steady her spinning head. The light that slanted through the windowpanes cast a pattern of rectangles on the carpet. Looking at them, she thought of playing hopscotch when she was a child. Her hair then had been so blond that it was almost white, though it had turned brown by the time she started school. And now her hair, the few tufts of it that remained, was white again. Somehow, that seemed to mean something. But what?

Henry pushed his wire glasses back up his nose and looked at her. "You look a little pale," he said.

"Tell me something," she said, closing her eyes.

"I don't know what to say."

"Anything. Say anything. Just make it something you've never told me before. Not me or anyone else."

"You're serious?"

She didn't answer. Silence, she knew, was the best answer. All her life she had used it to make him listen to her.

He cleared his throat and clicked his dentures again. She wanted to tell him to please please please stop making those noises, but she didn't. She just waited for him to speak.

"It was during the war," he finally said, and cleared his throat again.

She opened her eyes. "I don't want to hear about that woman," she said. "Tell me something else."

"No," he said. "This doesn't have anything to do with her. Or any other woman. Just you."

She lifted her head and looked at him. "*Were* there other women?" She almost hoped he'd say "Yes," just so she'd have some other pain to distract her.

He shook his head. "No. Not one. And that's the truth, Emma."

She laid her head back down on the warm pillow. Her head seemed to keep on sinking even after it had stopped, as if something inside her brain were spiraling ever downward. "Go on," she said, and closed her eyes again.

Once more he cleared his throat. And then he started. "You were working in town, then, at Tubby's—only it was called the Main Street Cafe then, remember? By the time I'd finish the morning chores, you'd have already taken the kids to school and gone on to work yourself. I'd come in the kitchen those mornings and make myself a pot of coffee and sit there at the table and I'd—"

She opened her eyes to see why he'd stopped. He was rubbing his forehead with a finger and thumb. "I don't know why I'm telling you this," he said.

"Because I asked you to," she said, and was immediately embarrassed: she'd said it like a young girl, a coquette, sure of the power of her charms.

"No," he said. "What I mean is, I could tell you anything. I don't know why I picked this."

"Just tell me."

"Okay," he sighed, and clicked his dentures. "I'd be sitting there in the kitchen, thinking about everything I had to do that day— bed the barn, mend fence posts, shovel grain in the silo, all that— and then I'd start thinking about you and wondering what you were doing down there at the cafe. I'd imagine you talking to customers, bringing them platters of bacon and eggs and French toast, and I'd wonder what you were thinking about while you talked to them, if it was me or the kids or if you just forgot about all of us while you were there, away from us and the farm. And I'd wonder if you liked being at work more than at home."

"Henry," she said, in the voice she'd always used to calm the children.

"Sometimes I was sure you were happier there. I believed you'd have left me if it weren't for the kids. We were having trouble then, you remember. That was a few months after—well, you know."

He couldn't say anymore. He didn't have to.

"I forgave you," she said. "You knew that."

"I know," he said. "But that's not the point."

She wanted to ask what the point was, but just then a pain flared in her side, and she had to clench her fingers and curl her toes for a few seconds, until it was gone.

"Are you all right?" he asked, his big warm hand on hers.

She nodded, and her head felt loose, as if it might roll off.

He stood up abruptly then and paced to the end of the bed. "And now here you are"—he looked around the room, his watery blue eyes scanning the blown roses on the wallpaper, the family portrait hanging over the blond mahogany dresser, the bedside tray with its overturned cellophane-wrapped water glass and its Styrofoam pitcher. "Here!" He shook his head. "Before me! *I* should have been the first." He turned his back to her and she watched his shoulders work.

She said, "Dear. Don't think like that."

"It wasn't supposed to be this way," he said.

"You'll be fine when I'm gone," she assured him. "You have your friends. The children'll visit a lot. And you can go see them, spend time with all the grandkids and their children."

"No," he said. Nothing else.

"Don't say that," she said, and tried to raise herself up onto her elbows. But the pain spun up from her side into her head and she fell back. Somehow, the fall seemed to take a long time, or to happen over and over—she wasn't sure which.

He took a deep breath. Then, his back still to her, he continued, "One morning I started out to the barn but I just couldn't bring myself to go in. I stood there for a long time, just thinking, and then I got into the pickup and drove into town. First I went by the school, hoping I'd see the kids out on the playground for recess, but they weren't there. So I headed downtown and parked a couple of blocks away from the cafe, where you wouldn't see the pickup. Then I went into the Rexall across the street and stood in one of the aisles near the front and watched you through the window. You were walking back and forth from the kitchen to the tables, carrying plates and pouring coffee and taking orders, and you were smiling and laughing with everybody." He turned around then and faced her. "It'd been so long since I'd seen you smile," he said.

She cleared her own throat now, and as she did, she wondered if it bothered him the way all of his noises bothered her. She said, "How long did you watch me?"

"I don't know. Five minutes. Ten. I'm not sure. But then I got back into the pickup and drove out to the farm. And when you came home that night, I didn't say anything. I wanted to tell you I'd been watching you, but I didn't know how to say it, or even why I'd done it. And I didn't know what you'd say, whether you'd be mad or not even care." He paused. "I don't know why, but I've never been able to forget that day. Every now and then I find myself thinking about it. I see you there, walking back and forth behind that plate glass window in your blue and white uniform, a smile on your face, your hair done up the way you wore it then, pinned on top in a bun. And I see myself, across the street, hiding, spying on you, like some kind of peeping tom, and I feel ashamed."

He sat on the edge of the bed. Down the hall in one of the rooms a telephone rang. They listened to it until it stopped.

"Why didn't you come into the cafe and talk to me?" she asked then.

He looked at his hands. "I didn't want to see that smile leave your face."

For a long time, she didn't say anything. She was trying to imagine that morning, trying to look through the cafe window and see her husband in the drugstore across the street, trying to make herself smile at him. She closed her eyes to try to see it better. Then she said, "Thank you."

"For what?" Henry asked.

"For telling me that story." She opened her eyes. For a second, she was surprised at how old he was. She almost didn't recognize him.

He cleared his throat. "I shouldn't have," he said.

"I'm glad you did," she answered.

"Why'd you want me to tell you something like that?"

"Because I'm not dead yet. And I was feeling like I was."

"Emma," he said. "Don't talk like that."

She closed her eyes again. "Now I want to tell you something," she said.

"You don't have to."

"Do you remember the day we first met?" she asked.

He hesitated a moment, then clicked his dentures. The sound made her think of a Geiger counter, the way it clicked whenever it came near something radioactive, and she laughed a little. After all the treatments she'd had, she probably was radioactive by now.

He looked at her. "What's funny?" he said.

"Nothing," she answered. "Everything." Then she said, "You don't remember, do you?"

He took a breath, then said, "It was so long ago."

She laughed again. "I don't remember that day either. I wish I could. I was someone else then, I had another life ahead of me—what, I don't know, or care, but another life just the same. And then we met and everything changed. And I can't remember that day. Where we were. What the weather was like. What we were wearing. What we talked about. It seems so important that I remember it, but I can't. Day after day I've laid here and tried to remember, but I can't."

He took her hand. "It doesn't matter," he said. "That was sixty years ago. A lifetime ago."

"A lifetime," she said.

He clicked his dentures once again. She wanted to tell him to stop it, but instead she smiled.

"Emma," he said, squeezing her hand. "I love you, sweetheart."

"I know," she answered. A pain was coming now, a big one, she could tell. She could feel it rising in her like a wave about to shatter itself against rocks, but she made herself keep on smiling until he finally smiled back.

# GLOSSOLALIA

That winter, like every winter before it, my father woke early
each day and turned up the thermostat so the house would be
warm by the time my mother and I got out of bed. Sometimes I'd
hear the furnace kick in and the shower come on down the hall
and I'd wake just long enough to be angry that he'd woken me.
But usually I slept until my mother had finished making our
breakfast. By then, my father was already at Goodyear, opening
the service bay for the customers who had to drop their cars off
before going to work themselves. Sitting in the sunny kitchen,
warmed by the heat from the register and the smell of my mother's
coffee, I never thought about him dressing in the cold dark or
shoveling out the driveway by porch light. If I thought of him at
all, it was only to feel glad he was not there. In those days my
father and I fought a lot, though probably not much more than
most fathers and sons. I was sixteen then, a tough age. And he
was forty, an age I've since learned is even tougher.

But that winter I was too concerned with my own problems to
think about my father's. I was a skinny, unathletic, sorrowful boy
who had few friends, and I was in love with Molly Rasmussen, one
of the prettiest girls in Glencoe and the daughter of a man who
had stopped my father on Main Street that fall, cursed him, and
threatened to break his face. My father had bought a used Ford
Galaxie from Mr. Rasmussen's lot, but he hadn't been able to make

the payments and eventually Mr. Rasmussen repossessed it. Without a second car my mother couldn't get to her job at the school lunchroom, so we drove our aging Chevy to Minneapolis, where no one knew my father, and bought a rust-pitted yellow Studebaker. A few days later Molly Rasmussen passed me in the hall at school and said, "I see you've got a new car," then laughed. I was so mortified I hurried into a restroom, locked myself in a stall, and stood there for several minutes, breathing hard. Even after the bell rang for the next class, I didn't move. I was furious at my father. I blamed him for the fact that Molly despised me, just as I had for some time blamed him for everything else that was wrong with my life—my gawky looks, my discount store clothes, my lack of friends.

That night, and others like it, I lay in bed and imagined who I'd be if my mother had married someone handsome and popular like Dick Moore, the PE teacher, or Smiley Swenson, who drove stock cars at the county fair, or even Mr. Rasmussen. Years before, my mother had told me how she met my father. A girl who worked with her at Woolworth's had asked her if she wanted to go out with a friend of her boyfriend's, an army man just back from the war. My mother had never agreed to a blind date before, or dated an older man, but for some reason this time she said yes. Lying there, I thought about that fateful moment. It seemed so fragile—she could as easily have said no and changed everything—and I wished, then, that she had said no, I wished she'd said she didn't date strangers or she already had a date or she was going out of town—anything to alter the chance conjunction that would eventually produce me.

I know now that there was something suicidal about my desire to undo my parentage, but then I knew only that I wanted to be someone else. And I blamed my father for that wish. If I'd had a different father, I reasoned, I would be better looking, happier, more popular. When I looked in the mirror and saw my father's thin face, his rust-red hair, downturned mouth, and bulging Adam's apple, I didn't know who I hated more, him or me. That winter I began parting my hair on the right instead of the left, as my father did, and whenever the house was empty I worked on changing my voice, practicing the inflections and accents of my classmates' fathers as if they were clues to a new life. I did not think, then, that my father knew how I felt about him, but now that I have a son of my own, a son almost as old as I was then, I know different.

If I had known what my father was going through that winter, maybe I wouldn't have treated him so badly. But I didn't know anything until the January morning of his breakdown. I woke that morning to the sound of voices downstairs in the kitchen. At first I thought the sound was the wind rasping in the bare branches of the cottonwood outside my window, then I thought it was the radio. But after I lay there a moment I recognized my parents' voices. I couldn't tell what they were saying, but I knew they were arguing. They'd been arguing more than usual lately, and I hated it—not so much because I wanted them to be happy, though I did, but because I knew they'd take their anger out on me, snapping at me, telling me to chew with my mouth closed, asking me who gave me permission to put my feet up on the coffee table, ordering me to clean my room. I buried one ear in my pillow and covered the other with my blankets, but I could still hear them. They sounded distant, yet somehow close, like the sea crashing in a shell held to the ear. But after a while I couldn't hear even the muffled sound of their voices, and I sat up in the bars of gray light slanting through the blinds and listened to the quiet. I didn't know what was worse: their arguments or their silences. I sat there, barely breathing, waiting for some noise.

Finally I heard the back door bang shut and, a moment later, the Chevy cough to life. Only then did I dare get out of bed. Crossing to the window, I raised one slat of the blinds with a finger and saw, in the dim light, the driveway drifted shut with snow. Then my father came out of the garage and began shoveling, scooping the snow furiously and flinging it over his shoulder, as if each shovelful were a continuation of the argument. I couldn't see his face, but I knew that it was red and that he was probably cursing under his breath. As he shoveled, the wind scuffed the drifts around him,

swirling the snow into his eyes, but he didn't stop or set his back to
the wind. He just kept shoveling fiercely, and suddenly it occurred
to me that he might have a heart attack, just as my friend Rob's
father had the winter before. For an instant I saw him slump over
his shovel, then collapse face-first into the snow. As soon as this
thought came to me, I did my best to convince myself that it arose
from love and terror, but even then I knew part of me wished his
death, and that knowledge went through me like a chill.

I lowered the slat on the blinds and got back into bed. The
house was quiet but not peaceful. I knew that somewhere in the
silence my mother was crying and I thought about going to
comfort her, but I didn't. After a while I heard my father rev the
engine and back the Chevy down the driveway. Still I didn't get
up. And when my mother finally came to tell me it was time to
get ready, her eyes and nose red and puffy, I told her I wasn't
feeling well and wanted to stay home. Normally she would have
felt my forehead and cross-examined me about my symptoms,
but that day I knew she'd be too upset to bother. "Okay, Danny,"
she said. "Call me if you think you need to see a doctor." And
that was it. She shut the door and a few minutes later I heard the
whine of the Studebaker's cold engine, and then she was gone.

It wasn't long after my mother left that my father came home. I
was lying on the couch in the living room watching TV when I
heard a car pull into the driveway. At first I thought my mother had
changed her mind and come back to take me to school. But then
the back door sprang open and I heard him. It was a sound I had
never heard before, and since have heard only in my dreams, a
sound that will make me sit up in the thick dark, my eyes open to
nothing and my breath panting. I don't know how to explain it,
other than to say that it was a kind of crazy language, like speaking
in tongues. It sounded as if he were crying and talking at the same
time, and in some strange way his words had become half-sobs and
his sobs something more than words—or words turned inside out,
so that only their emotion and not their meaning came through. It
scared me. I knew something terrible had happened, and I didn't

know what to do. I wanted to go to him and ask what was wrong, but I didn't dare. I switched off the sound on the TV so he wouldn't know I was home and sat there staring at the actors mouthing their lines. But then I couldn't stand it anymore and I got up and ran down the hall to the kitchen. There, in the middle of the room, wearing his Goodyear jacket and work clothes, was my father. He was on his hands and knees, his head hanging as though it were too heavy to support, and he was rocking back and forth and babbling in a rhythmic stutter. It's funny, but the first thing I thought when I saw him like that was the way he used to give me rides on his back, when I was little, bucking and neighing like a horse. And as soon as I thought it, I felt my heart lurch in my chest. "Dad?" I said. "What's wrong?" But he didn't hear me. I went over to him then. "Dad?" I said again, and touched him on the shoulder. He jerked at the touch and looked up at me, his lips moving but no sounds coming out of them now. His forehead was knotted and his eyes were red, almost raw-looking. He swallowed hard and for the first time spoke words I could recognize, though I did not understand them until years later, when I was myself a father.

"Danny," he said. "Save me."

Before I could finish dialing the school lunchroom's number, my mother pulled into the driveway. Looking out the window, I saw her jump out of the car and run up the slick sidewalk, her camel-colored overcoat open and flapping in the wind. For a moment I was confused. Had I already called her? How much time had passed since I found my father on the kitchen floor? A minute? An hour? Then I realized that someone else must have told her something was wrong.

She burst in the back door then and called out, "Bill? Bill? Are you here?"

"Mom," I said, "Dad's—" and then I didn't know how to finish the sentence.

She came in the kitchen without stopping to remove her galoshes. "Oh, Bill," she said when she saw us, "are you all right?"

My father was sitting at the kitchen table now, his hands fluttering in his lap. A few moments before, I had helped him to his feet and, draping his arm over my shoulders, led him to the table like a wounded man.

"Helen," he said. "It's you." He said it as if he hadn't seen her for years.

My mother went over and knelt beside him. "I'm so sorry," she said, but whether that statement was born of sorrow over something she had said or done or whether she just simply and guiltlessly wished he weren't suffering, I never knew. Taking his hands in hers, she added, "There's nothing to worry about. Everything's going to be fine." Then she turned to me. Her brown hair was wind-blown, and her face was so pale the smudges of rouge on her cheeks looked like bruises. "Danny," she said, "I want you to leave us alone for a few minutes."

I looked at her red-rimmed eyes and tight lips. "Okay," I said, and went back to the living room. There, I sat on the sagging couch and stared at the television, the actors' mouths moving wordlessly, their laughs eerily silent. I could hear my parents talking, their steady murmur broken from time to time by my father sobbing and my mother saying "Bill" over and over, in the tone mothers use to calm their babies, but I couldn't hear enough of what they said to know what had happened. And I didn't *want* to know either. I wanted them to be as silent as the people on the TV, I wanted all the words to stop, all the crying.

I lay down and closed my eyes, trying to drive the picture of my father on the kitchen floor out of my head. My heart was beating so hard I could feel my pulse tick in my throat. I was worried about my father but I was also angry that he was acting so strange. It didn't seem fair that I had to have a father like that. I'd never seen anybody else's father act that way, not even in a movie.

Outside, the wind shook the evergreens and every now and then a gust would rattle the windowpane. I lay there a long time, listening to the wind, until my heart stopped beating so hard.

Some time later, my mother came into the room and sat on the edge of the chair under the sunburst mirror. Her forehead was creased, and there were black mascara streaks on her cheeks. Leaning toward me, her hands clasped, she bit her lip, then said, "I just wanted to tell you not to worry. Everything's going to be all right." Her breath snagged on the last word, and I could hear her swallowing.

"What's wrong?" I asked.

She opened her mouth as if she were about to answer, but suddenly her eyes began to tear. "We'll talk about it later," she said. "After the doctor's come. Just don't worry, okay? I'll explain everything."

"The doctor?" I said.

"I'll explain later," she answered.

Then she left and I didn't hear anything more until ten or fifteen minutes had passed and the doorbell rang. My mother ran to the door and opened it, and I heard her say, "Thank you for coming so quickly. He's in the kitchen." As they hurried down the hall past the living room, I caught a glimpse of Dr. Lewis and his black leather bag. It had been years since the doctors in our town, small as it was, made house calls, so I knew now that my father's problem was something truly serious. The word *emergency* came into my mind, and though I tried to push it out, it kept coming back.

For the next half hour or so, I stayed in the living room, listening to the droning sound of Dr. Lewis and my parents talking. I still didn't know what had happened or why. All I knew was that my father was somebody else now, somebody I didn't know. I tried to reconcile the man who used to read to me at night when my mother was too tired, the man who patiently taught me how to measure and cut plywood for a birdhouse, even the man whose cheeks twitched when he was angry at me and whose silences were suffocating, with the man I had just seen crouched like an animal on the kitchen floor babbling some incomprehensible language. But I couldn't. And though I felt sorry for him and his suffering, I felt as much shame as sympathy. *This is your father*, I told myself. *This is you when you're older.*

It wasn't until after Dr. Lewis had left and my father had taken the tranquilizers and gone upstairs to bed that my mother came back into the living room, sat down on the couch beside me, and told me what had happened. "Your father," she began, and her voice cracked. Then she controlled herself and said, "Your father has been fired from his job."

I looked at her. "Is that it?" I said. "That's what all this fuss is about?" I couldn't believe he'd put us through all this for something so unimportant. All he had to do was get a new job. What was the big deal?

"Let me explain," my mother said. "He was fired some time ago. Ten days ago, to be exact. But he hadn't said anything to me about it, and he just kept on getting up and going down to work every morning, like nothing had happened. And every day Mr. Siverhus told him to leave, and after arguing a while, he'd go. Then he'd spend the rest of the day driving around until quitting time, when he'd finally come home. But Mr. Siverhus got fed up and changed the locks, and when your father came to work today he couldn't get in. He tried all three entrances, and when he found his key didn't work in any of them, well, he threw a trash barrel through the showroom window and went inside."

She paused for a moment, I think to see how I was taking this. I was trying to picture my father throwing a barrel through that huge, expensive window. It wasn't easy to imagine. Even at his most angry, he had never been violent. He had never even threatened to hit me or my mother. But now he'd broken a window, and the law.

My mother went on. "Then when he was inside, he found that Mr. Siverhus had changed the lock on his office too, so he kicked the door in. When Mr. Siverhus came to work, he found your dad sitting at his desk, going over service accounts." Her lips started to tremble. "He could have called the police," she said, "but he called me instead. We owe him for that."

That's the story my mother told me. Though I was to find out later that she hadn't told me the entire truth, she had told me enough of it to make me realize that my father had gone crazy. Something in him—whatever slender idea or feeling it is that connects us to the world—had broken, and he was not in the world anymore, he was outside it, horribly outside it, and could not get back in no matter how he tried. Somehow I knew this, even then. And I wondered if someday the same thing would happen to me.

The rest of that day, I stayed downstairs, watching TV or reading *Sports Illustrated* or *Life*, while my father slept or rested. My mother sat beside his bed, reading her ladies magazines while he slept and talking to him whenever he woke, and every now and then she came downstairs to tell me he was doing fine. She spoke as if he had some temporary fever, some twenty-four-hour virus, that would be gone by morning.

But the next morning, a Saturday, my father was still not himself. He didn't feel like coming down for breakfast, so she made him scrambled eggs, sausage, and toast and took it up to him on a tray. He hadn't eaten since the previous morning, but when she came back down awhile later all the food was still on the tray. She didn't say anything about the untouched meal; she just said my father wanted to talk to me.

"I can't," I said. "I'm eating." I had one sausage patty and a few bites of scrambled egg left on my plate.

"Not this minute," she said. "When you're done."

I looked out the window. It had been snowing all morning, and the evergreens in the backyard looked like flocked Christmas trees waiting for strings of colored lights. Some sparrows were flying in and out of the branches, chirping, and others were lined up on the crossbars of the clothesline poles, their feathers fluffed out and blowing in the wind.

"I'm supposed to meet Rob at his house," I lied. "I'll be late."

"Danny," she said, in a way that warned me not to make her say any more.

"All right," I said, and I shoved my plate aside and got up. "But I don't have much time."

Upstairs, I stopped at my father's closed door. Normally I would have walked right in, but that day I felt I should knock. I felt as if I were visiting a stranger. Even his room—I didn't think of it as belonging to my mother anymore—seemed strange, somehow separate from the rest of the house.

When I knocked, my father said, "Is that you, Danny?" and I stepped inside. All the blinds were shut, and the dim air smelled like a thick, musty mixture of hair tonic and Aqua Velva. My father was sitting on the edge of his unmade bed, wearing his old brown robe, nubbled from years of washings, and maroon corduroy slippers. His face was blotchy, and his eyes were dark and pouched.

"Mom said you wanted to talk to me," I said.

He touched a spot next to him on the bed. "Here. Sit down."

I didn't move. "I've got to go to Rob's," I said.

He cleared his throat and looked away. For a moment we were silent, and I could hear the heat register ticking.

"I just wanted to tell you to take good care of your mother," he said then.

I shifted my weight from one foot to the other. "What do you mean?"

He looked back at me, his gaze steady and empty, and I wondered how much of the way he was that moment was his medication and how much himself. "She needs someone to take care of her," he said. "That's all."

"What about you? Aren't you going to take care of her anymore?"

He cleared his throat again. "If I can."

"I don't get it," I said. "Why are you doing this to us? What's going on?"

"Nothing's going on," he answered. "That's the problem. Not a thing is going on."

"I don't know what you mean. I don't like it when you say things I can't understand."

"I don't like it either," he said. Then he added: "That wasn't me yesterday. I want you to know that."

"It sure looked like you. If it wasn't you, who was it then?"

He stood up and walked across the carpet to the window. But he didn't open the blinds; he just stood there, his back to me. "It's all right for you to be mad," he said.

"I'm not mad."

"Don't lie, Danny."

"I'm not lying. I just like my father to use the English language when he talks to me, that's all."

For a long moment he was quiet. It seemed almost as if he'd forgotten I was in the room. Then he said, "My grandmother used to tell me there were exactly as many stars in the sky as there were people. If someone was born, there'd be a new star in the sky that night, and you could find it if you looked hard enough. And if someone died, you'd see that person's star fall."

"What are you talking about?" I said.

"People," he answered. "Stars."

Then he just stood there, staring at the blinds. I wondered if he was seeing stars there, or his grandmother, or what. And all of a sudden I felt my throat close up and my eyes start to sting. I was surprised—a moment before I'd been so angry, but now I was almost crying.

I tried to swallow, but I couldn't. I wanted to know what was wrong, so I could know how to feel about it; I wanted to be sad or angry, either one, but not both at the same time. "What *happened?*" I finally said. "*Tell* me."

He turned, but I wasn't sure he'd heard me, because he didn't answer for a long time. And when he did, he seemed to be answering some other question, one I hadn't asked.

"I was so arrogant," he said. "I thought my life would work out."

I stood there looking at him. "I don't understand."

"I hope you never do," he said. "I hope to God you never do."

"Quit talking like that."

"Like what?"

"Like you're so *smart* and everything. Like you're above all of this when it's you that's causing it all."

He looked down at the floor and shook his head slowly.

"Well?" I said. "Aren't you going to say something?"

He looked up. "You're a good boy, Danny. I'm proud of you. I wish I could be a better father for you."

I hesitate now to say what I said next. But then I didn't hesitate. "So do I," I said bitterly. "So the hell do I." And I turned to leave.

"Danny, wait," my father said.

But I didn't wait. And when I shut the door, I shut it hard.

Two days later, after he took to fits of weeping and laughing, we drove my father to the VA hospital in Minneapolis. Dr. Lewis had already called the hospital and made arrangements for his admission, so we were quickly escorted to his room on the seventh floor, where the psychiatric patients were kept. I had expected the psych ward to be a dreary, prisonlike place with barred doors and gray, windowless walls, but if anything, it was cheerier than the rest of the hospital. There were sky blue walls in the hallway, hung here and there with watercolor landscapes the patients had painted, and sunny yellow walls in the rooms, and there was a brightly lit lounge with a TV, card tables, and a shelf full of board games, and even a crafts center where the patients could do decoupage, leatherwork, mosaics, and macramé. And the patients we saw looked so normal that I almost wondered whether we were in the right place. Most of them were older, probably veterans of the First World War, but a few were my father's age or younger. The old ones were the friendliest, nodding their bald heads or waving their liver-spotted hands as we passed, but even those who only looked at us seemed pleasant or, at the least, not hostile.

I was relieved by what I saw but evidently my father was not, for his eyes still had the quicksilver shimmer of fear they'd had all during the drive from Glencoe. He sat stiffly in the wheelchair and looked at the floor passing between his feet as the big-boned nurse pushed him down the hall toward his room.

We were lucky, the nurse told us, chatting away in a strange accent, which I later learned was Czech. There had been only one private room left, and my father had gotten it. And it had a *lovely* view of the hospital grounds. Sometimes she herself would stand in front of that window and watch the snow fall on the birches and park benches. It was such a beautiful sight. She asked my father if that didn't sound nice, but he didn't answer.

Then she wheeled him into the room and parked the chair beside the white, starched-looking bed. My father hadn't wanted to sit in the chair when we checked him in at the admissions desk, but now he didn't show any desire to get out of it.

"Well, what do you think of your room, Mr. Conroy?" the nurse asked. My mother stood beside her, a handkerchief squeezed in her hand.

My father looked at the chrome railing on the bed, the stainless steel tray beside it, and the plastic-sealed water glasses on the tray. Then he looked at my mother and me.

"I suppose it's where I should be," he said.

During the five weeks my father was in the hospital, my mother drove to Minneapolis twice a week to visit him. Despite her urgings, I refused to go with her. I wanted to forget about my father, to erase him from my life. But I didn't tell her that. I told her I couldn't stand to see him in that awful place, and she felt sorry for me and let me stay home. But almost every time she came back, she'd have a gift for me from him: a postcard of Minnehaha Falls decoupaged onto a walnut plaque, a leather billfold with my initials burned into the cover, a belt decorated with turquoise and white beads. And a request: would I come see him that weekend? But I never went.

Glencoe was a small town, and like all small towns it was devoted to gossip. I knew my classmates had heard about my father—many of them had no doubt driven past Goodyear to see the broken window the way they'd drive past a body shop to see a car that had been totaled—but only Rob said anything. When he asked what had happened, I told him what Dr. Lewis had told me, that my father was just overworked and exhausted. Rob didn't believe me any more than I believed Dr. Lewis, but he pretended to accept that explanation. I wasn't sure if I liked him more for that pretense, or less.

It took a couple of weeks for the gossip to reach me. One day during lunch Rob told me that Todd Knutson, whose father was a mechanic at Goodyear, was telling everybody my father had been fired for embezzling. "I know it's a dirty lie," Rob said, "but some kids think he's telling the truth, so you'd better do something."

"Like what?" I said.

"Tell them the truth. Set the record straight."

I looked at my friend's earnest, acne-scarred face. As soon as he'd told me the rumor, I'd known it was true, and in my heart I had already convicted my father. But I didn't want my best friend to know that. Perhaps I was worried that he would turn against me too and I'd be completely alone.

"You bet I will," I said. "I'll make him eat those words."

But I had no intention of defending my father. I was already planning to go see Mr. Siverhus right after school and ask him, straight out, for the truth, so I could confront my father with the evidence and shame him the way he had shamed me. I was furious with him for making me even more of an outcast than I had been—I was the son of a *criminal* now—and I wanted to make him pay for it. All during my afternoon classes, I imagined going to see him at the hospital and telling him I knew his secret. He'd deny it at first, I was sure, but as soon as he saw I knew everything, he'd confess. He'd beg my forgiveness, swearing he'd never do anything to embarrass me or my mother again, but nothing he could say would make any difference— I'd just turn and walk away. And if I were called into court to testify against him, I'd take the stand and swear to tell the whole truth and nothing but the truth, my eyes steady on him all the while, watching him sit there beside his lawyer, his head hung, speechless.

I was angry at my mother too, because she hadn't told me everything. But I didn't realize until that afternoon, when I drove down to Goodyear to see Mr. Siverhus, just how much she hadn't told me.

Mr. Siverhus was a tall, silver-haired man who looked more like a banker than the manager of a tire store. He was wearing a starched white shirt, a blue-and-gray striped tie with a silver tie tack, and iridescent sharkskin trousers, and when he shook my hand he smiled so hard his crow's-feet almost hid his eyes. He led me into his small but meticulous office, closing the door on the smell of grease and the noise of impact wrenches removing lugs from wheels, and I blurted out my question before either of us even sat down.

"Who told you that?" he asked.

"My mother," I answered. I figured he wouldn't lie to me if he thought my mother had already told me the truth. Then I asked him again: "Is it true?"

Mr. Siverhus didn't answer right away. Instead, he gestured toward a chair opposite his gray metal desk and waited until I sat in it. Then he pushed some carefully stacked papers aside, sat on the edge of the desk, and asked me how my father was doing. I didn't really know—my mother kept saying he was getting better, but I wasn't sure I could believe her. Still, I said, "Fine."

He nodded. "I'm glad to hear that," he said. "I'm really terribly sorry about everything that's happened. I hope you and your mother know that."

He wanted me to say something, but I didn't. Standing up, he wandered over to the gray file cabinet and looked out the window at the showroom, where the new tires and batteries were on display. He sighed, and I knew he didn't want to be having this conversation.

"What your mother told you is true," he said then. "Bill was taking money. Not much, you understand, but enough that it soon became obvious we had a problem. After some investigating, we found out he was the one. I couldn't have been more surprised. Your father had been a loyal and hardworking employee for years, and he was the last person I would've expected to be stealing from us. But when we confronted him with it, he admitted it. He'd been having trouble making his mortgage payments, he said, and in a weak moment he'd taken some money and, later on, a little more. He seemed genuinely sorry about it and he swore he'd pay back every cent, so we gave him another chance."

"But he did it again, didn't he?" I said.

I don't know if Mr. Siverhus noticed the anger shaking my voice or not. He just looked at me and let out a slow breath. "Yes," he said sadly. "He did. And so I had to fire him. I told him we wouldn't prosecute if he returned the money, and he promised he would."

Then he went behind his desk and sat down heavily in his chair. "I hope you understand."

"I'm not blaming you," I said. "*You* didn't do anything wrong."

He leaned over the desk toward me. "I appreciate that," he said. "You don't know how badly I've felt about all of this. I keep thinking that maybe I should have handled it differently. I don't know, when I think that he might have taken his life because of this, well, I—"

"Taken his life?" I interrupted.

Mr. Siverhus sat back in his chair. "Your mother didn't tell you?"

I shook my head and closed my eyes for a second. I felt as if something had broken loose in my chest and risen into my throat, making it hard to breathe, to think.

"I assumed you knew," he said. "I'm sorry, I shouldn't have said anything."

"Tell me," I said.

"I think you'd better talk to your mother about this, Danny. I don't think I should be the one to tell you."

"I need to know," I said.

Mr. Siverhus looked at me for a long moment. Then he said, "Very well. But you have to realize that your father was under a lot of stress. I'm sure that by the time he gets out of the hospital, he'll be back to normal, and you won't ever have to worry about him getting like that again."

I nodded. I didn't believe him, but I wanted him to go on.

Mr. Siverhus took a deep breath and let it out slowly. "When I came to work that morning and found your father in his office, he had a gun in his hand. A revolver. At first, I thought he was going to shoot me. But then he put it up to his own head. I tell you, I was scared. 'Bill,' I said, 'that's not the answer.' And then I just kept talking. It took me ten or fifteen minutes to get him to put the gun down. Then he left, and that's when I called your mother."

I must have had a strange look on my face because the next thing he said was, "Are you all right?"

I nodded, but I wasn't all right. I felt woozy, as if I'd just discovered another world inside this one, a world that made this one false. I wanted to leave, but I wasn't sure I could stand up. Then I did.

"Thank you, Mr. Siverhus," I said, and reached out to shake his hand. I wanted to say more but there was nothing to say. I turned and left.

Outside in the parking lot, I stood beside the Chevy, looking at the new showroom window and breathing in the cold. I was thinking how, only a few months before, I had been looking through my father's dresser for his old army uniform, which I wanted to wear to Rob's Halloween party, and I'd found the revolver tucked under his dress khakis in the bottom drawer. My father had always been full of warnings—don't mow the lawn barefoot, never go swimming in a river, always drive defensively—but he had never even mentioned he owned this gun, much less warned me not to touch it. I wondered why, and I held the gun up to the light, as if I could somehow see through it to an understanding of its meaning. But I couldn't—or at least I refused to believe that I could—and I put it back exactly where I found it and never mentioned it to anyone.

I didn't tell my mother what I had learned from Mr. Siverhus, and I didn't tell anyone else either. After dinner that night I went straight to my room and stayed there. I wanted to be alone, to figure things out, but the more I thought, the more I didn't know what to think. I wondered if it was starting already, if I was already going crazy like my father, because I wasn't sure who I was or what I felt. It had been a long time since I'd prayed, but that night I prayed that when I woke the next day everything would make sense again.

But the next morning I was still in a daze. Everything seemed so false, so disconnected from the real world I had glimpsed the day before, that I felt disoriented, almost dizzy. At school, the chatter of my classmates sounded as meaningless as my father's babble, and everything I saw seemed out of focus, distorted, the way things do just before you faint. Walking down the hall, I saw Todd Knutson standing by his locker, talking with Bonnie Zempel, a friend of Molly Rasmussen's, and suddenly I found myself walking up to them. I didn't know what I was going to say or do, I hadn't planned anything, and when I shoved Todd against his locker, it surprised me as much as it did him.

"I hope you're happy now," I said to him. "My father *died* last night." I'm not sure I can explain it now, but in a way I believed what I was saying, and my voice shook with a genuine grief.

Todd slowly lowered his fists. "What?" he said, and looked quickly at Bonnie's startled, open face.

"He had *cancer*," I said, biting down on the word to keep my mind from whirling. "A tumor on his brain. That's why he did the things he did, taking that money and breaking that window and everything. He couldn't help it."

And then my grief was too much for me, and I turned and strode down the hall, tears coming into my eyes. I waited until I was around the corner and out of their sight, then I started running, as fast as I could. Only then did I come back into the world and wonder what I had done.

That afternoon, my mother appeared at the door of my algebra class in her blue uniform and black hair net. At first I thought she was going to embarrass me by waving at me, as she often did when she happened to pass one of my classrooms, but then I saw the look on her face. "Excuse me, Mr. Laughlin," she said grimly, "I'm sorry to interrupt your class but I need to speak with my son for a moment."

Mr. Laughlin turned his dour face from the blackboard, his stick of chalk suspended in mid-calculation, and said, "Certainly, Mrs. Conroy. I hope there's nothing the matter."

"No," she said. "It's nothing to worry about."

But out in the hall, she slapped my face hard.

"How *dare* you say your father is dead," she said through clenched teeth. Her gray eyes were flinty and narrow.

"I didn't," I answered.

She raised her hand and slapped me again, even harder this time. "Don't you lie to me, Daniel."

I started to cry. "Well, I wish he *was*," I said. "I wish he was dead, so all of this could be over."

My mother raised her hand again, but then she let it fall. "Go," she said. "Get away from me. I can't bear to look at you another minute."

I went back into the classroom and sat down. I felt awful about hurting my mother, but not so awful that I wasn't worried whether my classmates had heard her slap me or noticed my burning cheek. I saw them looking at me and shaking their heads, heard them whispering and laughing under their breath, and I stood up, my head roiling, and asked if I could be excused.

Mr. Laughlin looked at me. Then, without even asking what was wrong, he wrote out a pass to the nurse's office and handed it to me. As I left the room, I heard him say to the class, "That's enough. If I hear one more remark . . ."

Later, lying on a cot in the nurse's office, my hands folded over my chest, I closed my eyes and imagined I was dead and my parents and classmates were kneeling before my open coffin, their heads bowed in mourning.

After that day, my mother scheduled meetings for me with Father Ondahl, our priest, and Mr. Jenseth, the school counselor. She said she hoped they could help me through this difficult time, then added, "Obviously, I can't." I saw Father Ondahl two or three times, and as soon as I assured him that I still had my faith, though I did not, he said I'd be better off just seeing Mr. Jenseth from then on. I saw Mr. Jenseth three times a week for the next month, then once a week for the rest of the school year. I'm not sure how those meetings helped, or even if they did. All I know is that, in time, my feelings about my father, and about myself, changed.

My mother continued her visits to my father, but she no longer asked me to go along with her, and when she came home from seeing him, she waited until I asked before she'd tell me how he was. I wondered whether she'd told him I was seeing a counselor, and why, but I didn't dare ask. And I wondered if she'd ever forgive me for my terrible lie.

Then one day, without telling me beforehand, she returned from Minneapolis with my father. "Danny," she called, and I came out of the living room and saw them in the entryway. My father was stamping the snow off his black wingtips, and he had a suitcase in one hand and a watercolor of our house in the other, the windows yellow with light and a thin swirl of gray smoke rising from the red brick chimney. He looked pale and even thinner than I remembered. I was so surprised to see him, all I could say was, "You're home."

"That's right," he said, and put down the suitcase and painting. "The old man's back." Then he tried to smile, but it came out more like a wince. I knew he wanted me to hug him and say how happy I was to see him, and part of me wanted to do that, too. But I didn't. I just shook his hand as I would have an uncle's or a stranger's, then picked up the painting and looked at it.

"This is nice," I said. "Real nice."

"I'm glad you like it," he answered.

And then we just stood there until my mother said, "Well, let's get you unpacked, dear, and then we can all sit down and talk."

Despite everything that had happened, our life together after that winter was relatively peaceful. My father got a job at

Firestone, and though for years he barely made enough to meet expenses, eventually he worked his way up to assistant manager and earned a good living. He occasionally lost his temper and succumbed to self-pity as he always had, but for the rest of his life, he was as normal and sane as anybody. Perhaps Dr. Lewis had been right after all, and all my father had needed was a good rest. In any case, by the time I was grown and married myself, his breakdown seemed a strange and impossible dream and I wondered, as I watched him play with my infant son, if I hadn't imagined some of it. It amazed me that a life could break so utterly, then mend itself.

But of course it had not mended entirely, as my life had also not mended entirely. There was a barrier between us, the thin but indestructible memory of what we had been to each other that winter. I was never sure just how much he knew about the way I'd felt about him then, or even whether my mother had told him my lie about his death, but I knew he was aware that I hadn't been a good son. Perhaps the barrier between us could have been broken with a single word—the word *love* or its synonym *forgive*—but as if by mutual pact we never spoke of that difficult winter or its consequences.

Only once did we come close to discussing it. He and my mother had come to visit me and my family in Minneapolis, and we had just finished our Sunday dinner. Caroline and my mother were clearing the table, Sam was playing on the kitchen floor with the dump truck my parents had bought him for his birthday, and my father and I were sitting in the living room watching "Sixty Minutes." The black pastor of a Pentecostal church in Texas was talking to Morley Safer about "the Spirit that descends upon us and inhabits our hearts." Then the camera cut to a black woman standing in the midst of a clapping congregation, her eyes tightly closed and her face glowing with sweat as she rocked back and forth, speaking the incoherent language of angels or demons. Her syllables rose and fell, then mounted in a syntax of spiraling rapture until finally, overcome by the voice that had spoken through her, she sank to her knees, trembling, her eyes open and glistening. The congregation clapped harder then, some of them leaping and dancing as if their bodies were lifted by the collapse of hers, and they yelled, "Praise God!" and "Praise the Lord God Almighty!"

I glanced at my father, who sat watching this with a blank face, and wondered what he was thinking. Then, when the camera moved to another Pentecostal minister discussing a transcript of the woman's speech, a transcript he claimed contained variations on ancient Hebrew and Aramaic words she couldn't possibly have known, I turned to him and asked, in a hesitant way, whether he wanted to keep watching or change channels.

My father's milky blue eyes looked blurred, as if he were looking at something a long way off, and he cleared his throat before he spoke. "It's up to you," he said. "Do you want to watch it?"

I paused. Then I said, "No," and changed the channel.

Perhaps if I had said yes, we might have talked about that terrible day he put a gun to his head and I could have told him what I had since grown to realize—that I loved him. That I had always loved him, though behind his back, without letting him know it. And, in a way, behind *my* back, too. But I didn't say yes, and in the seven years that remained of his life, we never came as close to ending the winter that was always, for us, an unspoken but living part of our present.

That night, though, unable to sleep, I got up and went into my son's room. Standing there in the wan glow of his night light, I listened to him breathe for a while, then quietly took down the railing we'd put on his bed to keep him from rolling off and hurting himself. Then I sat on the edge of the bed and began to stroke his soft, reddish blond hair. At first he didn't wake, but his forehead wrinkled and he mumbled a little dream-sound.

I am not a religious man. I believe, as my father must have, the day he asked me to save him, that our children are our only salvation, their love our only redemption. And that night, when my son woke, frightened by the dark figure leaning over him, and started to cry, I picked him up and rocked him in my arms, comforting him as I would after a nightmare. "Don't worry," I told him over and over, until the words sounded as incomprehensible to me as they must have to him, "it's only a dream. Everything's going to be all right. Don't worry."

DAVID JAUSS is the author of two previous collections of short stories, *Black Maps* and *Crimes of Passion*, two collections of poems, *You Are Not Here* and *Improvising Rivers*, and a collection of essays, *On Writing Fiction*. He has also edited or co-edited three anthologies: *Strong Measures: Contemporary American Poetry in Traditional Forms*; *The Best of Crazyhorse: Thirty Years of Poetry and Prose;* and *Words Overflown by Stars: Creative Writing Instruction and Insight from the Vermont College of Fine Arts MFA Program*. His short stories have been published in numerous magazines and reprinted in such anthologies as *Best American Short Stories*, *Prize Stories: The O. Henry Awards*, and, twice, *The Pushcart Prize: Best of the Small Presses*, as well as in *The Pushcart Book of Short Stories: The Best Short Stories from The Pushcart Prize*. He is the recipient of a National Endowment for the Arts Fellowship, a James A. Michener/Copernicus Society of America Fellowship, three fellowships from the Arkansas Arts Council, and one from the Minnesota State Arts Board. His collection *Black Maps* received the Associated Writers and Writing Programs Award for Short Fiction. He teaches creative writing at the University of Arkansas at Little Rock and in the low-residency MFA in Writing Program at Vermont College of Fine Arts.

For 31 years, cover artist JACK L. GEISER worked as a professional photographer. His work covered industrial, legal, advertising and commercial fields. His assignments included working with many politicians, sports figures, dignitaries, celebrities and famous people as diverse as Mother Teresa and Bob Hope.

The last five years Jack has been artistically exploring the realms of digital photography on his own through Photoshop and the Internet. His work now covers texture, surrealism, abstraction, and realism. His day-to-day rambling artistry can be seen at www.flickr.com/photos/jg_photo_art/

Jack lives in Omaha, Nebraska, with his wife Shelly, who is a published poet and is currently working on her first novel. They run a small business together and try to spend time, when possible, with their four children and five grandchildren.

CPSIA information can be obtained at www.ICGtesting.com
Printed in the USA
BVOW08s1405310114

343203BV00003B/10/P